Tell Me Tomorrow

ASHLYN HARMON

Moonwake Books, LLC

979-8-9900117-1-7 (eBook)
979-8-9900117-0-0 (Paperback)

Published by Moonwake Books, LLC

Book Cover by Yummy Book Covers

Edited by Earley Editing, LLC

To the 2012 and 2016 Olympic Swim Team (especially the men's team).

Thanks for all the memories. And the inspiration.

Dear Reader,

As an author, my goal is to provide readers with real and relatable characters. Stories they can see themselves in. Just like in real life, my characters don't live in a sunny, constantly perfect world.

This novel includes the following content that could potentially trigger some readers: discussions of mental health issues, body image issues, fat-shaming, and characters discussing the public outing of a bisexual character (this is not shown). As always, please take care of yourself.

Love you all,

Ashlyn.

Glossary

Here is a quick reference guide for all the swimming terminology used within this book.

- Age Group Swimmer: A swimmer who trains and competes in a program that groups athletes according to age, gender, and capability. During meets, they compete with swimmers of a similar age and ability, providing fair competition to younger athletes.

- Championship Meet: A meet held at the end of the season and usually requires athletes have qualifying times to compete. It can serve as a selection meet for a national team.

- Clinic: A scheduled program that is specifically used for instruction.

- Event: A race of any given distance. (i.e. the 200-meter freestyle, the 200-meter individual medley, etc.)

- Heat: The preliminary sessions in the morning of a meet are composed of heats. When there are too many swimmers to compete in an event at the same time, it's broken into heats based on seed times posted by each swimmer.

- Heat Sheets: A listing of every swimmers seed times in the events at a meet. Coaches submit these times weeks in advance, and the meet uses them to inform spectators of the order of events, the competing swimmers, and the general timeframe for the session.

- Individual Medley (IM): All four strokes together in one race. Order is butterfly, backstroke, breaststroke, freestyle. Equal distance must be swam in each stroke.

- Olympic-size Pool: Also called a long course pool. It's 50 meters in length with a minimum depth of 6 ft 7 in, recommended to be 9ft 10 in deep. Consists of ten lanes.

- Olympic Trials: A sanctioned long course meet held the year of the Olympic games to determine which swimmers will represent the USA on the team. Fifty-two athletes are named to the team, 26 men and 26 women.

- Warm/cool down: A recovery swim that's done after a race so the swimmer can rid their body of excess lactic acid that's generated during the race.

Warm-up: A period of practice and chance for swimmers to loosen up prior to the start of a meet or their event.

Prologue

June 2023

"Come on, pick up," I mutter into the phone, anxiously tapping my foot. "Seriously, Bryce, answer the damn phone!"

The ringing stops.

"Hey, what's up?"

I release a long breath before talking. "So, you know how you imploded your love life, again, and quit your job?"

Bryce groans. "Obviously. Are you seriously calling to remind me how much of an idiot I am for losing her, again?"

"No, but I can if you need a reminder." The last time my best friend had lost Josie Martin, I'd bitten my tongue. I'd been nothing more than the supportive best friend I knew he needed me to be, but to lose the same girl twice, he was a dumbass. And I was happy to make sure he knew it. "I'm always happy to call you a dumbass."

"Absolutely not, Carter," he replies. "Why'd you call if not to annoy the hell out of me about this?"

"Were you serious when you said you wanted to leave Omaha the other night?"

He hesitates; a sure sign he's weighing the pros and cons of what it would mean to do so. It would be a way to leave Josie behind, once and for all, but we both know he's not ready to say goodbye. "I don't know. Why?"

I pick at the hem of my sweatshirt. "I might have done something stupid."

"When in the history of ever has it been a good idea to start a sentence like that, Carter? What did you do?"

"I bought a pool."

Silence. Dead silence follows my declaration. It's such a stuttering silence, I pull the phone from my ear to make sure the call hasn't disconnected. It hasn't.

"What do you mean you bought a pool?" The question comes out slowly. "Like you bought a plastic pool your new dog can play in, but you also forgot to mention you got a dog?"

Part of me wishes it were something that adorable. "No, dude, I bought a club. It's in South Carolina."

"How did you even find out about a pool in a completely different state?"

I don't want to admit the truth, but I know I have to. Plus, if there is anyone who can understand what I'm going through, it's him. "I was doom scrolling the other night, feeling lost as to what will come next. You know, the usual."

"You have a year until the Olympics, Carter." There's a sympathetic note to his voice. "You don't need to be worrying about that right now."

"You and I both know it's easier said than done," I challenge. "It's going to fly by and then I'll be done. It'll be over."

I've dedicated my whole life to this career, to be an Olympic swimmer. I not only made it happen once, but twice, and am trying one more time. If I make it to Paris next summer, it'll be my final Olympics. It'll also be the only one I ever compete in without Bryce. Thirty years of hard work will come down to mere moments, and then I'll find myself staring into the abyss.

Bryce hasn't said anything.

"I want to have a plan," I continue. "I want to know what's coming next, like you did."

His laugh is bitter. "Oh, yeah, I totally knew what I was doing. I came to Omaha, took a job in sales I hate, broke the heart of the woman I love, and quit my job. It's been a productive four months for me."

"So that job didn't work out, but this one could."

"What one could?" He presses.

Oh, right. I need to tell him about my plan.

"Which is why I called," I explain. "I bought this pool in South Carolina; it needs some work, but I figured we could run it together, dude. You understand all the business stuff. I studied sports management—we could make this work. We could build a great team here and host professional meets. Give kids the chances we had."

"I haven't even seen the place, and you want me to move across the country to run it?" The way he asks the question tells me he's already made up his mind. And he's in. "How many pools are there?"

"Two. One indoor and one outdoor," I rattle off, ready to answer any question he has. "They're both long course."

He hums and I wonder if he's taking notes. "Does it have a gym facility?"

I consult the notes laid out on the cluttered kitchen island before me. "Yes, but it'll need a lot of work."

"How much work are we talking here, Carter?"

"We'll need to hire someone." Getting the place up and running probably won't happen before the Olympics, but we could get started. Especially if he was out there while I stayed in Georgia to train.

"You really already bought it?"

"Yes," I confirmed. "I saw it online, drove out one weekend, and signed the papers on the spot."

"Why didn't you tell me about this?" The question isn't accusatory, but I can hear the worry in his tone. He's trying to figure out where I am.

What he's failing to remember is the fact I've gone to therapy since I was in college and was always the one who had a good grasp on his mental health. "You were busy with Josie, and I needed to decide for myself. If you don't want to do this, I can find—"

"And miss the chance to run a club with you? Hell no."

A grin overtakes my features. "You're in?"

"Hell yeah I am," Bryce assures me. "When do you want me out there?"

"Mid-July?" I ask. "We'll need to get you added to the deed and all the paperwork before I head to training camp before Worlds."

I hear him clicking away at something and, for the first time, wonder if he's at work. Maybe I should feel guilty about bothering him, but what can he really get done in the last two days of employment? It's not like he has anything to lose. "I can do that."

"Sweet! I need to get back to the pool, but we'll talk more about this later?"

"Sure," he agrees. "Hey, Carter?"

I was about to hang up when he grabbed my attention. "Yeah?"

"Whatever happens over the next twelve months, you're going to be fine." My cheeks heat up at his ability to read me so well. After nearly twenty-five years of friendship, it makes sense. "Even without this backup plan, you'd figure it out, and you'd be fine."

"But this is a great backup plan, right?" I press, not wanting to talk about my fears. "It's going to work out?"

"It's going to be great, Carter," he assures me.

I deflate against the counter I'm leaning on. There is no one I'd rather do this with than him. "You know what this means, right?"

"What?"

"You have right around three weeks to get Josie to forgive you and convince her to move out here with you."

"Oh, fuck off," he groans. "Go to practice, you ass."

I laugh, feeling pleased with myself for throwing him so off-kilter. "Later, man."

The call disconnects and I stare down at the paperwork still spread across the counter, a weight lifting off my shoulders. There's only so much about the next twelve months that I'll be able to control, but this, this is something that's all mine. It is something I can hold on to when it feels like everything is drifting out of my gasp.

It is the lifeline I need.

Chapter 1

August 2023

"This place is a mess."

I glance over at Bryce and try not to wince. His eyes scan every aspect of the building we're standing in, and I know what he's thinking. *What the hell did Carter rope me into?* But I also know he sees it; the same way I saw it the first time I stepped in here. There is potential.

We can make this place into something great. We can give other young, hopeful swimmers the same opportunities we had growing up. Neither one of us is vain; we both know we wouldn't be anywhere without the coaches we had along the way.

"There is no way we'll get this up and running before the Olympics." Bryce steps closer to peer down into the pool, which is currently a mess of rotting wood and chipped concrete. He wrinkles his nose. "And what is that smell?"

I shrug, but am still desperate to have him on my side for this. "This place was cheap, man. They were eager to sell."

"Yeah, I can see why," he comments, moving to head upstairs toward the locker rooms and offices.

I trail after him like a lost puppy. "We know what a pool like this needs, Bryce. It's going to take a lot of work, but we can do this."

He turns to look at me for the first time since stepping inside the building, a pinched look on his face. My heart is thrumming in my chest, beating so rapidly I feel a slight shortness of breath. What if I'd made a huge mistake? Buying this place, dragging him into it, him bringing Josie into it, and knowing it'll all be on them until after the Olympics. I'm a certifiable jerk.

"Obviously we can do it, man." Just like that, all the tension deflates from me like a balloon. I wonder if he can hear whatever sound it's making. "I have no idea how we're going to do it, how long it's going to take, or how much it's going to cost, but we can do this."

I fight the urge to pump my fist in the air I like I did when we were kids. I settle for a grin. "You haven't seen the outside pool yet."

His eyebrow arches. "After this, I'm a little afraid to see it."

I shrug, owning up to overselling the pool when I first pitched the idea to him. "It's not nearly as bad as this. It should be up and running soon. You might be able to offer some private coaching or even tryouts before long, which will help the cost of everything."

"Can you even swim outdoors in Columbia during the winter?"

That is another question I don't know the answer to. Over the last couple of months, I've been too busy to focus on all the things I didn't think through with this decision, but now that I'm standing in this mess of a building with Bryce, I'm freaking out a bit.

"Oh, look!" Bryce's voice drags me from my anxious thoughts. He's leaning into the open doorway of one of the small offices. "It looks like we have at least one usable room."

Before I can jump into all the reasons this place is great, even though it's literally falling apart in places, Bryce grins at me. He's joking. I marginally relax. "I'm glad you'll have somewhere to sit down, dude. That was the top of my priority list when I went looking for a pool to buy."

"Did you tour more than one?"

"Nope," I replied, stuffing my hands further in the pocket of my sweatshirt. "I think Josie would call it serendipitous or something like that."

He chuckles. "And then Mia would declare that to be bullshit. Nothing happens for a reason."

"Or everything does."

Neither one of us says anything else as we move through the rest of the building. Taking a couple of moments to absorb it all. It's more overwhelming to be walking through it this time. I haven't been here since the first time, but now I feel like I'm seeing it with a whole new set of eyes. This isn't someone else's potential mess, it's my mess—our mess—and I'm leaving Bryce to be the one who mostly deals with it.

I was shocked, but elated, when he told me he had taken my advice to heart and Josie was coming with him. Despite my anticipation to get things moving on the pool, I gave them a chance to breathe. They'd both uprooted their lives—Josie for the first time—and moved out here to do this with me. The least I could do was give them a few of weeks to get settled before I sprung how bad things were on them.

Our focus turned to getting Bryce on all the necessary paper-work. Then, before I knew it, I was headed to Budapest for World Championships while they hung back and figured out their lives in

Columbia. Now, here we are, with Worlds behind us, and a huge mess in front of us.

"Okay, you weren't wrong." Bryce is walking the deck along the outside pool, the last thing we need to see. "This isn't nearly as bad as the rest of it."

The bleachers probably needed to be replaced for safety reasons. The pool would need to be repainted and minor repairs made. We'd need new starting blocks, but otherwise, it wasn't in too bad of shape. "I think it'd be great to host meets out here."

There's a glint in Bryce's eyes as he looks around. I can tell he's imagining it like I'd done. "Yeah, it'd be cool if we could get some pro meets out here."

"Now who's getting ahead of themselves?" I taunt, earning a laugh from my best friend. "You ready to get out of here?"

He takes one more look around the pool before nodding. "Yeah, let's grab lunch."

We settle on Brick Tavern, a local bar and restaurant known for their burgers, according to Bryce, at least. Apparently, this place came to the rescue for him and Josie when they first moved here and found themselves too exhausted from unpacking to cook.

Honestly, I wasn't hard to please when it came to food. As long as someone else was making it—because I can't cook to save my life—I'm good.

Brick Tavern is a modern place with an industrial vibe, all dark wood and metal accents. TVs showing various sports hang throughout the place, but the volume is low and the music fades into the background, making it more suitable for a lunch crowd. There are even university students studying with empty plates at the corners of their books.

Eventually, this city will be my home, or I hope it will anyway. Right now, I feel like a visitor who didn't do enough research before picking a destination.

"We should come up with some sort of plan," he says.

It doesn't surprise me that Bryce immediately gets down to business as soon as we placed our orders and we each have a draft beer in front of us. He has always been the kind of guy who liked to know the objective, the one who kept me steady and focused when my excitement got ahead of me.

If he'd been there when I first saw the pool, we would have had this plan in place before we even made an offer on the building.

I nod, fiddling with my beer. "And we obviously can't do any of the repairs ourselves. We'll have to hire someone to come in, do a design, and orchestrate the rebuild or remodel—whatever it's called."

"I'm sure we can find a company to do everything. It'll mostly be Josie and I handling it. How soon do you want to have it up and running after the Games?"

"Within a couple of months. The timeline won't matter if I don't make the team, though." Bryce presses his lips together, a sure sign he wants to yell at me. "My times were shit at Worlds. You know it's true."

"They were not shit. You walked away with three medals."

"Only one of which was gold," I shoot back. We've been doing this most of our lives, building each other up while we tear ourselves down. It's a game we are rather good at by now. "I'm not promised a spot on the team, and you know it."

"I also know you'll be training your ass off for the next several months, Carter. That's why I'm here, because you bought this thing, and it's going to be great, but you can't deal with it right now. So do what you need to do and trust me to do the rest."

My brow arches. "I cannot ask you to do that."

"You're not asking me, dude." He sighs. "I'm not even offering. We're business partners, and this is what business partners do. They step up when the other one can't take something on. Do you really think I moved here thinking you'd be available every day to make decisions? No way. You'll be here when it counts and, in the meantime, go finish your shit."

Finish my shit.

That's what I'm doing. I'm on the last leg of a career I dedicated my entire life to, worked day in and day out for. I won't even be thirty until this July, but I was already facing the r-word. Retirement. It's something every swimmer expects, to be retired far younger than any of our non-swimmer friends, but the meaning is different for us.

Retirement, to me, feels like I'm saying goodbye to my life's work. It's not the end of hard work, more the shift to something I haven't allowed myself to think about yet. I know it's time. I considered retiring when Bryce did, but I felt like I still had more things to accomplish. Things I'm not sure I'll be able to see through now that they're staring me down. Less than one year until Trials, and it feels like the ticking of a bomb.

"Does it ever get easier, man?"

Bryce looks up from his phone, brows furrowed in confusion. I don't say anything. I don't need to. A second later, he's setting his phone down on the table and giving me his full attention. "I don't know if easier is the right word, but it's not as daunting, I guess."

I almost tease him about his word choice. I've never heard him use the word "daunting" before. Maybe living with a writer is helping with his vocabulary.

"I didn't deal with it the same way you did, though," he argues. "I didn't pick an Olympic year and decide that was when I'd be done. Maybe I did initially, but I had an injury I couldn't bounce back from, and I just knew it was time."

"But how?" I stress. "What if I'm not ready to say goodbye? What if I should have said goodbye years ago?"

"Well, it's too late to change the past," he replies. "You can change the future. You haven't made it officially known you're planning to retire. If you get out there and decide you want to go for another year, or two, or three, then you do it. It's your life, dude."

"I bought a pool," I pointed out.

"And signed your best friend on as a co-owner." He waves me off. "If you decide to keep going, then I'll find another washed-up swimmer who can help me coach. My phone is full of numbers, Carter. Stop worrying about the what-ifs. I've got your back."

I know it's true, but that knowledge isn't necessarily going to be enough to make me believe there's nothing to worry about. I'd never felt so untethered from my life before, and it was freaking me out. All of Bryce's advice came from a genuine place of care, because he can't tell me how to live my life, but I find myself wishing someone would tell me what to do.

Being an adult sucks.

The server arriving with our food prevents me from continuing down the spiral I was rapidly heading toward. Despite knowing

Bryce would be more than willing to listen and offer advice, I felt like I'd laid enough on him now. I was set to go back to Georgia tomorrow morning, already hitting the grind in preparation for the Olympic year just months away. For now, I just want to hang out with Bryce.

True to his word, Bryce is handling it.

A week after our walkthrough at the pool, I have an email waiting for me after a weight training session with the subject line: Josie says we can't use power tools. Laughing to myself, I open the email and scan the list of companies that will manage everything from design to overseeing the construction process. He also added several notes about the general length of time we could expect to spend on this and a general budget.

The projected budget—from his research—nearly made my eyes bug out of my head. I knew it'd be expensive, but damn. I'm going to have to win several gold medals to pay for this.

He requests I scan through the companies and let him know which ones to start calling. He'd handle all the initial interactions, he informs me, and then we'll get together to go over the quotes and make our decision as a team.

The weight lifts off my shoulders at the realization I'm not alone in this. Bryce was serious that day in the bar—he can handle it. He wants to handle it. He'll take care of everything in Columbia, and I'll stay back in Georgia, trying to make my last team.

I can figure out the rest of my life later.

Chapter 2

October 2023

Head down, I push into the crowded conference room. My colleagues crowd around a table set up with coffee and pastries from the bakery across the street. The smell is enticing, but I know better than to head to that table.

It's bad enough I'm the only female contractor in this misogynistic frat house, but God forbid the girl with curves eats a baked good. It was a lesson I learned the hard way and have no interest in ever repeating. Instead, I keep to myself as I slip into an empty chair, not too close to the front, but not too far away, either. I scan the agenda already laid out before me, then pretend to be engrossed in something on my phone.

Of course, I'm not actually looking at anything. I don't have any active projects right now and the only person who would maybe text me is my boyfriend. However, I'm sure Will is sleeping after a long overnight shift at the hospital. Besides, after being together for two years, we've moved past the honeymoon phase of needing to text each other throughout the day.

A few minutes later, Thomas Dalton enters the room with his assistant Nadine, the only other female in the office, trailing behind him. "Take a seat, everyone."

Thomas might look like your typical southern gentleman who's used to hard work, but it couldn't be further from the truth. Don't be fooled by the jeans and casual button-down. Thomas inherited a dynasty and has only continued to build it up in the years since he took over. Dalton Enterprises is responsible for some of the biggest builds South Carolina has seen in the last eighty years and has even been known to take on private homes and housing communities.

No project is too big or small. Let us build your dream. That's our motto.

It doesn't matter if no one here actually cares about the clients we work with, it's all about the appearance and reputation we have. If we appear to be one big, happy family, the community will buy into it and trust us to help build it up. We'll make money, we'll get our name in the media, and we'll keep growing until we're the only name that comes to mind for design and construction.

If I had it my way, we'd focus more on family homes and giving back to the community who has given us so much.

Not that it matters. I'm just the stepdaughter. I'll never take this company over. Thomas has his eye set on a few of my male colleagues for the role. Right now, I'm lucky I have a job. I'm even luckier if I'm given one project a quarter—I'm never given more than one at a time, and they're usually short-term, and so ridiculously easy I can do them in my sleep.

I'm the most disposable employee in this entire office, but he knows he can't get rid of me.

"Let's get this meeting started." Thomas calls the room to attention with only his tone of voice as everyone takes their seats. "We have a number of proposals to get through today, but I think we should start with the one no one will want: a sports complex in Columbia."

Everyone around me groans.

"Why didn't you pass on this one, boss?" Brent, the office asshole but one of Thomas's favorites, asks. "You had to know how we'd all react."

"But why?" I speak up, earning several surprised looks. I tend to wait to be spoken to in these meetings. Now that I have everyone's attention, I have to finish my point. "What's the big deal? We haven't even heard what all it'll entail."

Brent leers at me, eyes sparkling with amusement. There's nothing this guy loves more than being able to mansplain something to me. "This happens every four years or so, Katrina, typically in conjunction with the Olympics. Everyone gets the sports bug and wants to open the complex their community so desperately needs. These projects are rarely seen through, or they end up falling apart and being abandoned a year after opening. They're a waste of time."

"This one might not be," Thomas breaks in, bringing everyone's attention back to him. "It's owned by two Olympic swimmers, Bryce Clark and Carter Abrams. One of them is retired, the other will be retiring at the conclusion of the 2024 Games. They want a full natatorium they can coach a team out of. That means there will be two pools, a full gym, seats for spectators, offices, and fully equipped locker rooms. This one has the potential to pull through. They want it open by next fall."

Brent leans back in his seat. "Which is why we're taking this one, because it's tied to two big names? I'm still not taking the job, boss."

Thomas picks up a small packet full of the project details. "Well, it's a good thing I was going to have Liam take the design lead on this one."

Embarrassed anger flushes Brent's cheeks as I hold back a snicker. I can see Nadine doing the same thing out of the corner of my eye, and it takes everything in me not to turn to share a commiserating look with her.

Brent thinks he's God's gift to women and architecture, but the reality is he's more of a walking red flag in both areas. His designs are modern, cold, and impersonal. He wouldn't know what natural light and color was if it smacked him in the face. Just like he wouldn't know what basic human decency is if his life depended on it. The longest relationship he's had since I've known him was a total of five months, and he believes Nadine and I are here for his visual and physical entertainment.

Liam will be a good fit for a project like this. Based on the little information Thomas has shared with us, I get the sense these two athletes are passionate about what they're doing, and Liam will take that into consideration with his designs. He's the only architect on the team I enjoy working with. He's a good guy, who listens to his clients, and succeeds in bringing their vision to life. It's not about putting his name on a shiny new building for Liam; it's about building things that matter.

"I'd be happy to take this on, Mr. Dalton." Okay, so maybe Liam is a bit of an ass-kisser, but he's only been here for a year. He's still trying to get on Thomas's good side—if one exists—and he's one of the younger architects here. "Who's the lead contractor going to be?"

Groans and sounds of protest echo from every single man on my team.

And I don't get it. I don't know what a project like this will look like, but someone has to take it on. Maybe this could be a chance for me to prove myself. I'll have all the plans drawn up by Liam, who I know is exceptionally good at his job. All I have to do is oversee the renovation, which is literally my job, and I'm damn good at it. Despite my stepfather's inability to see it.

"I can take it." The words come tumbling out of my mouth before I can stop them, and every head turns to look at me once again.

I fight the urge to sink back in my seat, pretending I hadn't said anything.

Thomas arches a brow. "I'm not sure this project is the right one for you, Katrina."

Now I do feel myself sinking under his amused look.

"Why not?" Liam speaks up from across the table. He grins in my direction when I look at him. My heart is erratic in my chest. "In fact, I would prefer to work with Katrina on this one."

His encouragement gives me motivation to fight for myself, too. I sit up straighter. "You already know Liam and I work well together; every project you've paired us up for has been completed on time and under budget. No one else wants to take it on, but you clearly don't want to lose it. Let me take this job."

I can practically see the wheels turning in Thomas's head. Yes, this is a big project, but there's really no way I can mess it up. He would get everything he wants. Dalton Enterprises would be associated with a couple of Olympians, and he'd have me out of his hair for several months. It's shocking for him to take so long to say yes.

"All right, the job is yours, Katrina." He finally relents, but he lifts his chin until he can stare down his nose at me. "However, I expect weekly updates. Also, the clients have been extremely strict about staying on budget. It's a nonnegotiable to them."

I hold my head a little taller. "I'll get it done on time and under budget." It's a tall promise to make, especially since I haven't seen a single thing on the project, but I'm committed to see this chance through. No one will be disappointed. "Whatever updates you want, I'll provide them."

Thomas doesn't look impressed, but he also doesn't change his mind. "Nadine, please get both Liam and Katrina the full file. Liam will need to meet with them to go over plans and be sure to secure an appropriate rental for Katrina to stay in during the project."

Unable to hide her own grin, Nadine nods, and takes notes. I'm suddenly more anxious for this meeting to end than I was before it started. I want to get my hands on the file. I want to talk to Liam about any preliminary plans he has. I'm itching to get started on a project for the first time in literal years. My desire to dive headfirst into a project is back, and it's exhilarating. I'm ready to work on building something that will matter to someone.

More than that, I'm ready to finally prove my worth to every person in this goddamn room. Prove to them I deserve to be here and not only because of who my stepfather is.

He has never given me much of anything, despite what so many people think. I was twelve when he came into my life and never really left, but never became a part of it either. He remained on the sidelines as my life continued. When he married my mother a year later, he gave me his name. I didn't have much of a say in that matter. She wanted us to appear like a united front, a perfect little ready-made family. So that's what we became.

The well-respected developer and doctor, with the well-behaved daughter that never caused them any issues. It was the role we all needed to play, and we did it well. The only reason I have this job now is because of the way my mother wants society to view us. All Thomas had to do was hire me. He didn't need to give me any real authority or duties. The sexist asshole made sure a woman's name wasn't on anything important.

Until now. I'm not naïve enough to think he won't be taking credit for most of my work, reminding me of where my last name came from, but it's a start. I'm not sure I need the credit and the glory; I want enough space to be able to do my job. If I screw this up, I'll never have this chance again. Hell, it'd probably end up being the one thing he could use to get rid of me, like he's always wanted.

So, I better not screw this up.

By the time I get back to my desk, I'm feeling confident in my ability to make this project a success. The quick pep talk from Nadine and Liam has me floating on cloud nine, my confidence at an all-time high. It's a feeling I don't have all that often, so I want to keep riding it as long as I can.

As per my usual routine of things, I scan through the brief on the request for a proposal, taking note of the contact information of the two owners. Their emails are personal ones, not tied to business accounts, which makes me relax even more. They have as much to lose if this doesn't work out as I do.

Well, maybe not just as much. After all, they're Olympians, and I'm only a contractor from South Carolina, who desperately wants to get out from underneath her family's overbearing thumb. Still, we're practically one and the same.

Next on my to-do list is an introductory email. The three of us won't meet until it's time to break ground, but I always prefer to let clients know who's on their team right up front. That way, there are no surprises. I move my mouse until my computer comes to life and click into my email, starting a new draft:

```
Dear Mr. Abrams and Mr. Clark,

My name is Katrina Dalton and I'm a
contractor with Dalton Enterpris-
es. I am reaching out to intro-
duce myself as the second half of
your design team. Once you approve
the design elements with Liam,
I'll take over the construction
process.
To oversee the project to the best
of my ability, I'll be temporarily
relocating to Columbia and will
be available to assist in any
way I can. I'm looking forward to
getting to work with you both to
bring your vision to life. I'll
```

be working closely with Liam to
ensure all your expectations are
met.
Our current timeline has us scheduled to break ground on January
2, 2024, following the holiday.
This will allow us to keep up
with your proposed timeline and
give us extra time should the need
arise, though I don't anticipate
it will. If you have questions,
please don't hesitate to reach out
to me or Liam. We will be more than
happy to assist you. All my contact
information is listed below.
I look forward to working with you!

Best,
Katrina Dalton
Contractor
Dalton Enterprises

As soon as I send the email, I switch my focus to the project folder Liam has already set up and sent through to me. There's not much in there, though—just some preliminary photos of the property, a document of notes, and some research he's done on other natatoriums around the country. I open the folders first.

The moment I do, my stomach drops. This place is a mess. It's not the worst I've seen, but it's not the easy turnover I was expecting to see based on what I was told in the meeting. Just looking at the first picture, a sinking feeling has me doubting my ability to keep this under budget and on schedule, which is another one of the mottos of Dalton Enterprises. Honestly, for a company who doesn't give a shit about people, we have a lot of those.

I'm still on the first picture when I reach for a legal pad and pen to jot down my own notes. There is only so much I can tell about this place from the photos, but there are areas I'll want to focus on. With each picture I click through, my notes get more extensive.

Over the hour, I become fully engrossed. I can start to see this project coming together. Liam's designs will heighten the appeal that's already there and we'll be able to pull together a really great place—lots of natural light and comfortable seating for those enjoying the pools. It can be a great place; I can see why the owners wanted it.

An incoming email pulls me from my daydreaming. It's from Mr. Abrams.

```
Hello Katrina,
Thank you for reaching out. Bryce
and I are looking forward to work-
ing with you both on this project
as well. I appreciate your willing-
ness to relocate for the duration
of the rebuild. It shows a level
of commitment we're used to but

rarely see in other people.
With that being said, I'm not sure
how often our paths will cross. You
```

will primarily be working with,
and getting approval from, Bryce.
He'll be the one on site, as I'll
be remaining in Georgia to continue training for the Olympics. I'm
sure I'll be around occasionally,
but he will provide most of the
updates to me.
If something important does come
up, or you need me specifically,
I can be available, so please
don't hesitate to reach out when
needed. All I ask is for your
understanding, since my schedule
might not allow me to have a prompt
response time.
Let us know if you need anything
else from us,
Carter Abrams.

I'm caught off guard by the email. Thomas had told us one of them was still swimming, but there was no mention of him not being available during the construction process. Most of the time, I'm fairly hands off with the clients but with a project this large, and me relocating for it, we'll end up sharing the same spaces at least every so often. I'm sure they'll want to utilize any of the rooms they can during the construction, as they're trying to grow a business. Which is fine, as it means they're easily available when I need to run something by them, but it's not helpful when only one owner is present.

And what did he mean his schedule doesn't allow him to have a prompt response time? He's a swimmer! What more could he possibly need to do other than swim? I know I'm out of my element with this job, but come on, even I'm not that dense.

At least he told me I could reach out to him if I need to. I know better than to rely on only one owner to make decisions. Someone always ends up mad when we end up cutting the one thing they were dying to have. Communication is key in business, and I'll be damned if Carter isn't part of this and ends up disappointed with the results. He's not messing this chance up for me because he's too busy to answer a phone call or email.

Chapter 3

Katrina

November and December 2023

"Hello, ladies," Liam greets, sliding into the empty chair across from me. "Mind if I join you?"

"Can we say no if you're already sitting down?" Nadine teases, earning a playful glare from him. "Don't look at me like that! I can still be a jerk if you want me to."

"You a jerk? Never."

As their playful banter continues, I watch with a small smile on my face. They don't need me to participate. The two of them have been heading toward something since they first met. Neither of them is willing to make the first move. For now, I get to enjoy watching it all unfold. I don't intervene, confident that one day they'll figure it out on their own.

We might have to wait a lifetime for it to happen, though.

"We're finalizing the plans for the Columbia project next week." Liam pulls me back into the conversation moments later, unwrapping his burrito as he does. "Then everything should be good on my end, until something inevitably comes up."

I don't even try to hide my surprise. "Wow, that was fast. Did they not want to make a lot of changes?"

In all actuality, it's not that surprising. How many ways can you change designs for a swimming complex? Besides, Liam is damn good at his job. I'd be more surprised if they did have a lot.

"Not too many," he admits. "Some things we had to compromise functionality over design on, but I'm used to that happening."

I make a face at the mention of my least favorite aspect of the job. There's nothing worse than having a beautiful design torn to shreds because the structure of the building won't allow it to happen. Usually, I'm the one giving Liam news like that. It's kind of nice not to be the bad guy this time around.

"Wow, and I haven't even gotten in there yet." It's my turn to tease him as I stab at my salad with my fork. It's not that it's bad, it's just his burrito looks—and smells—better. "Just wait until that happens."

Groaning, he turns to Nadine. "Do you see what she does to me? Kat loves to ruin my best plans. I'll never forget the first time we worked together. She was in there for one day and I had to change my whole design."

I gasp, pointing at him with my fork. "That is not my fault! You didn't even attempt to see if that was load bearing, and it clearly was. It was the first thing I noticed when I walked in the door. After that, everything else unraveled."

Nadine grins, looking between us. "To me, it sounds like Kat is good at her job."

I beam at her. "Thank you!"

Liam playfully rolls his eyes. "I should have known you'd take her side."

"Women need to stick together!" She nudges me with her elbow, and I nod in agreement. "Especially in a men's club like this."

He shakes his head. "Do not lump me in with those assholes, please." He knows neither one of us ever would. He's nothing like the rest of the guys who work here. Which should be obvious because he's eating with us, not with them. "In all seriousness, Kat, their changes aren't that big of a deal and have more to do with their functionality than the buildings. Which is probably a good thing, because we're kind of out of our element here, right?"

Still picking at my salad, I frown at him. "How do you mean?"

"Neither one of us knows what to do with a pool! I have no idea what a training center ran by professional swimmers needs. Sure, I can do research, but it's not the same thing as actually knowing."

I look at him like he's crazy. "What are you talking about? You've worked on sports complexes before."

"Baseball stadiums and football fields, not a pool," he argues.

"All they need is a pool, and you already said that." I wave him off. "The rest is detail. Right, Nadine?"

"Actually, there are a lot of things a well-equipped natatorium would need that you might not be thinking of."

Her tone is so quiet, so reserved, that I'm not sure I even heard anything she said, but then the realization dawns on me that she knows something about this sport. At least, something more than both Liam and I combined. He and I exchange a look of surprise. Then I focus back on Nadine, who's focused on her lunch.

"What are we missing, Nadine?" I press, wanting whatever wisdom she can offer us.

"And how do you know anything about this?" Liam adds, his surprise more evident in his tone than mine. "Are you a swimming fan or something?"

Looking up, she looks between the two of us and nods. "I used to swim in high school and college. I do some volunteer coaching and lessons at the community center downtown."

When I look back at Liam, I can see it clear as day. The incoming insult, meant to be a joke, is visible on his face before it can come tumbling out of his mouth. I try to catch his eye, clear my throat—anything to stop him before he makes a huge mistake.

But it's too late.

His brow arches as he takes in her body, looking her up and down as if he is seeing her for the first time. "You used to swim? What happened?"

I kick him in the shin, ensuring the slight heel of my bootie is the thing making impact from under the table. He hisses, glaring at me.

"Damn, Kat," he whines, bending down to rub his leg. "What the hell was that for?"

I nod to Nadine, but the damage has already been done. In the time it took me to kick him, she's stood and gathered all her stuff. Her head is ducked, but I can see the heat coating her cheeks. Realization dawns on Liam's features as he stands, attempting to stop her. She barely looks at him as she takes a step to the side and walks back toward her desk.

Leaning back in my seat with my arms crossed over my chest as I glare at the only good guy in this whole damn building.

His shoulders sag as he takes his seat again. "Kat, please don't. I know, okay, and I'm sorry."

"I'm not the person you should be apologizing to." My tone is icy, my view of Liam changing right before my eyes. "Fatphobia isn't funny, and it's not cute."

He looks like he's ready to make an excuse or say something to argue with me, but he doesn't. "I know," he sighs out instead. "And I know I owe her an apology. I promise I'll make it up to her."

"If she lets you," I challenge back, standing to gather my things. "You were supposed to be the one who's different, Liam."

"I am! I messed up," he pleads. "Are you seriously that mad at me, Kat?"

I shake my head. "Not mad, disappointed."

I'm disappointed in the way I am when people turn out to be something other than what I thought them to be. Disappointed to know my friend was crushing on a man who could make cruel jokes. I don't want her in a relationship like that, don't want her in a relationship like the one I have. I can handle mine, because I've developed thick skin, but I never want her to have to do that.

"You know, it's really not that hard to not be a dick," I tell him. "You've done such a good job up until now."

"I'm going to make this up to her—prove to you both that I'm not that kind of guy," he insists. "I made a mistake."

I shrug. "Mistakes have consequences, Liam, and now you have to face them."

There's soft music playing as I stand at the stove, focusing on the chicken breasts I'm searing in the pan. My boyfriend, Will, sits at the island, reading something on his phone. He hasn't said much since he got to my apartment, except asking when dinner will be ready. I'd barely been home for five minutes when he walked in asking the question, so my response had been a little snippy. I should have known it'd cause him to go quiet.

In less than two months, I'll be heading to Columbia for the next six months and I haven't told him yet. I know him well enough to know he's going to be mad. Angry about how I made the decision without talking to him, but we haven't seen much of each other in the last few weeks, so I'm not sure when I would have had time to say anything.

Besides, it's not like I'm going to a different state. Columbia is less than two hours away from Charleston, which is an easy distance to visit each other. Although, I have the feeling I'll be the one making the drive the most often, as Will's job as a resident at the best hospital in the city keeps him occupied. It's not like I'm moving away. I'll still have my tiny guest house on the back half of Thomas and my mom's lot, and he'll still have his apartment.

We could do long distance. Hell, sometimes I feel like most of our relationship has been long distance, despite living in the same city. We've never been the couple who constantly need to be around one another.

"I have some news I want to share with you!" The smile on my face is as big as it can be when I glance over at Will, who doesn't give a single indication he's heard me. "Hello? Earth to Will?"

At my raised voice, his gaze snaps up from the phone with a scowl. "Yes, Katrina? I was reading something."

Every fiber of my being is itching to start a fight with him, but I resist and keep on smiling. "And I'm trying to have a date night with you. Couples usually use this time to talk and catch up with life."

"Don't be a petulant child." He, surprisingly, puts his phone down to give me his full attention. "What is it you want to tell me?"

I'm more used to his condescending remarks than I should be, but they still sting. He uses them all the time, almost like they're his love language. Every time he says one, I hear the old cliché about how if a boy is mean to you, it's because he likes you. Will obviously likes me. We've been together for two years, but I was hoping he'd eventually stop talking to me this way.

"Thomas has given me a new project to oversee," I explain, turning the temperature down on the chicken. "And it's a big one this time. It'll take several months."

Now I have his undivided attention. "Yeah? What is it?"

"A natatorium." The word, which I didn't even know existed until a couple of weeks ago, still feels weird on my tongue, making it painfully obvious I don't know what I'm talking about. "You used to swim in college, right?"

"I had a scholarship." He shrugs like it's no big deal. Which is fine, because maybe it's not a big deal to get a scholarship for swimming. I don't know anything about the sport. It's not something Will keeps up with, at least not to my knowledge, and I only found out about it because I came across a medal while cleaning. "Who's the design lead on the project?"

"Liam." The scowl is back, and I sigh. "I don't understand what your problem with him is. He's only ever been nice to you and he's literally the only decent guy I work with."

"He's too invested in you and hasn't gotten the hint to back off."

The notion that Will feels threatened by Liam is laughable to me. Especially because he's clearly into Nadine, if he can get his foot out of his mouth and make it up to her.

"That's ridiculous. He's not into me or anything like that, trust me. We work together, and we do it well. He'll finish the design aspect and I'll be in Columbia to oversee the project."

"How long will you be in Columbia?"

"They gave us seven months, but we'd ideally like it to be six," I say.

"You'll be building as the Olympics are happening?" Will asks. I shrug because I guess. I'm not even sure when the Olympics are. I just know they're sometime soon. "Do you know who's opening the natatorium? They must not be competing now."

"Apparently they're both Olympians," I explain, flipping one of the chicken breasts in the pan. "One of them, Bryce, is retired. The other one, Carter, is going to Paris, or something."

"It won't be guaranteed until June." I'm not sure what Will means by that, exactly, but he's interested in what I'm saying now. "Are you talking about Bryce Clark and Carter Abrams?"

My jaw drops open. Do all swimmers know each other? "Wait, are you friends with Olympians?"

He rolls his eyes like I'd asked something ridiculous. Who knows? Maybe I did. "That's not how it works, Katrina. We're not friends. I swam against them in college. So, our paths crossed that way."

"Do you not like them? I haven't met them yet. Are they nice?" I was suddenly desperate to know something, anything, about the people I'd be working with for half a year. "Liam says they're cool, and they've seemed nice—"

"I don't know, Katrina!" he snaps, jaw clenched. "I haven't seen them in eight years, and we never talked. We were rivals."

I know better than to keep pestering him, I do, but this is a side of Will I've never seen. The snark and annoyance, yes, but not the side that's willingly talking about swimming. Something he's always seemed a little embarrassed to be part of. "Come on, Will, there has to be something you can tell me."

"They're jocks, Katrina." He rolls his eyes. "They never had a plan to be anything but a professional athlete, no drive to make anything more of themselves. It looks like they accomplished that, but I'm sure they're as shallow as they've always been. I'm going to take a shower now."

He's out of his chair so quickly I barely have time to register what he says before he's already heading toward the bathroom. I glance down at the chicken that's done. "But dinner is literally done, Will."

"I'll eat when I'm done," he calls back. "Don't wait for me."

Something in me crumbles as I hear the door shut behind him. Looking over at the table I'd set up, I realize it was, once again, for nothing. It doesn't matter how hard I try to rekindle whatever flame we once had, he would be there to blow it out. Date night means nothing more to him than a chance to have someone else feed him. There's no connection anymore and I'm not sure how to get it back.

Maybe this project in Columbia came at the perfect time. This time—and distance—apart might be good for us. It could be what we need to save our relationship.

⌒

I arrive in Columbia on the twenty-sixth of December, which gives me more than enough time to get settled in my rental before we break ground on January second. I'm meeting with Bryce and Carter on the twenty-ninth to go over the schedule and do the walkthrough with the two of them from a contractor's perspective. Everything I would normally do during this free time has already been done. The demo crew is going to be on-site bright and early on the second. I've triple checked with all my subcontractors for the first phase, and I have Liam's plans memorized, complete with areas I worry we might run into trouble.

Which means I have a few days off to relax.

My rental is a cute little townhome, not too far from the pool, and I'm instantly pulled into the quaintness of it. Unsurprisingly, it's much bigger than anything I would need. I knew Nadine would find me a nice place, complete with a room for Liam should he need to be on-site for anything. I'm going to be more than comfortable for the next several months.

Hell, there might even be a part of me that never wants to leave.

Once I put my stuff down, I snap some photos of the place and send them to Nadine and Will. To Nadine, I compliment her on her choices and thank her for making sure I had a place I'd feel comfortable in. To Will, I want my boyfriend to see the nice place I'm staying at, stressing that he can come and spend some nights with me. He responds with how it would depend on his schedule. I've been with Will long enough to know that means no. If I want to see him, I'm going to have to go and see him in Charleston. He won't be coming to me.

Lying back against the couch, I'm overcome with the reality that this is the first time I've ever been alone. All through college, I lived at home with Thomas and my mother. Now, as an adult with a job at my stepfather's company, I'm still living on their property, where my mother can appear out of nowhere to comment on my life. At work, Thomas has only ever given me local jobs. So, for the first time, I am truly on my own in a city I don't know.

The fear creeps in then, making me realize that if something were to happen, the people I'm closest to are two hours away, minimum. At nearly thirty, this is a feeling I should have experienced by now, but it's all new to me. The eerie quiet, the reality that no one will appear at my front door unannounced. Part of me hates it, part of me is terrified of it.

But there's another part of me, a bigger part, I think, that is loving it. Independence is something I've longed to have my whole life but have been denied time and time again. The realization of how big this chance is dawns on me. Not only am I proving myself from a work standpoint, but I'm also proving to my family that I can be on my own. I don't have to have someone to depend on.

It's scary, sure, but it's more of a thrill than anything else, and I owe it to myself to take this opportunity for what it is.

Chapter 4

Katrina

December 2023

The first thing I notice when I pull into the pool's parking lot is that the building doesn't look nearly as bad as I remember it being.

Last month, as Liam worked with the owners to finalize the plan and budget, he and I had done a walkthrough on our own. The inside was a chaotic mess, complete with an unpleasant odor that wasn't residual chlorine. I hadn't paid too much attention to the concrete exterior, tucked snuggly into a wooded area, too focused on what I'd find inside. Now, I'm beginning to think I let the inside taint the outside in my memory.

The second thing I notice is that someone else is already here. Just one car, though, not two. Then again, the owners could have driven here together.

I pull into one of the many empty parking spaces, but the one that leaves one between myself and the shiny black car. It's nothing special, standard, and functional, but definitely new. And certainly not the flashy car I'd expect an Olympian to drive. As I cut my engine, the other driver exits his car.

And boy, is he tall. He stands well over six feet, with shoulders so broad I wonder how they even manage to fit in a car like that. He's styled his dirty blond hair to be slightly disheveled. He's dressed the way I expect a professional—or former professional—athlete to dress. In nice black joggers, sneakers, and a dark green, long-sleeved shirt that shows off his well-defined arms.

I glance down at my outfit, feeling a bit overdressed. My white T-shirt, jeans, sneakers, and gray blazer isn't anything too special, but it's more than I typically wear to a job site. Especially when considering I'm wearing makeup and my hair is done. I wanted to make a good impression, and impressions start with appearances.

Grabbing my stuff, I exit my car with a warm smile, ready to dazzle. "Hi there! I'm Katrina Dalton."

Hi there? Internally, I cringe. I just made myself sound like either an old southern grandma or an overly chatty soccer mom. Neither of which I am. Clearly.

He takes a few steps toward me to shake my outstretched hand, his smile more reserved than mine. "Bryce Clark, nice to meet you."

"Nice to meet you, Mr. Clark." I glance around the parking lot. There's still no one else here. "Is Mr. Abrams already inside, or is he joining us later?"

Bryce's brow furrows. "No, he won't be joining us at all. He's training in Georgia. He told me he'd sent you an email months ago explaining this."

I fight to keep the smile on my face. "Yes, I did receive that email. However, he also mentioned he'd be available should the need be pertinent. I expected he'd be here for this meeting."

Bryce is shaking his head before I even finish my thought. "I apologize for any misunderstanding, but he and I both agreed this meeting isn't one he needed to be involved in."

"I'm sorry?" I question, trying not to sound as offended as I suddenly feel.

"That came out wrong. I'm sorry." He goes to backpedal. "It's just that we've already approved Liam's plans, which was something he needed to be involved in. The season is about to kick off, and with his first meet next week, we both agreed he didn't need to be here to go over a construction schedule. I figured you and I were more than capable of handling this, correct?"

Keep smiling, girl, I tell myself. "Absolutely! We should get started then."

The layout of the building is a tad strange, at least to me, but it works for the purpose the property is serving. Structurally, there shouldn't be anything major we have to change, and I'm grateful for that. It's laid out like a large L with the indoor aspects taking up the larger side and the outdoor pool shooting out toward the back behind the lobby. The lobby leads into both pools and the locker rooms while the upstairs houses the offices and full gym. Overall, it didn't feel like a complex project, it just has a lot of moving parts.

Which is why I wanted to have this meeting. It's my chance to walk the property with the client and get their input on everything. The more questions I asked, the smoother the construction would go once we get started. What I wasn't expecting was for Bryce to have just as many questions as me.

"I'm excited to get more natural light in here." The indoor pool is dark and a little depressing. Liam's design features more natural light and a wall of windows in the gym that'll overlook the pool. "I think it'll add a great element to this space."

Although Bryce nods, he doesn't look convinced. "Hopefully, the humidity won't make it pointless. I like the idea, but I also don't see the point in spending a bunch of time and money on something that doesn't even matter."

"What makes you think it wouldn't matter? They won't be fogged over all the time. I'm sure the people using the pool will find it wonderful."

"Or it'll blind them," he argues. "It doesn't matter which side of the pool the windows are on, the sun will directly hit them at least once a day. I want to make sure no one is blinded during meets—coaches or spectators."

My frustration is growing by the minute with him. Will's words from the last night at my place flutter to the front of my mind, reminding me this man doesn't know how to be anything other than an athlete. He's not thinking like a business owner who needs to consider the design of his building. He's being cocky, acting like he knows more than me because he's been to the Olympics. I can't let him undermine my authority or knowledge at every turn.

"I understand your concern, but there's not always going to be a meet here," I point out with a tight, professional smile. "You need to think about all the people who will be using this space."

Bryce stands straighter, squaring his broad shoulders. "This is a training center, Katrina. When we're not hosting meets, swimmers will be training for hours a day. I need to make sure you understand this isn't a fun pool for families to come and hang out at."

Ready to get my point across, I place a hand on my hip and pin him with an unwavering look. "Do you really expect me to believe this building will never be open for recreational swimming?" His slight hesitation is all the answer I need. "You need to think about everyone who'll use this pool, Mr. Clark."

"Bryce," he corrects. "Look, it will probably be open to some recreational swimming, especially in the beginning, but it's not the primary use for this. We'll have serious swimmers using this space more often than not."

Deciding to let him believe he's a little in control of this meeting, I nod sagely. "Yes, serious swimmers, I understand. That's who the design is catering to, and I'll make sure it isn't lost. Shall we continue upstairs?"

He doesn't look convinced, but he relents, stepping aside to let me take the lead. As we exit the indoor pool, I look back at it, picturing the wall of windows I know will be in there soon enough, and imagine what it'll look like bathed in natural light with the sun reflecting off the water. I might even have to go swimming once it's all done. It'll be great.

About an hour later, Bryce and I come to a stop at the disheveled desk in the lobby area. I set the portfolio folder I brought with me on the counter, flipping it open to make sure there isn't anything else I needed to go over with him. "That's all I have to go over with you today. Are there questions you want to ask me?"

Hands stuffed in the pockets of his sweatpants, he shakes his head. "Not at the moment. You've covered everything I wanted to discuss with you."

This is one of those moments I wish Thomas were here for, so he can see firsthand how good I am at my job. I am transparent with the clients we work with, and build a relationship of trust and commitment, so I can anticipate their needs before they arise. I know it doesn't matter. Nothing I do will ever be enough to make him understand how capable I am.

"Great!" I snap the folder closed, a little more forcefully than I mean to, and reach down to stuff it in my bag. "Are you sure you want to be present to help with the cleanout and demo? Just because I offer the option to my clients doesn't mean I expect everyone to take me up on it. It's up to you."

"Why do you offer it if you don't expect them to take you up on the offer?"

It's something I started offering after I worked on a few home remodels. There was something grounding about them getting the chance to get their hands dirty. They wanted to be an active part of their project. I never expect businesses to take me up on it, mainly because if they're fresh builds, there is no demo. But with Bryce, I had the feeling he'd take me up on the offer, as he already seems connected and protective of this place.

"It can be rather cathartic," I explain as I hoist my bag on my shoulder. "It helps the transition phase and makes you feel like you're getting a fresh start."

The grin that overtakes his features is open and honest. It's something I had yet to see, and it's a little disarming. "That's why I'll be here. This is a clean slate for Carter and me, in ways you couldn't possibly understand."

I want to ask questions. Statements like that mean there is more to the story than I know, but I hold back my curiosity. He's a client, not a friend, and that would involve me crossing so many professional boundaries. Boundaries I can't afford to cross if I'm trying to impress Thomas and every other asshole in his office.

"Great! I'm always grateful for an extra set of hands."

The two of us make small talk as we head out for the day, Bryce locking the door behind us. During this meeting, I have found myself wondering how this project might unfold. Bryce and I have already started butting heads over little things and he seems more stubborn than me, which is saying something. But now I think we can reach an understanding—I know what a building needs, and he knows what to do with it once we're done.

"I'll see you next week then," he says once we reach our cars.

Both of us are awkwardly standing there, hovering by the driver's side doors of our respective vehicles. So I nod. "Yes, have a happy New Year's Eve and Day, Bryce."

"Same to you." He nods before unlocking his door and sliding into the driver's seat.

By the time I get comfortable behind the wheel of my car, Bryce is already pulling away with a slight wave. I offer one back, unsure if he can even see me as he pulls out of the parking lot. For a moment, I lean back, taking a deep breath, and going over everything from the meeting we'd just had. I can't shake the feeling that Carter should have been there, and the annoyance I feel surrounding it. I'm worried Bryce won't be giving him all the updates he needs—that if something happens, or a decision needs to be made, that Carter doesn't like, it'll reflect poorly on me.

Normally, I trust my clients to be honest with me, but something about this feels a little weird to me. Carter is a professional swimmer who might live a state over, but can make the drive within a couple of hours. This is his business; it's not a silent partner situation. He's going to have an active part in it. He should know things, and he should be part of the important meetings, like today.

My phone is in my hand a second later and I'm drafting a quick email to Carter about everything that we talked about during the walkthrough. By the time I've covered everything, the email is long, but I don't care. Yes, it's me going over Bryce's head, but it's also me covering my ass. I'm the one whose job and position are at stake here, whether they know it or not. I hit send before tossing the phone in the passenger seat and start my car.

I don't look at my phone again until I'm back at my rental, food in hand, and exhaustion creeping up in my bones. The silence of the townhouse is a little overwhelming, as I'm reminded that I'm alone. If I was back home, nothing would be different about what's happening now. I wouldn't go wandering into my parent's house looking for conversation, they either wouldn't be there or wouldn't want to talk. Yet there's comfort in knowing someone is close by if I need them.

I reach for my phone, thinking I'd text Nadine or Liam, giving them both an update on what's been happening, and that's when I see the email from Carter waiting in my inbox. I'd almost forgotten I'd sent that, but click into it and scan his response. He thanks me for all the updates, informs me that Bryce had given him them as well, but appreciates hearing from me. Then, at the bottom of the email, is his phone number. Which I already have but have felt weird using without permission, but now I have it.

I'm horrible at email, he informs me. Please feel free to text me.

Clearly, he wants me to keep updating him on the project, so I save the number and make a mental note to only email when something is too ridiculously long for a text message. I also make a mental note not to let Bryce know I was going over his head, but I stand by what I think: Carter should be part of this.

Chapter 5

Katrina

January 2024

I'm at the pool bright and early on Demo Day and get to work. I was too excited to get much sleep last night, despite the long and taxing day I knew I had ahead of me. I was worried I wouldn't want to get up after falling asleep, but it ended up not being a problem. I was up way before my alarm, which allowed me to fit in a quick yoga workout before I had to get breakfast started and then get ready.

I dressed in clothes I can move easily in and don't mind getting dirty, blonde hair tied back in a messy ponytail, and out the door fifteen minutes early.

When I pull into the parking lot, I find another car sitting there. Dumpsters line one curb, but no one else is here and we still have hours before the demo crew is supposed to arrive. It isn't the same car Bryce had driven to our first meeting. This one is a dark green Jeep, a lot closer to the kind of vehicle I'd been expecting him to drive. Clearly, he has two. What a lovely disposable income he must have.

Grabbing my backpack and the emotional support water bottle I filled before I left, I exit my car and make my way into the building, using the key Bryce had given me last time. I drop my stuff by the reception desk, noting the two—barely touched—iced coffees sitting there. Carter Abrams must have finally decided to grace us with his presence.

No one is around, though, so I take a moment to pull my laptop out of my bag and check emails. There are also a few contracts I want to check the status of. Just like normal, I quickly become so engrossed in my work and I don't notice someone else enter the lobby until they clear their throat.

When I look up, I see a redhead with messy, wavy hair standing there in leggings and a loose-fitting Team USA shirt. "Hi, you must be Katrina, the contractor?"

My brow arches at this stranger who knows my name. "Yes? I'm sorry, but should I know who you are?"

Her eyes roll in a frustrated sort of way. "Of course he didn't tell you." She steps closer until she's smiling down at me over the edge of the desk and I'm more confused than I remember ever being in my life. "Joslyn Martin, but you can call me Josie. I'm Bryce's girlfriend."

"Oh!" I stand to shake her hand. "He didn't tell me you'd be joining us today. It's nice to meet you, Josie."

Her smile is gentle, warm, and welcoming. "Nice to meet you too, Katrina."

"Call me Kat, please."

I don't normally tell strangers to call me by a nickname I can't even get my boyfriend or family to use, but something about her makes me feel comfortable. Maybe it's the warm smile or the messy hair, but it's evident she's comfortable in her own skin. Which is something I'm trying to be better about. They say to surround yourself with the energy you want in your own life, after all.

Josie steps around the counter, collapsing into the only available seat beside me. She reaches for one of the coffees. "I have to tell you; I am so beyond excited to have another woman around. I love Bryce, but he's been the only person I've spent time with since moving here."

Instantly, I know what she means. While I may not have a lot of friends, I would go crazy if Nadine weren't at Dalton Enterprises. She is one of the few people I see outside of work and consider a real friend. Maybe it's out of necessity, being the only women in the office, but I don't care. I'm grateful to have her as a friend. So, I get it.

"Happy to be here," I say with a small smile. "When did y'all move here?"

"July." Her answer surprises me. I hadn't expected them to move for the pool, but why else would they have moved so close to the purchase date? "It was all a bit surprising and a little rushed, given the circumstances."

I tilt my head with a slight frown. "The circumstances?"

"Yeah, Carter bought the place kind of out of nowhere," she tells me. "He had a small panic about what he was going to do after he retires, saw this place for sale, and just went for it."

Brent's words from the meeting months ago ring in my mind. This place could end up failing a year after it opens, especially if it was bought out of the blue. If that happens, it would be a waste of my time and resources. Even worse, it would make Dalton Enterprises look bad, and Thomas will surely blame me for that.

Unaffected by my internal panic, Josie continues. "He called Bryce, who honestly needed something like this, and asked him to run it with him. We packed everything up and moved out here from Omaha in a matter of weeks."

"Wait, hang on," I reply. "Bryce wasn't part of the initial buying process, but he's the one here dealing with the remodel?" She nods, taking a sip of coffee. "They must be good friends or Bryce has a lot of trust in Carter. Did he know what the plan was before he moved out here?"

"He had a general idea. They talked it all through before Bryce agreed. I'm honestly glad this came up. It's right in line with what I always saw the two of them doing after they retired. I knew Bryce wouldn't be happy in a corporate setting forever."

Now that was something I absolutely could not picture. "How long did they swim for?"

She looks over at me, an appraising glint in her eyes. I wonder if she can tell I'm not part of this world, that I'm clueless about this sport. That maybe I'm not the right person for this job. "Their whole lives, almost. They grew up in club and age group swimming. Then they both swam through college before turning pro. Bryce swam professionally until 2022 and Carter's still going."

"Until after the upcoming Olympics," I finish, basing my answer on the little bit of information I know about the owners. "Then he's retiring, right?"

She downs the rest of her coffee with a shrug before standing. "Maybe. It's what he says."

My eyes track her movements as she tosses the cup in the recycle bin. "What do you mean?"

"He could change his mind. He's not even thirty yet, isn't battling an injury. He might decide he's not quite done yet. It's happened with other athletes before."

Brent's words come floating back again. "What will happen to this place if he decides to keep going?"

"Bryce will run it," she replies. "Speaking of him, I need to go find him. It was nice to meet you, Kat! I'll see you when it's time to break shit!"

I can't help but laugh as she waves at me over her shoulder. "We'll start in an hour!"

I'm left in silence once again, allowing the whirlwind of information to swirl in my mind. I'm not sure what to make of it. It's already bad enough Carter isn't here for the remodel and decisions are going to have to be made without his input sometimes, but now there's a chance it could be years before he's even part of this business. The chance of success seems to be slipping further and further away.

None of that can matter. I need to focus on the project and the information I have on hand. At the end of the day, my job is to finish this rebuild on time and on budget. Preferably early and under budget, but that can't happen if I get caught up in whatever is going on with the owners.

Hours later, I am so exhausted I can't even sit down because I am terrified I won't be able to get up again. For the most part, all the random crap in the building has been cleaned out. Josie and I had tag-teamed the locker rooms and offices while Bryce and some of my crew worked on getting the bigger things out. All the dumpsters we had on-site were full, with piles of random lumber and other equipment that needed to be taken away or donated. The parking lot looked as chaotic as the building looked this morning, but it felt good to see proof of our hard work.

Josie calls my name as I enter the indoor pool, snapping pictures of the progress to include in the email I send Thomas. I look over to find her sprawled out on one of the bleachers, looking uncomfortable but unwilling to get up. Bryce and two of the other guys are in the pool, cleaning out the debris. We would definitely need to replace the pool, as the cracks were a lot worse than I initially thought.

"Girl, you need to sit down," Josie decides when I come closer. "I don't think I've seen you sit down once since we started."

She isn't wrong. I barely ate lunch, deciding to take my share of the pizza I'd ordered in an office with me as I made notes on things that will need extra focus and what will need to be tackled tomorrow. It was easier to work through the hard, long days, and then collapse into an exhausted mess when I got back to the rental. I snap some pictures of the area before taking a seat next to Josie. I don't let myself relax to the same degree as her, though.

"Bryce is going to have to carry me home." She's still staring up at the ceiling when she makes her declaration. "And then I'm not moving for a week."

"You're not coming tomorrow? There's more demo to be done." I'm barely paying attention as I send some pictures to Liam, letting him see everything unfold.

Josie lets out a groan, followed by a tired whimper. "I can't do it. I'm so tired."

I laugh, turning to look at her. "But tomorrow is the fun day. Tomorrow we get to break shit. I have some concrete that needs broken up and a few of walls that need to come tumbling down."

She lifts her head just enough to peer at me, her brow furrowed. "Are you lying to me?"

I shake my head. "I got a sledgehammer with your name on it."

Glee fills her gaze. "I think I can rally enough to be here tomorrow."

"That's very brave and considerate of you," I reply. "I can't thank you enough for the help you'll be giving me."

"If I'm not allowed to use power tools, should you be allowed to use a sledgehammer?" I look up to see Bryce approaching the two of us, water bottle in hand. "If you ask me, that seems just as unsafe."

"Who says you're not allowed to use power tools?" I ask.

"Me." Josie takes his outstretched hand, allowing him to pull her into a seated position. When he sits beside her, she sinks against him. "He's an amazing swimmer, graceful in the water—fast and strong—but he will hurt himself if he uses a power tool. I just know it and I don't need to find out how good his insurance is yet."

I laugh, but don't know what to say to that. It's late enough that I've already sent some of the crew home for the night, and there's no reason for them to stick around. So, I tell them they're free to go.

"Are you sure?" Josie asks, but Bryce has already stood. "Is there anything you need our help wrapping up?"

"Nope," I assure her. "I just need to wrap up and send two quick emails, then I'll head out, too."

"Great!" Bryce is already tugging Josie to her feet. "We'll see you tomorrow, Kat."

As Bryce leads Josie to the exit, she waves at me over her shoulder. The remaining members of the crew have also cleared out of the pool area, and I'm left in total silence. It's a weird sort of echoing silence that makes me realize just how big a space like this is, big and empty.

I take a deep breath. Day one is done, and it'll only be uphill from here thanks to my planning.

I look down at my phone to find a message from Liam, telling me how good the place looks so far and thanking me for the update. The message makes me realize there's someone else who might want an update. I'd never even considered texting a client, but it's what Carter asked for.

So, without thinking about it too much, I find his contact, and send him a quick message with some photos of the place. It's more than I send Liam, but hopefully it's not overkill.

To my surprise, he replies a second later:

> It looks great, Katrina! Thanks for the update. You got a lot of work done today. Make sure to get some rest!

And I don't know why—I'm not sure I can even begin to find the words to explain it—but his response has me smiling.

⌒

"That all needs to go!" I motion to the bleachers lining one side of the outdoor pool. "There are a bunch of safety concerns and they're old as hell. We're getting new ones."

Carl, one of the guys on the crew, glares at them with an annoyed grunt. "Are you sure? They're bolted in there pretty good; it might set us back a day or two."

Stretching my shoulders back, I place my hands on my hips and shake my head. "Absolutely not. This demo needs to be done by the end of the week. The deck is getting redone too, so bring in whatever equipment you need to take them down. I want them out of here by tomorrow afternoon, Carl."

He grumbles under his breath more but doesn't argue as he ambles away to tell a few of the other guys leaning against the bleachers what we'd just talked about. I know the moment he tells them the bad news because they all start groaning, but I don't care. I'm here to do a job and get it done on time. I'm not meant to be anyone's best friend.

Looking around the deck, I slide my phone out of my pocket and snap some pictures of the progress. Most of them would go into the update I send Thomas on Friday, but I send a couple to Carter with a quick note about where we are in the demo process. Since that first day, I'd taken to sending Carter a couple of messages throughout each day, just updating him, and keeping him in the loop. Every time I send something, he seems grateful, so I keep going.

"Okay, how do you get them to listen to you like that?" I turn to see Josie walking toward me, looking impressed. "I worked in a corporate office for years and could never get any of the guys in sales to meet deadlines or take me seriously. You must have a superpower."

"A lot of practice and patience," I admit, sliding my phone back into my pocket. "Definitely not a superpower. I just make my expectations clear. I've worked with a couple of these guys before; they know I won't put up with bullshit."

"It's still impressive, and a skill I never managed to learn." She comes to a stop in front of me.

I shrug, not sure what the big deal is. It's not confidence or even a skill. It's me simply knowing I have a job to do and that I'll only be able to do it well if people take me seriously. "Just doing my job."

"Yes, that's all you're doing." She rolls her eyes in what looks like annoyance, but her tone is teasing. "Anyway, I came over to see what you are up to tonight."

The question catches me off guard, but the answer is an easy one. "Going back to my rental and binge watching some shitty reality show. Why, what are you up to?"

Her nose crinkles in displeasure. "Well, I was hoping we could hang out. That new rom-com that just came out is playing tonight at eight-thirty. Want to go with me?"

Instinct tells me she'd rather go with Bryce, but then I think back to our first conversation nearly two weeks ago. Despite how much she cares about him, she's excited to have another woman around. To be honest, I was trying to come up with an excuse to go out tonight, so this feels perfect. Plus, I know exactly what movie she's talking about, and I've been dying to see it.

"That sounds great." Her smile is infectious. "Did you want to grab dinner first? I have nothing to cook at the house."

She nods enthusiastically. "That sounds perfect! Does six o'clock work for you? I can pick you up."

"Sounds great. I'll text you the address."

"Perfect! Now I get to go tell my boyfriend he's on his own tonight."

She looks a little too giddy at the prospect before turning to do just that. I bite back a laugh as she practically skips away from me, but I can't help wondering what that's like. They're so secure in their relationship, they can admit to one another when they need space, and it doesn't feel like a big deal. It's not something I've ever had with Will. Usually, it feels like I have to beg him to spend time with me at all.

My phone vibrates in my back pocket. Pulling it out, I see a text from Carter. Before I focus on that, I send Josie the address, knowing if I don't do it now, I will forget. Then I switch back to the thread with Carter, fighting yet another smile.

Looking good! Can't wait to see the finished product. Don't work too hard, Dalton.

Not a chance! I'm hanging out with Josie tonight, so I'll need to leave early to ensure I don't smell like whatever this place smells like.

God dammit! Bryce told me that smell is gone.

I'm glad you're hanging with Josie. She's good people.

Me too! I'm excited to spend time with her. The smell has mostly gone, but there's still some lingering.

It's going to plague us forever, isn't it?

> Maybe you'll just be known as the pool with the weird smell forever

Do not even joke about that. Please.

> lol

> Sorry, you're right. I shouldn't joke about it. I'll be sure to get some air freshener or something.

I don't think that would help. I just got to the gym, so I'll talk to you later. Thanks for the update.

His last message has a picture of a rack of weights with it. I can see his shadow, but nothing else. I wish he would have tilted the camera ever so slightly so I could see a sliver of his reflection in the mirror. It feels weird to be talking to someone when you don't know what they look like. I'd considered googling him or looking up social media, but it feels like an invasion of privacy.

At the end of the day, he's my client, and this weird friendship is already crossing lines I never thought I'd cross. Looking him up would be too much for me.

Yet, I can't help but wonder what he actually—

"Katrina!" I snap out of my mind, stuffing my phone in my pocket like I'd been caught looking at something I shouldn't be. Carl is standing several paces down the deck, pushing against one of the bleachers, barely paying attention to me despite being the one who called my name. "We need you down here."

I take a deep breath, pushing all thoughts of Carter Abrams from my mind. "I'm coming," I say and focus back on my job.

Chapter 6

Carter

January 2024

Just as I expect, January is a month of utter chaos from the moment it starts.

Coach wasted no time kicking us into gear for the upcoming Olympics, already training us harder than he did the previous year. The sets were harder, the practices longer, and I felt the exhaustion at the end of it all deeper in my bones. It's all an old routine to me now, knowing that I must make every moment between now and the Games count more than anything, and I can't waste them. There won't be such a thing as a day off for months.

On top of all the training and the stacked schedule of meets I have color-coded in a calendar on my phone, there's also a storm of media requests. People are starting to care about swimming and pay attention to it again. As we amp up for Paris, the realization that a lot of their favorite swimmers have retired since they last cared has created a lot of questions about whether Team USA can hold on to the legacy we've had for years. What better way to show spectators that Team USA is in good hands than to interview veterans hoping for one more Olympics and the brightest up-and-coming stars the sport has to offer?

I fall into the first category.

This has always been my least favorite aspect of being a professional in the sport. I'm always worried I wear my heart too much on my sleeve for this and setting boundaries feels strange. Unlike Bryce, I never mastered the poker face he could give the media. He had a talent for giving them just enough and never bringing his personal life into it. My personal life has been in it longer than I care to admit.

Then there's the pool. While I'm having cameras shoved in my face and being questioned about things that happened ten years ago, Josie and Bryce are in Columbia dealing with a mess I handed them. Construction started on schedule, but Katrina has been pestering me about little details here and there. I don't know if she doesn't believe Bryce when he tells her he's already talked to me about something, but she feels the need to follow up with me. It should be annoying, especially since we specifically told her I'd be busy, but so far, it's been having the opposite effect.

It's been a good distraction from everything else going on. Bryce has been keeping me updated by sending me photos of everything as it happens, but has mostly kept things spaced out as to not bombard me with constant messages. I know it's to keep me from getting distracted, but I wish he'd give me more information as it came. Katrina's questions and updates have been making me feel like I'm still part of it.

The more we text, the more I find myself wanting to know more. Although we haven't shared anything too personal yet, I feel this draw to her that I can't quite explain. I'm sure it has everything to do with the fact that it's been years since my last serious relationship, something I'd rather not dwell on too deeply. The last break up hurt, no matter how mutual it was, and nothing else seemed to go anywhere. I can blame it on my priorities being elsewhere, but the reality is no one seems to want serious with a professional athlete; and I've never been one for flings.

I certainly have no interest in a long-distance, pen pal like relationship with our contractor who I know nothing about. No matter how happy seeing flickers of her personality shining to otherwise professional text messages makes me.

As soon as I drop my bag by the door, my phone goes off with a text. I pull it from the pocket of my sweatshirt to find a text from Katrina. A smile pulls its way across my face, but before I can even open the message, a call comes in from Bryce.

I answer the call. "Fuck you."

Bryce responds with a shocked laugh. "Hello to you, too. Why am I on your shit list today?"

I move into the kitchen to grab a drink. "Because you're retired. Why couldn't you hold out until we both could have retired?"

Another laugh. "I'm guessing the interview today went well?"

I collapse onto the couch with a groan. "They asked me if you are going to make a comeback four times. Then, when they'd exhausted that question, it was all about whether I could hack it without you. Like I didn't make it to Worlds without you."

"Damn." He whistles. "I'm sorry, Carter. You have the right to be mad at me."

Sighing, I sink further back into the cushions. "No, I don't. It's not your fault people can't come up with unique questions."

"No, but you can't be mad at them. So be mad at me. I can handle it."

I swallow against the sudden lump building up in my throat. I miss doing this with him. I'm one of the oldest athletes trying to make the team; I'm tired; I hate dealing with the media. All those things would have been so much easier to face with Bryce by my side.

I don't blame him for wanting to retire. He was ready to move on, and his body was ready for him to quit, too. In a lot of ways, Bryce had the choice taken from him. An injury he couldn't fully bounce back from was the final nail in the coffin of his career. In those last few months, it was hard to watch him struggle through meets and recovery that took four times as long.

I get to make the choice. I can go or stay—it's up to me and it's not fair for me to put any blame on him.

"How about I don't get mad at anyone?" I offer. "It doesn't do any good for me to be mad at them or you, especially when the decision is fully up to me."

I hear some slight shuffling in the background, Josie's voice muffled as she talks to someone else. "Are you having second thoughts? Is that why you haven't made an official announcement?"

"No," I insist, "I'm done."

"I was serious when I told you we'd make it work if you want to keep going."

"And I'm serious when I say I'm done. I'm tired, Bryce. This has been my whole life for so long. Emotionally, mentally, and physically—I'm tired."

"I get it." I know he does; he was already starting to feel that way when he got hurt. "I just want to make sure you know there are choices."

Choices he didn't have. Choices he wants to make sure I've thought about before giving up the one thing I've ever really worked toward.

"I promise I know that," I assure him. "And I know you have my back."

"Always."

It's been like this for as long as I can remember; inseparable childhood best friends who chased a crazy dream together. Bryce Clark has been one of the few people who have stayed by my side without question. He was the first person I came out to when I was fifteen and he was by my side when I told my family a year later. They were great, but I knew he was ready to intervene if it had gone the other way. That I'd always have a place at the Clarks, and no one was going to question who I am or make me explain myself.

Carter and Bryce. Bryce and Carter. We'd always been those kinds of friends and it wasn't going to change.

"Katrina has been sending me updates on how everything is going." I change the subject from focusing on the past and present, shifting it to what's coming next. "It looks like a completely different place now that it's all cleaned out."

"I'm just happy the smell has mostly gone away." He chuckles. "She shouldn't be sending you updates, though. I've told her how busy you are and that I can handle it. I'll tell her to back off again."

"No." Maybe the word comes out too fast. Maybe there's too much force behind my insistence, but I can't take it back now. "She's not bothering me or asking me a million questions. It's fine, seriously."

I don't want to tell him how out of the loop I'm feeling. How I wish I could just throw in the towel and move to Columbia, let my focus be on what's coming. I've never been good when it comes to staring down a goodbye, and I know this is going to be the hardest one yet. Despite how ready I am, I'd rather just skip past the hard part.

"If you're sure, man." He knows there's something I'm not telling him. I can tell by the way he hesitates, pausing to see if I'll tell him anything else. "Just let me know if it gets to be too much."

"Yeah, of course." I fight against a yawn. "I need to take a nap, Bryce. Morning practice kicked my ass and coach wants us back for a weight session after dinner."

"There's something else I want to talk to you about if you can wait a couple more minutes." Bryce informs me before I can even think of hanging up. "It's something I'm not going to do without talking to you first."

Well, that has my attention. "Yeah, what's up?"

"Remember how Mia offered to help us market the club?" I find myself nodding, despite knowing he can't see me. "I think we need to do more than just take her up on the offer. We need to hire her."

Technically, it's in the budget, but the salary is nowhere near to what she's making now. "You know Mia will say yes if we offer it to her, and we can't afford her, man. I'm not making her accept a job she doesn't want because we're her friends. That'll be setting her career back."

"I know, and I would never take advantage of her like that, but I think she needs a legitimate reason to leave Charlotte and we can give it to her."

If there's one thing I know about Mia Sheridan, it's that she doesn't run away from anything. If she's looking to leave, there has to be more to the story. "What happened?"

"Bianca happened," Bryce replies. "Or, at least, she is happening."

I don't know much about Mia's ex, just that she'd left and hadn't returned after a fight. Mia was heartbroken, not knowing what to do about the lack of communication. It'd left a strong impact on her. She'd used her own experience to convince Bryce not to abandon someone you care about when things get hard.

"Part of their fight was Bianca wanting her parents to buy them a house and fund a marketing business for them. I'm sure you can imagine how Mia took that."

I could picture it clearly. Mia believes in hard work and not having anything handed to her. She wants to know she deserves the things she gets. Plus, Josie told me she loves working for the firm she's at right now. "So, they fought about it?"

"Yup. Bianca got mad, accused her of secretly hating her for having parents who care about her, and left. About a month ago, I guess some of Mia's clients got poached by a new firm out of nowhere."

My blood ran cold, anger bubbling up inside me. "No."

"Turns out, Bianca's parents still funded that business for her and are helping her offer clients amazing perks for signing with her. In the process of it all, she's tanking Mia's reputation and credibility in Charlotte." The tone in Bryce's voice tells me he's clenching his fists, fighting against the same anger I'm feeling. "Since the firm Mia works at caters to local small businesses, they're talking about firing her because they don't want to be affiliated with someone who has a bad reputation."

"What the hell?" I sit up straighter, suddenly feeling wide awake. "That's so fucked up. None of that is her fault, and they should be focusing on doing something about Bianca. She's the one ruining reputations here."

"That would include potential legal issues they don't want to be wrapped up in." Bryce's tone is mocking as he parrots whatever was said to Mia.

"That's bullshit." I'll never understand how businesses can decide what battles to fight, especially at the expense of their employees.

"I know," Bryce agrees. "Look, Josie doesn't know I'm telling you this, and I don't think Mia knows I know."

"I won't say anything," I promise, "but Mia's not an idiot. Don't insult her intelligence. She knows you and Josie tell each other everything."

He laughs awkwardly. "Yeah, I guess you're right. My point is, Mia won't agree to the job if she thinks I'm offering it to her out of pity. I want to make sure you're in on it and agree with me before I tell her about it."

"Of course I am." There's not a single doubt in my mind about this decision. Mia would add an element to the club that neither Bryce nor I could bring. Their blog hadn't failed because they weren't good, it just wasn't what the sport necessarily needed at the time. "I don't have a clue how to market a place like this."

"Great, that's what I'll tell her when I pitch it to her." He's basically talking to himself now, working through a plan on how to present this idea to Mia in a way that shows we're more authentic in our request than wanting to offer her help she'd never asked for. "Hopefully she won't look at it like it's a handout."

"Because that's not what it is. We need her and maybe she needs out of Charlotte. It's just friends looking out for one another."

He groans. "I hope she sees it that way. Maybe I should have Josie pitch it to her."

"No," I protest. "She'll see it the way we want her to. Besides, you're a good friend, Bryce." I hear him scoff in the background. "I'm serious, dude. You're the type of friend who's always looking out for his friends. Standing up for them, opening a club with them, finding ways to get them out of shitty situations. It's who you are."

"Mia and I are not friends," he argues. "She hates me."

"Keep telling yourself that." If Mia hates him, I'm not sure he'd be house hunting with her best friend right now. "I'm serious. I need to take a nap and you have a phone call to make. Let me know what she says?"

"Uh, yeah, I'll text you. Get some sleep, dude."

We wrap the conversation up from there and I stand from the couch, my stiff and sore muscles protesting at the movement. My bed is calling my name.

I grab my drink off the coffee table and head into my room, checking Katrina's message as I go. She sent me a quick video of Josie beating the shit out of a wall with a sledgehammer, the message simple: Everyone should fear her.

I laugh, wondering if Bryce has seen this video. I quickly type out a reply, confirming she's right before making sure my alarm is set and plugging my phone in. I don't pull the blinds shut, too exhausted for the extra ten steps. Instead, I just pull my T-shirt over my head, drop it on the floor, and face plant into my bed. Sleep instantly overtakes me.

Chapter 7

Katrina

January 2024

When I enter the lobby from the indoor pool, I find Josie sitting cross-legged on a chair at the desk in the lobby, laptop open and resting in its rightful place—her lap. As I approach, she looks up and smiles at me before removing an earbud. I can hear music pumping from it, the volume probably turned up to drown out some of the work going on outside. "Hey, Kat."

"Hey," I greet, glancing down at the copy of Liam's design in my hand. "Have you seen Bryce?"

"He's up in his office." She points to the door with a scowl. "I was up there, too, but he kicked me out. Apparently, singing Taylor Swift under your breath doesn't help your boyfriend focus on writing a business plan."

I grin as she playfully rolls her eyes, but I'm already heading toward the stairs. "Do you want me to yell at him for banishing you to the dungeons?"

She nods firmly. "It's what any good friend would do."

I laugh, shaking my head as I push through the doors. She and I both know I won't do it, though. While Josie and I have gotten close over the last few weeks, hanging out together at least a few times a week and even having a girl's night at my rental when Bryce had to go to Georgia to help Carter with something, Bryce and I are practically strangers. We've never crossed the line of professionalism that blurred with Carter and Josie. He's here to remodel a pool and I'm here to execute his vision. There's nothing more to it than that.

As I approach the office, I notice his door is barely propped open despite the sound of muffled machinery. I rap a knuckle against the splintered wood. He glances up. "Hey, do you have a second? I have a question."

The look he gives me is wary, but he still nods. I step into the small room that somehow feels smaller now that there's only an old metal desk in it, Bryce, and myself. I set the papers down on the desk, pointing to the problem area I spotted. "What's this?"

His brow arches. "The plans for the remodel," he deadpans. "The ones Liam drew up and Carter and I signed off on. I'd think you'd want to ask me a real question, Katrina."

I want to roll my eyes at his sass, but somehow refrain, and dig my finger into the paper with more force. "These are the plans for the main pool." He finally looks to where I'm pointing. "Are you seriously telling me you don't see any issues with them?"

He shakes his head and says, "No. Nothing has changed on those."

"Bryce, you have seating taking up one entire wall." The wall is covered in basic stadium style plastic seats and there's no room for anything else on that side. "They're taking up valuable space. Not everyone will want to sit here. You need room for some tables and chairs."

He balks at that. "This isn't the type of pool you lounge by, Katrina. Patio seating isn't practical. How many times do I have to tell you this?"

"What about parents who are watching their kids during lessons or practice?" I can tell I'm pushing his buttons, but I'm not convinced he's thinking past his own daydream. He needs to be realistic. "Do you think they'll want to sit on hard plastic chairs all the time?"

"I'm not building this place for the parents," he shoots back. "Anyone who has ever gone to a swim meet knows comfortable seating is not happening. It's part of the charm of the sport."

I bring my hands to my hips, ready to stand my ground like I would with any person under my command I work with. "Now you sound ridiculous. Why are you sacrificing comfort?"

Bryce glares right back at me. "There is plenty of space on that side of the pool," he points to the opposite side, "for the athletes to relax and be comfortable. That's what matters to me. Why can't you just listen to me? I know what this place needs. I've spent my whole life in pools like this."

"Just because something has been one way for all your life doesn't make it the only right way," I challenge. "Nor does it prohibit you from making changes."

He releases an exasperated sigh. "Oh, I'm sorry. I was under the impression that Liam was the design lead on this project, not you. Why are you trying to change something you have no part in? It's been approved, Katrina."

It feels like my stomach drops to my feet at his words. Suddenly, embarrassment flooding my cheeks, I realize I can't find any of my own. Desperate to get out of there, I snatch the plans back off his desk and leave the same way I just came. "Forget it!"

"Great talk," he calls before the door swings shut behind me.

I storm down the stairs, the sound of my shoes hitting the concrete echoing. When I push my way back into the lobby, the heavy metal door clangs shut behind me, startling Josie. Her eyes widen as she looks at me.

I raise my hand to keep her from saying anything because I just can't right now. "Your boyfriend is impossible to work with!"

"Wait!" she calls after me, but I continue to the front door. I need a minute. "What did he do this time?"

The door swings shut behind me, providing a literal wall between me and the thing—person—causing me so much stress. I just have to pull myself together and reiterate to myself that I can pull off this job. That I'm not going to let someone like Bryce Clark get under my skin. I'm good at my job and my instincts are solid, even if he refuses to see it. I just need one of them to listen to me.

Not knowing what else to do, I pull my phone from my pocket and scroll through the contacts until I find the one I'm looking for. I dial the number, purely on instinct, then press the phone against my ear. The longer it rings, the more frustrated I become.

He told me he'd be available if something important came up and now that there was something, he's not answering. Bryce probably got to him before I could—

The ringing cuts off. "Hello?"

I freeze at the sound of his voice. I'm not sure what I expected Carter Abrams to sound like, but I was unprepared for this. His voice is deep, heavy with something that could be exhaustion, but it's warm and smooth. I feel like his voice could wrap me up in a hug that I'd never want to go free from.

Some girls are attracted to biceps. Some girls are attracted to smiles. I'm a sucker for an attractive voice, and this man has one.

"Hello?" he questions, and I swear a shiver runs down my spine. Pull it together, Katrina! "Miss Dalton?"

"Katrina," I dumbly correct, not even sure how the word manages to come out. "I'm sorry to bother you, I just need to run something by you and it's a bit of a time sensitive issue."

"It's no problem," he assures me. "I was just taking a nap."

The anger comes back in me like a firecracker, snapping and sparking to life in a flurry of activity. He's taking a nap in the middle of the afternoon while I'm here with his business partner, working our asses off to remodel a pool he foolishly bought. Now I'm not sure who to be madder at: Bryce, or him.

"Well, I'm sorry to wake you," I snark. "This should be quick and then you can get back to your nap."

He must not hear the ire in my tone because he laughs. He has the nerve to laugh, which sends another zip of something down my spine. "I needed to get up any—"

I don't want to hear his excuses. "I want to talk to you about the main pool. The plan Liam drew up, and you approved, has an entire wall of stadium seats."

"Yes," he confirms. "Bryce and I are hoping to have the opportunity to host a lot of meets, maybe even some professional ones. What's the problem? Are we unable to get the stands installed on time?"

"No, there's no problem with the supplies. The problem is with the plan. I need you to talk to Bryce. I don't know if he's being all that realistic with this design element. You don't just want to cater to those participating in the sport, you should be considering other people who will use this space. Having an entire wall of stands is a waste of valuable space."

"I'm sorry, but what are we talking about here? Do you want to make a change to the design that was already finalized?" The reason they're best friends is suddenly starting to make a lot more sense. "Katrina, I understand your concern, but the type of place Bryce and I are running isn't going to be for leisure swimming. Yes, we'll do lessons, and have open swimming, but people aren't coming here to lie by the pool and read."

He's not being rude or chastising me the way Bryce had, but it feels just the same. It feels like neither one of them is taking me seriously enough. I may not understand what this sport needs, but I do understand what the public will want from a pool.

"Everyone keeps saying that, but I can't imagine you'd possibly need that much space."

There's a sharp inhale on Carter's side of the phone. "Look, I know you're not familiar with this sport, but it is more popular than you'd expect. When meets are going on, those seats will be full. We need you to trust that we know how to accommodate the people who will be using this facility the most."

There's the chastising. "And I really need both of you to under-stand I'm just trying to do my job."

"And you're doing it fantastically, but we're just doing ours, too."

"Bryce is doing yours," I snap back.

"Excuse me?"

"Bryce is doing your job, Carter." I take a deep breath through my nose. "You're in Georgia swimming."

"I'm in Georgia doing my job," he stresses, but I just roll my eyes. "Miss Dalton, do you think I'm just sitting in Georgia doing nothing?"

I cringe at the use of my last name, knowing I'd crossed a line I can't step back from. I might as well drive my point home. Maybe one of them will finally listen to me. "Not at all, Mr. Abrams. I think you're in Georgia being a professional swimmer. Now, if you'd excuse me, I need to get back to my job."

I don't give him the chance to argue or say anything more. I end the call and turn to go back inside. When I step through the door, I'm still fuming, but now it's for a whole other reason. Josie isn't at the desk when I get inside, and I take that as a blessing in disguise. As close as we're becoming, I don't need her eternal optimism right now. If Carter and Bryce won't take my job seriously, why should I take theirs seriously?

—

"Katrina!"

I glance up from the paperwork I'm looking over to see Bryce storming toward me, phone clenched in his hand. Sighing, I drop the pen and turn to face him, readying myself for battle. "What can I do for you, Bryce?"

"Did you call Carter to try to get him to agree with you about the stands after we talked this morning?"

I shrug, because what else can I do? "I wanted to make sure you were both on the same page with this. Neither one of you wanted to listen to me, so if you end up hating them, please remember they're not easily removed."

My words just make him angrier. "You can't keep doing this. If I tell you we're keeping something the way it is, that's all you need. Stop calling him."

I cross my arms over my chest. "You're not the only one who owns the building, Bryce. He's your business partner. He should be part of the decision-making process."

The last two conversations I've had with Bryce and Carter were nothing but disappointing. Bryce has spent the last month making excuse after excuse for Carter, but my phone call with him this morning just proved how pointless it all is. He's not busy, he's taking mid-morning naps.

"I'm the one in charge while he's training. We've told you this," he snaps. "If there's something he needs to be looped into, I'll make the call. He doesn't need to answer every little question you have."

I fight back a scoff, wanting to make some joke about how easy the life of a professional swimmer seems to be. Bryce keeps insisting Carter has this packed schedule, but what more is there to it than swimming and occasionally smiling at a camera? "Oh, please, stop making excuses for him."

Bryce gawks at me, eyes wide. "I . . . uh . . . what?"

"I know it's not my place to say this, but it's kind of bullshit that he's left this all to you. He's a professional swimmer, right?" Bryce nods, still looking shocked. "So, he swims. I can't imagine he's all that busy. Besides, the Olympics aren't for months. He has time to be here."

I think I might have broken Bryce.

He stands there, mouth opening, and then closing without a single word coming out. There's something in his eyes, though, and the way he's looking at me makes me shift uncomfortably. I can't tell if he wants to scream at me or fire me. Maybe both.

He takes a deep breath through his nose, hand clenching at his side. "You have to know there's more to it than swimming laps and showing up at the Olympics."

I hold his gaze as my brow creases. My confidence in what I'd just said wavers slightly. "No."

He huffs. "Most professional swimmers train a minimum of six days a week. They're in the pool twice a day, swimming at least six miles a day, but it's usually closer to ten. That doesn't even consider the dryland workouts, the recovery, or the nutritional side of things."

Six to ten miles a day? Holy shit! No wonder he was taking a nap.

Guilt claws up my chest as I take a step back. I'm even more clueless about this sport than I realized and Will certainly hasn't helped matters any. No matter how many times I ask him questions, wanting to get insight, he changes the subject. I've tried asking Nadine, but she shut down after the conversation with Liam last month. As a result, I've been walking around here looking like an idiot who thinks she knows everything when she hasn't got a clue.

"And the Olympics are not the only major meet for professional swimmers!" Now that Bryce has gotten started, I'm not sure he's stopping anytime soon. Something tells me this isn't the first time he's given this lecture. "It might be the only one to get any real media coverage, but it's not the be-all and end-all of swimming. My point is, this is his job, Kat. Even if you don't see it that way."

"Whoa!" I raise my hands to calm him down. "I never said I don't see it—"

"Your actions implied it." My mouth snaps shut, heat flushing my cheeks because he's right. "Let him do his job while you and I do ours."

I nod once before Bryce turns to go up to his office, leaving me standing there in the aftermath of my embarrassment. Heat still ignited my cheeks. I've been doing to Carter and Bryce, the same thing I'm fighting against in my own career. Belittling what they do, not trusting the work they put into it, and pretending like I know more than they do about what's going on.

I pull my phone from the pocket of my leggings, going to the message thread I have with Carter, but I don't send him anything. Instead, I stare down at the last message he sent for several seconds before I pocket the phone again. Bryce is right; I shouldn't be bothering Carter with unnecessary details and, even though I just want to apologize for wasting his time, this doesn't feel like the right time.

Besides, I'm too mortified to even think about reaching out to him right now. I'd been so unprofessional when I was on the phone with him this morning. Even worse, I'd been cruel. I'd acted immaturely over the fact I wasn't getting what I wanted. Even if I felt like I wasn't being heard, I'd been so wrapped up in doing this job well, I'd failed to do the one thing I always promised myself I'd do: listen to the clients.

The last thing I need to do is embarrass myself further. I'll finish for the day and go home, maybe do some research, and see what else I can figure out about professional swimming. To be honest, that should have been the research I did months ago instead of looking at pretty pictures of pools.

Chapter 8

Katrina

End of January

I'm sitting at the desk in the lobby on Friday morning when Bryce and Josie come in, both wearing matching scowls. They'd gone house hunting yesterday and, by the looks on their faces, it didn't go well.

"How did it go?" Bryce grunts, grabbing the notebook he keeps in the desk. Josie's unpacking her laptop as she gives me a grim smile. "That good, huh?"

Bryce doesn't answer me. We haven't spoken much since our argument the other day. Instead, he grumbles out something about needing to make some calls. He's halfway out the door leading into the main pool, the quietest place right now, before he backtracks. In a few strides, he's closing the distance between him and Josie. Something twists in the pit of my stomach as he kisses her forehead, murmuring something, and then kissing her lips. Without another word or look in my direction, he's out of the room.

Their relationship is so easy and natural. I can't help but feel a little jealous. It's not fair that some people just have it come so easily to them.

Josie slumps in the chair beside me, legs crossed with her laptop open on them. She checks something on her phone, frowning down at it.

The silence is awkward and tense. I need it to be broken, now. "Did you guys really not find anything you liked?"

She startles at the sound of my voice, but shakes her head once she recovers. "It's been such a mess, Kat. We found a couple we love, but they're so far out of our budget. Bryce doesn't want to rent, which I understand, you know? We're putting roots down; this is supposed to be the start of the rest of our lives. We might not have much of a choice. At least not until the club is up and running, giving us a steadier stream of income."

I rework my question. "You didn't find anything you like in your budget at all?"

"Technically, we did, but it'd need work done." She hands me her phone, which is open to a house listing. "We love it, but Bryce doesn't want to take on another project like this right now."

When I look down at the phone, I am pulled in by a quaint two-story brick home. The front lawn looks like it needs some work, and the small porch needs a new staircase and a fresh coat of paint, but it's in good condition overall. I flip through the pictures, listening to her rattle off all the reasons they've both decided this was a no. Despite Josie clearly loving it.

The closer I look at the pictures, the more I believe my initial reaction is correct: the house needs updating and remodeling, but it's not in terrible shape. There's some wallpaper that needs to go, a room full of wood paneling that's giving me a headache, and a kitchen that needs a whole remodel, but those are easy fixes. At least not daunting enough to pass on a house they love.

It was also the kind of house I can picture them in, especially after making it their own. There are plenty of windows, character without being too quirky, and a large backyard for hosting friends. It really is perfect for the two of them.

"Josie, the house isn't bad." Her mouth snaps shut at my interruption, turning to look at me with wide eyes. "Obviously I can't say for sure without getting in there myself or having an inspection done, but most of the updates look like they'd be cosmetic."

"Really?" Her tone is so full of hope, I instantly make up my mind to help her. The hope is gone as soon as it's there, though. "Bryce has a point. We have enough going on with his place to balance another renovation."

"What if you have help?"

She's shaking her head. "I could never ask you to do that, Kat. You have your hands full with the club."

"You aren't asking, I'm offering." I shrug. "Besides, this is my only project right now, so I can juggle multiples. I have a lot of contacts in Columbia, so I'm sure we can get everything set up. You said it was in your budget?"

"Under, actually," she admits. "We have about fifty grand to work with. Do you think that'd be enough?"

I glance down at the phone, wondering just how much money professional swimmers make. "That should be more than enough."

"Bryce hates how small the kitchen is."

It's a feeble argument, and I know she's looking for a reason not to get too excited.

"We can look into building onto it. It looks like there's space," I comment, flipping back to the floor plan. "That's not something you'll need to worry about."

"Oh, my god," Josie breathes as I hand her back the phone. She looks down at the pictures and her eyes practically have hearts in them. "You have no idea how happy you're making me right now. I love this house!"

I laugh lightly. "Don't get too excited. You still need to get Bryce on board. We both know I'm not his favorite person."

A look of determination crosses her features, a glint of something in her eye. "Leave him to me."

Just like that, I know what I've signed up for. There's no way Bryce will say no to Josie and his behavior when he got back suddenly makes a lot more sense. He's disappointed he can't give her what she so clearly wants, but he can. Josie deserves to be happy here, just like Bryce, and I want to be part of that. I want her to start a new life with something she loves, something she can grow into. If that happens to be this house, well, that's exactly why I went into this business. Unlike Thomas, I mean it when I say I want to help people bring their dreams to life.

～

I'm packing up my bag to head home when Bryce finds me, hands stuffed in the pocket of his hoodie, biting down on his bottom lip. "Do you have a minute to talk?"

The front door is less than twenty feet away, and he's not blocking my path. Theoretically, I could grab my bag and make a run for it. I didn't have to face this conversation or the consequences of my actions over the last four weeks, but I do owe him an apology.

I'm woman enough to know when I fuck up and I need to apologize for it. That's what needs to happen, so I nod.

"Josie told me about you offering to help with the house," he begins. "I just want to thank you for that. I could see it on her face. She loves it and I want to make her happy."

This isn't the opening I was expecting. It's not the two of us revisiting the last conversation we had. Instead, he's giving me an opening and I'm going to take it. "I think it's a great house, Bryce, and you're right about her loving it. I'm more than happy to help. I've already got some ideas."

"I called our realtor." His gaze keeps shifting around the room, refusing to settle on anything. "We put in an offer. Apparently, the owners are eager to sell, so she's hopeful we'll find out in the next couple of days and then we'll do the inspection."

"Sounds great." I smile softly, wanting to ease his awkwardness. He's not comfortable. "Look, Bryce, I owe you an apology."

Gray eyes finally meet my gaze, his brow furrowed in confusion. "For what?"

I fiddle with the ends of my ponytail, debating whether I want to bring up something he isn't ready to talk about, but I know I can't avoid it forever. "About earlier?"

"Wait." He frowns, shaking his head. "You seriously want to talk about that?"

"Of course I do! I was a jerk to you. I've been nothing but a jerk the whole time I've been here and, not to mention, unprofessional."

"Whoa, Kat, hold on." He's giving me an amused grin, making him look boyish. "I'm not sure I'd go that far. You're just out of your element here; just like I am. I don't know anything about building things."

"But you're not questioning my ability to do my job, or my knowledge," I contradict. Now that the apology has started coming out, it can't be stopped. "You're the professional athlete—you know what a place like this needs. I know how to build it, that's it. I'm not even the one who came up with the design."

The amusement drops from his face. "Hey, no. Don't sell yourself short. Liam might be the one who came up with the design, but you're the one bringing it to life. We literally can't do this without you."

Part of me wants to bring up the fact that I'm not even doing that, not really. I'm overseeing and managing the people bringing it to life. But something in Bryce's demeanor stops me short.

"That's the last thing I wanted to talk about, Katrina. I thought that was done and over with, but maybe I'm shit at communication." He chuckles, like there's some inside joke. "Actually, I know I'm shit at communication. Just ask my girlfriend and best friend."

A smile tugs at the corners of my lips. "I'm not sure anyone is great at it all the time."

"I'm working on it." I'm not sure if he's reassuring me or himself. "I had something else I needed to talk to you about. Can you hang out a minute more? This is related to work."

I try to keep up with the slightly abrupt change of subject with a nod, shifting my weight from one foot to the other. "Sure, what's up?"

"Starting in early February, there's going to be someone else around a lot more."

There's a swoop of something in the pit of my stomach at the thought of someone else being around, because who else could it be? Maybe Carter decided he wasn't going to try for the Olympics anymore. Or maybe there's a pool here he can train at instead. There have to be a million different reasons for him to be moving here permanently early, right?

Why is the thought of him being here all the time terrifying?

Over the last month, I've created this fantasy version of Carter Abrams from the phone calls, emails, and text messages we've shared. We haven't talked about anything important, but he's been easy to talk to. We'd crossed professional lines I'd set for myself more often than I care to admit, making it somehow different. There's something pulling me toward him—an impulse that makes me want to know more. It's a dangerous feeling, one I've spent weeks trying to ignore, and if he's here, I doubt I'd be able to ignore it at all.

"Mia Sheridan is moving here." The little Carter centric bubble pops around me. "She's Josie's best friend. Maybe she's talked to you about her? Carter and I hired her to work on marketing the club. She wants to get started as soon as possible and use the construction process to help us build some hype."

Now a whole new sense of worry crashes around me. He's right, Josie's told me about Mia, but I didn't necessarily think I'd ever meet the woman. I know it's ridiculous to worry that my new friend will ditch me, but it's there. Building friendships hasn't ever come naturally to me, and I tend to feel protective of the one I have with Josie.

"Is that a problem?"

Bryce is staring intently at me as I snap out of my thoughts. I blink up at him for a moment. "No, of course not. Why would it be?"

"I don't know, but you were being weirdly quiet about it."

Embarrassed, I look away. "Sorry, it's been a long day." I grab my bag, hosting it over my shoulder, hoping Bryce gets the hint that

I'm ready to get out of here. "Josie's told me about her. I'm looking forward to meeting her."

"She's excited to be here," Bryce confirms. "I think the change of pace will be good for her. But I've kept you long enough. I'll let you go."

As I flash him a grateful smile, my stomach lets out a growl that has us both laughing.

"Okay, that clearly means I have to go."

"One last thing." I nearly let out a groan. How many more last things could there possibly be? "I'm serious. I just want to go back to your apology. There's nothing to apologize for. Let's just trust that each of us knows what we're talking about and go from there. Sound good?"

Gripping the strap of my bag, I nod. "That's what I should have been doing from the beginning."

He nods. "Then we're good. Have a good night, Kat."

"You too Bryce."

A couple of hours later, I find myself sinking into the comfy couch in my living room as the sound of the phone ringing echoes through the otherwise empty space. It takes several rings before Will answers, the video call connecting a moment later. On instinct, I smile as his image comes into focus, but it diminishes with the blank look on his face.

"Hey!" My voice is overly perky, even to my own ears. He smooths a hand over his short, reddish-brown hair, which he must have recently buzzed again, because it wasn't like that last week when we did this. "Are you okay?"

"Fine. Tired." Those two words are the only response he offers, staring expectantly.

"Have your shifts been long?"

I can hear him tapping against the table impatiently. "I'm an ER doctor at a trauma hospital in a major US city, Katrina. What do you think?"

I sink further back into the couch, cheeks flushing. "Right. Stupid question."

He snorts. "You think?"

Biting my lip, I glance around the living room to find something to focus on. Something that will keep the tears at bay.

He notices, though, because he lets out a groan. When I look back at the phone, he's rubbing at his temples. "Don't cry. I shouldn't have snapped like that."

It's not an apology, but it's the closest I'll ever get. "It's fine."

Fine. God, I hate that word. Everything in my life is fine. My job is fine. My relationship is fine. They're all stagnant and fine. Except, for the first time in a long time, I'm feeling the itch beneath my skin to change that. To make my life better than fine, even if I'm not sure how.

"How's the project going?" I'm not surprised that he changes the subject instead of offering me any comfort or trying to fix what he'd done. "Have you finished demo?"

I play with the edge of my sweatshirt as I nod. "They've already started replacing the outdoor pool, since that's the area we're focusing on first. That's the first step and then we'll build everything out around it. That should be done by the end of February, weather permitting."

He nods while his gaze is focused somewhere else. Maybe his computer or tablet is off the screen. "That's good."

Nothing else, no further questions asked. I guess I have to keep talking. "It's been nice having Bryce's girlfriend around. I have someone to talk to and hang out with on the weekends."

He looks at the camera. "Are you and Clark not getting along?"

Will and I haven't talked since the disastrous fight earlier in the week, and I don't feel the need to bring it up now. It's been taken care of. The only person I need to talk things out with is Carter, and I'm still not sure how to approach that conversation. "We get along fine. We just tackle things differently."

"He's a jackass," Will scoffs.

If he had asked me a week ago, I would have agreed with Will, but now I'm not so sure. There's something about Bryce Clark that I can't put my finger on, but I think he cares deeply about his friends. The way he jumped to Carter's defense was more about being his friend than an athlete, and the whole thing with Mia seems weird. Josie has told me how much Mia enjoys her job in Charlotte. To suddenly have her moving here, working for them, makes me think there's more to the story than I'm being told.

"I wouldn't say that. I think he just knows what he wants." It isn't a lie because Bryce isn't afraid of letting his opinion be known. "He and his girlfriend are looking for houses here in Columbia. They want to settle down and start establishing some roots. I offered to help while I'm here."

His focus was on something off camera again. "How much are they paying you for that?"

"Nothing." The thought of asking for money for this never even occurred to me. "I'm not doing it for the money. I'm doing it to help friends out."

He's shaking his head. "That's your problem, Katrina. You don't know the difference between work and fun. They're not your friends, they're clients. If they have another project they want your assistance on, then you should be compensated for that."

I fist my hand in the sleeve of my sweatshirt, gritting my teeth. "It's not like that, Will. I'm doing it for his girlfriend. She's been wonderful."

"What will your father say when he finds out?" Will questions. "You're still being a representative of Dalton Enterprises."

"Stepfather," I grit out. I might not have a clue who my biological father is, but Thomas Dalton has never been my father. Not the way he should have been, and I refuse to claim him as such now. "And I don't care what he thinks."

Will's laugh sounds as mean as he intends it to. "Keep telling yourself that, Katrina."

"I need to go, Will," I snap, fighting back the urge to cry and be sick. Why did he have to call out all my insecurities? "I have to get some sleep."

He doesn't press me. Doesn't mock the fact that I don't usually sleep all that well and can never fall asleep before midnight like I expect him to. Instead, he just smiles, like he's accomplished all he wanted to. "Sounds good. I'll talk to you later."

I nod. "I lov—"

He disconnects the call.

Chapter 9

Katrina

February 2024

The next morning, I'm awoken by a phone call at six o'clock. A whole hour and a half before my alarm is even supposed to go off. After my phone call with Will, I hadn't slept at all. I spent most of the night tossing and turning, thinking back on our relationship, wondering if there was ever a time I was happy. If I ever felt loved or desired in his presence. The answer made me want to be sick. The rest of the night, seeping into the early morning hours, was spent trying to figure out what to do with that realization.

The answer ended up being a disappointing nothing because I couldn't just end a two-year relationship out of nowhere. Especially when he got along with Thomas and my mother so well. He is the first boyfriend I've ever had, and I knew he'd probably be my last. My only. My mother's statements hold some weight: not everyone is going to want me, so maybe I need to hold on to the one who does.

No matter what.

It doesn't help that the deep, smooth voice of Carter Abrams has infiltrated my dreams. My imagination hasn't even attempted to conjure up images of what the man could look like, instead allowing me to float in a blissful slumber, surrounded by a voice I haven't been able to get out of my mind.

I've barely drifted off when Thomas calls, wrenching me from one of those very dreams. Thomas wants to have a one-month chat about the update to the pool. Bleary-eyed, I answer all his questions as I stumble into the kitchen to make coffee, which would have been easier if I'd remembered my glasses sitting on the nightstand. He drones on and on about timeline and numbers, everything I already had memorized, before he finally decided he should let me get to the job site.

Before I hang up, he tells me his opinion about helping Bryce and Josie with their house. My blood boils as I listen to him criticize me for not having my priorities straight and, if it should impact my progress on the pool, he'll pull me from the project and make me come home. I'd turned thirty less than a week into this project, but he talks to me like I'm a child.

By the time I finally get him off the phone, I'm going to be late. I send Bryce a text, knowing he'd be at the property to get some work done, before getting ready in a rush. A simple outfit of jeans and a crewneck sweatshirt is all I have time for, my hair going into a messy bun as I run out the door, a large travel mug of coffee in hand.

Bryce is standing at the lobby desk when I walk in. I can hear the faint sounds of the crew getting ready for the day on the pool deck. He barely looks up from some paperwork when I enter. "Morning. They said they might have to cut electricity today."

"No shit," I mutter, dropping my stuff by the desk. I can feel his gaze on me as I look through my bag for my laptop. "I told you they'd be working on some wiring out there today."

"And I'm just reminding you we could be plunged into total darkness at any moment," he replies evenly. "You know, since we work in a building that has a giant hole in it."

"I'm sorry," I groan. "I shouldn't have snapp—"

"You don't have to apologize to me," he cuts me off. "Look, I get it, you're still mad at me, but I thought—"

Now it's my turn to cut him off. "It's not that, Bryce. I meant what I said yesterday. We're good and I have nothing to be mad at you for. I had a shitty morning."

His brow arches, looking at me curiously. "Anything I can do to help?"

Sighing, I collapse into a chair and take a long sip of my coffee, laptop forgotten on the desk. "Unless you know how to convince my boss, who's also my stepfather, that I'm an adult who's good at her job and convince my boyfriend to care about my life. Oh, and for my boyfriend to stop telling my stepfather, who's also my boss, things I tell him in confidence, then no."

His eyes widen. "Wow, that's quite the morning."

"Some of the boyfriend stuff happened last night," I reply, flipping my hand dismissively. "But don't act so shocked, you asked."

"Right, I did." He takes the other seat, looking at me. I stay slouched in my own chair, looking at him expectantly over my mug. "When it comes to the boss thing, I can't really help. Besides coaches and sponsors, I've mostly worked for myself. I lasted a grand total of three months in a corporate job, but hated it so much I quit and moved halfway across the country to open a club with my best friend."

"Which tells me you ultimately knew what you wanted. Even if you weren't ready to accept it. All I know is this job, and I can't jeopardize it."

"I don't know who you've talked to, but I had no idea what I wanted." He chuckles. "That was the problem. I knew what I didn't want, but I wasn't ready to admit it to myself or anyone else, mainly because it was the logical next step."

"I . . ." I swallow thickly. I have more in common with Bryce Clark than I ever would have thought. "I did not know that. I kind of assumed."

"People have assumed things about me, and Carter, for years. We're used to it."

He's always seemed like the kind of guy who's nothing but sure and steady in his own confidence. He seemed to have his shit together—he's opening a business, met the love of his life, and he's done more in thirty years than I will ever achieve in my lifetime. Hearing that he's struggled just like the rest of the world is humbling. It's making me feel less uncertain and lonely.

"I worked my whole life for a career that was over in a matter of seconds, and it's not something most people care about." He motions to me like I'm the prime example, and I laugh. "After swimming was done, I did what I thought was the best next step, and I was wrong. I'll never regret it, because it got me Josie, but I wasn't happy."

I bite the corner of my lip. "What are you getting at here, Bryce?"

"Don't wait around hoping things will get better. You'll waste your life doing that. Your happiness is your own responsibility. Putting it in the hands of someone else will only lead to disappointment. Even if the person you trust it with is your stepfather or your boyfriend."

I see it now. For the first time in a month, I see what it's like to be Bryce Clark's friend and I realize I was right. He'd go to hell and back for other people, no matter how much it might hurt him. Tears sting the corner of my eyes, but I feel like I've just come from the most productive therapy session I've ever had. Therapy has never been as real to me as this conversation.

Maybe I need to add finding a new therapist to the list of things I need to do.

"You know, when you say things like that, I can almost see why Josie's interested in you." Teasing has always been my default when I don't want to accept whatever else I'm feeling.

Laughing, he stands up. "Trust me, I know I hit the lottery with her."

"Good." I grin back. "You'd be stupid to fuck it up."

"Never," he promises. "But Kat?"

"Hmm?" I question around a sip of coffee.

"What I said applies to the boyfriend, too. If he doesn't see you or care about you, maybe it's time to find someone who will."

No one has ever said it to me so plainly. I know Liam and Nadine both think Will is a dick, but neither one has ever said it. They tiptoe around it, avoiding him when we're at events together or when I bring him up in conversation. There have been so many signs. Signs telling me to abandon ship and look for higher ground, but I don't listen to them.

What if higher ground is just as unstable? What if this is the best I can get and I let it go? What if this really is as good as it gets for me?

There's a loud clank, followed by a horrid grinding sound from the outside pool. Both Bryce and I look panicked, but I'm grateful for the save. I stand up as well. "I should go see what that's about."

He nods. "Just think about what I said, okay?"

"I will," I promise, because I'm sure I won't be able to think of anything else.

Chapter 10

Carter

February 2024

> How much groveling do I have to do to get you to forgive me?

The text message has been sitting on read for days. Not because I'm avoiding her, but because I'm not sure how to respond to it. I can't pretend I wasn't stunned by the phone call, but she hadn't offended me. She doesn't know what she's talking about when it comes to the sport and the expectations placed on me, and I can't fault her for that. There are a lot of people who know nothing about swimming.

That has always bugged Bryce more than me. I get his frustration, but I don't see the point in fighting to get people to care about something that's important to me. The people who do care and matter are the ones who show up—that's a philosophy that has served me well in both my personal life and my career. Bryce sees it differently, though. Which is why he confronted her; he was looking out for me and the sport we love. I wish he would have let me handle it.

Kat might have stepped over some professional lines, but she shouldn't feel like groveling for forgiveness is the only way to fix it.

Which is why I ultimately decide to call her. I'm not sure she'll even pick up after I ignored her message for so long, but I have to try.

Eventually, the ringing cuts out. "Hey."

She sounds so tentative, so unsure of herself. I instantly hate it. Hate that she's not sure how to talk to me. "Hey, you had a question about groveling for forgiveness or something?"

"I texted you that days ago."

"I know," I reply, "and I shouldn't have waited so long to respond. I am sorry about that, but, Kat, there's nothing to forgive. You didn't do anything wrong."

"Are you crazy? Of course I did! I was rude and unprofessional."

Katrina Dalton could give Bryce Clark a run for his money. They're both ridiculously stubborn, which makes their weird feud at the start of this make a lot more sense.

"The way I see it, you were watching out for my business, and by extent, my best friend. You can't help what you don't know, and it sounded like I was taking advantage of Bryce. I would have had the same reaction if I were in your shoes."

I can't say I would have called someone out the way she did, but hey, we can't all have the same level of confidence.

"Well, I get it now," she assures me. "Or, at least, I get it more than I previously did. Bryce made sure of that."

I rub at my forehead. "He shouldn't have spoken to you that way. I was planning to talk to you about it."

"Don't be mad at him. I'm glad he did it. It's not just about you, Carter."

"Wow, way to make a guy feel special," I joke, mock horror seeped into every word.

It has the desired effect as she giggles into the phone, the sound melodic in my ear. "You know what I mean! I've been treating Bryce just as unfairly, questioning every design choice you guys made with Liam; he had a right to be mad at me, too."

"Like I said, it sounds like you were trying to make the remodel as successful as possible, and we can't fault you for that," I say. "I fully understand where you were coming from, and it'd make total sense for a pool that'll primarily be used for recreational purposes."

"But that's not what you and Bryce are trying to do here."

"No, it's not, but it's also not your fault for not understanding that. We could have done more to help you understand."

"I also could have done more research to understand the specs of the project better. I really am sorry. I want you to know that."

"I don't doubt it at all. We're good, Katrina. You're not in any danger of getting fired or having your boss called. You apologized and we're fixing it."

I hear a shaky breath on her side of the phone—something that I've always seen as a sign to move on from the topic of conversation. I have nothing left to say and am glad we've cleared the air. I wouldn't mind talking to her more, but before I get the chance, she's telling me she needs to go because her boyfriend is calling. She thanks me again for being so understanding and doesn't give me a chance to reply before she hangs up.

Boyfriend. The word pierces through my heart. It's ridiculous to be affected by the fact she has a boyfriend when I don't even know her, not really. Sure, she's fun to talk to, and she's been a immense help when it comes to getting my mind off my dwindling career, but it's not enough to establish a crush with. Yet, the minute she said boyfriend, it felt like one more thing I could cling to was floating away from me.

Then again, the last thing I should be doing is getting caught up in a fantasy. Especially with someone who has a significant other.

Two days after my phone call with Kat, I'm at the gym halfway through my workout when someone asks me if I need a spot. I turn to accept the offer and am shocked to see Bryce standing behind me, looking smug as hell. It'd been a couple of months. We've gone longer than that without seeing each other, but right now, he was the only person I wanted to see.

"What are you doing here?" I ask once we separate from the hug. "Is Josie here?"

"No, she and Kat are having a girl's weekend, whatever that means." I laugh at the uncertainty on his face. "So, I decided, you know what, I deserve a guy's weekend."

"Hell, yeah." I reach for my water bottle. "How long are you here for?"

"I told Josie I'd be back tomorrow." He looks around the gym, hands on his hips. That's when I notice he's dressed in jeans and a T-shirt. Not exactly the right apparel to workout in.

I raise my brow while I take a drink. "Are we working out? How did you even know I was here?"

"I thought you'd be swimming," he admits. "I found Coach, and he told me you were here. I mean, we can workout if you need to."

I shrug, knowing an intense workout is the last thing on Bryce's mind right now. "Or we could go get dinner and a beer."

"Oh, thank god." He relaxes, nodding. "Yes, let's do that."

Which is how we find ourselves sitting across from one another forty-five minutes later with cold beers paired with chips and salsa. Bryce fills me in on the latest developments at the pool and the budding friendship between Josie and Kat. I'm excited to hear they were getting along so well, figuring they could be good for each other during this whole thing. I am worried about what's going to happen when Mia joins the fray in a couple of days. I'm not sure Bryce can cope with the two of them together.

Then, somehow, the topic of conversation turns to swimming.

"I meant to tell you, that was a hell of a swim a couple weeks back in Indianapolis," he comments. "I think Josie broke my eardrum she was cheering so loud."

I knew which one he was referencing, my first place finish in the 400-meter IM at the first meet of the year. The time was seconds better than either me or my coach thought I'd be, and it felt like a good start to the year. "Thanks. I'm not sure where that came from."

"Bull," Bryce scoffs. "That's your training paying off, doing exactly what it should be doing. You're setting yourself up for a kickass season that'll end up with you going to your third Olympics."

I'm quiet for a second, not sure how I want to respond to that. I know what he's doing. We've been each other's hype team for as long as I can remember, but this is different. Yes, I'm posting solid times, but Trials are still months away and I'm not the only athlete with Paris on his mind. Hell, I'm not the only one who's looking at this like it's my last chance.

"You wanna tell me what's going on with you?" Apparently, I've done a piss-poor job of hiding my rising anxiety from him. He's watching me closely, a chip dangling in his hand. "I mean, I think I know, but I'd like to hear it from you."

I groan, dropping my head back against my chair. "Don't make me say it out loud, man."

"It helps when you do," he countered around a mouth full of chips. "Trust me."

I make a face, reaching for my beer. "Don't talk with your mouth full. What would your mother think?"

"If you don't want to be done after this, you can tell me," he says after he swallows. "I know I've said it before, but I'm going to keep reminding you. Don't quit until you're ready."

Swallowing the drink I'd just taken, I shake my head. "That's not it. I know I'm done after this; it's not the same as it was, and everything hurts more. I'm ready to be done."

Bryce frowns at me. "If you're not freaked out about retiring, then what's got you so freaked out? Is it about what happens after?"

"Yeah, obviously," I scoff. "Weren't you, dude?"

"That's not the same and you know it."

"It is, though!" I lean my arms against the table. "You settled for a job you knew you'd hate, I know that, and you figured out a way to make it work. I'm staring at a future that I want, but I have no guarantee it'll even work out. And, if it doesn't, I'll take my best friend and his girlfriend down with me. Two people who moved halfway across the country to do this with me."

"Take us down with you?" Bryce's tone is incredulous, eyes wide. "Carter, what the hell are you talking about?"

"You and Josie, obviously!" I wave my hand in front of me as if I can manifest his girlfriend to be here, too. "You guys gave up everything to come do this with me—what if it fails?"

"It's going to work out because we're all determined as fuck, Carter," he insists. "Besides, what do you mean we gave up everything to do this with you? I'd already sent my resignation when you called, and Josie was about to do the same; the only thing the two of us did with this was change locations and get fresh starts. Both as individuals and as a couple. That's something we'll always be grateful to you for."

"You say that now, but will that still be true if this whole thing goes up in flames?"

"Flames? You better be talking metaphorically, Carter. Listen to me, it hasn't even started yet, and you're already worried about this? That's ridiculous. We're not going to have immediate success. No one does, but we know what hard work does and we're willing to make it happen. Answer me this: Do you want to do anything other than what we're doing?"

"No," I admit. It's true. There's a reason I asked him to do this with me. There's a reason I found myself up late at night looking at cheap places we could remodel. I wanted this when I bought it and I want it more now.

"Me neither," he promises. "If I've learned anything, it's that we all make choices. I chose to do this with you, Josie chose to come with me, and Mia chose to take the opportunity we're giving her. If it fails, we're all equally responsible for the impact it'll have on us. It's not just on your shoulders."

I take a deep breath, looking across the table at him. I don't get the chance to say anything more, though, as the server brings our food. We're momentarily distracted as he makes sure we have everything we need, offering another round of beers and disappears for a moment before returning with them.

We're both several bites in when I break the silence again. "I'm sorry for just throwing all that out there, Bryce."

He swallows the bite he just took, reaching for his beer to wash it down. "Don't apologize, Carter. Just talk to me, okay? Or Josie. Literally anyone. You don't need to be a ball of anxiety over nothing. We're here for you."

I nod, picking at the fries on my plate. "And it's not going to fail."

"Not a chance in hell."

Somewhere, deep down in me, I believe him. I know the people involved in this are willing to do the work, to put in the long hours, and make this happen. Something in me says that ten years from now, we'll wonder why it was ever a question. We'll be loving our lives and it's all because of the choices we make now. It's hard to let yourself see the future when so many things can go wrong in the present. With the right people to lean on, maybe it doesn't have to be so scary.

Chapter 11

Katrina

February 2024

I hear the excited squealing before I have the chance to round the corner and enter the lobby. Once I do, I have no question as to what's going on. Across the room, Josie is embracing a taller woman while jumping up and down. This could only mean one thing: Mia Sheridan has arrived.

Off to the side, Bryce is rolling his eyes, but there's a fond smile on his face. His gaze drifts over to me as I approach from the outside pool I was just checking on. "You would think they haven't seen each other in years, right? We were literally in Charlotte last weekend helping her pack."

"Oh, my god! You must be Kat!"

With a slight jump, I glance over at Mia to see her smiling at me. Her bright and welcoming smile is almost a contradiction to the rest of the woman standing before me. She's tall, with long legs encased in dark, torn jeans, and a cute top exposing tattoos scattered along her arms and collarbones. Her dark brown hair is in a messy pile on top of her head, and light, natural makeup highlights her pale skin. Her lipstick is a deep, vibrant shade of red. And it's perfectly applied.

I'm instantly jealous of her makeup skills.

"Hi." I grin back when I remember she had spoken to me. I extend my hand toward her. "Yeah, I'm Kat. Nice to meet you."

"You too," she beams back, shaking my hand. "Josie has been keeping me updated on the construction—things are coming together beautifully."

A faint blush creeps up my cheeks. "Thank you, but it's easy to follow a plan."

She scoffs. "Oh, please. It's easy to come up with a plan, and hard as hell to execute one. Plus, we all know Bryce wouldn't be able to pull any of this off without you."

"Awe, I love you, too, Mia," he sasses back.

She pays him absolutely no mind. "From what Josie's told me, I think the two of us are going to get along great."

Stepping up behind Josie to wrap his arms around her, Bryce groans. "Oh god, there's two of them now. Why didn't I see that coming?"

Josie laughs, patting his arm. "I think you'll be fine."

"Easy for you to say. They both like you."

"You know you're my favorite of all her boyfriends, Clark!"

"That's not a compliment, Mia," he shoots back. Josie looks like someone just told her the secret to happiness at the two of them fighting. "I've heard everything about them, met one of them, and they were all assholes."

"Well, she's clearly not begging Josie to breakup with you, Bryce." I don't know where my teasing tone came from, but I'm saying the words before I even register them. I'm not used to bantering with him. I keep going. "I think that means it is a compliment."

Mia's smiling face turns back to me. "Yes, thank you! Jos, you were right. We're going to be great friends."

"You remind me of one another," Josie says from Bryce's arms.

And I think Josie is losing it.

I can't see a single thing I have in common with the woman in front of me, no matter how much I wish I could be more like her. Mia seems to be the embodiment of a female badass and might even come across a little unapproachable. That's not me at all.

"If we both love to give Bryce a hard time, we'll be great together," Mia declares.

"Yes, I'm so happy we hired you, Mia. Now I get to deal with you being mean to me every day."

"Honestly, it was the main selling point for me," she admits with a smirk.

I'm not sure what Bryce and Carter have to offer Mia in terms of a job, but I get the sense she was needing a fresh start. Bryce and Josie look out for the people they care about; that much has already become true. I'm learning that being their friend means someone always has my back. It's not something I'm used to, and not something I necessarily have now, but I feel myself getting closer to it. Believing I'm deserving of a something like that.

"How about Josie and Kat show me around?" Mia's question pulls me back to the present. "I'd love to see how everything's coming together."

Reluctantly, Bryce releases Josie. "That's fine. I have a clinic I need to get to at one of the schools."

"Clinic?" I question, unsure what he means by that.

"It's like a swim lesson for kids thinking about joining a team," Mia explains. "Bryce leads them in a series of sets and teaches them other techniques they can use and then runs them through some drills. A lot of schools and teams will jump at the chance to have someone like Bryce teach their kids."

I glance at Bryce, who shrugs. "It's a good way to get some money coming in until our club is up and running. Carter and I will also run some clinics or camps in the summer, so it's extra practice for that."

I don't know why, but I didn't think Bryce was earning an income right now. I thought all of this was being funded by the money he earned as a professional. Now that I know he's working, at least in some regard, it explains why he's rarely home on the weekends and why that's when Josie wants someone to hang out with.

"Okay, show me around!"

After showing Mia around the whole complex, Josie invites me to join the two of them for dinner. Desperate for a night out with friends, or at least people who could become friends, I readily agree. I can't remember the last time I'd gone out with people who weren't work colleagues or my boyfriend. Having a social life has never been a major concern of mine since I've been too focused on pleasing my mother and getting Thomas to take me seriously as an employee.

On the rare occasions I did go out with people my own age, they're usually Will's friends, and they made sure I knew I was the odd one out. I didn't have a medical degree or a fancy office in downtown Charleston. I didn't fit into whatever mold they thought a doctor's girlfriend should fit into. I haven't hung out with Will's friends for over a year, and he hasn't made a single comment about it.

Hours later, as I sit in a fun industrial bar with a margarita in front of me and the menu in my hand, I can't help but feel like I've missed out on something fundamental. Mia and Josie chat amicably about the menu with the easy confidence that comes with years of friendship that tells me they'd be perfectly comfortable in total silence.

Silence scares me.

My phone buzzes at my elbow with another text from Will. He'd called me while I was getting ready, wanting to complain about his day. He hadn't been too happy when I cut him off, telling him I had plans tonight. Especially because it was with people he doesn't know. I ignore it.

It buzzes five minutes later, once the server has taken our orders and collected the menus. I glare down at it, silently willing him to leave me alone. When I want to talk to him, he can't be bothered, but the first time I have plans, he wants to be involved.

"If you glare at that phone any harder, it might burst into flames."

A faint blush coats my cheeks as I flip the phone to rest face down on the table. When I look up, Mia is grinning at me over the top of her margarita. "Sorry, my boyfriend won't stop texting me even though I told him I'm out with friends."

I try not to cringe at my use of "friends". We probably weren't close enough for that, yet. Even Josie and I weren't quite there.

"I didn't know you have a boyfriend," Josie comments, looking intrigued.

"Sounds a bit possessive to me," Mia retorts.

I bite my lip, keeping my need to defend him at bay. Will has never come up in a conversation with Josie and me, despite the fact we've gotten closer. Despite the fact, I confided in Carter about him. Apparently, the news hadn't spread. And Mia's practically a stranger; she's only known me a few hours, but easily picked up on something I haven't been ready to admit to myself.

My phone buzzes again. Then once more.

I grab it and chuck it in my purse.

Mia arches a dark brow. "If that's his response to you hanging out with friends, you need to cut your losses and run. How long have you been together?"

"Two years. My mother's the head of emergency medicine at Charleston Hospital, and she introduced us during his final year as a resident. We've been together since."

I pick at the corner of my napkin, thinking back on our relationship. It was just another thing my mother orchestrated for me. Sure, Will is attractive, and he's generally a good guy, but is he the right person for me? I've been wondering that for longer than I care to admit. The way he treats me isn't what I want, and sometimes I realize I deserve better, but it's going out and getting it that scares me.

The fear of being alone keeps me with the easy choice.

"Do you want to talk about it, Kat?" Josie's question is gentle, gaze locked on mine. "You've got two great listeners right here, and we've both been through some shit when it comes to love."

"I just . . ." I struggle to find the right words. "Have you ever looked at someone one day and just knew it was going to end?"

"God, yes," Mia says with a snort. "My ex-girlfriend."

"Same," Josie admits. "With Bryce."

"And technically, that one happened twice," Mia points out.

My jaw drops open at the idea of Josie and Bryce ever being anything other than Josie and Bryce. The world's most adorable couple had been split up? Multiple times! If it happened to them, what does that mean for the rest of the world? "What?" I gasp. "No way! You two are—"

"Not always perfect," Josie cuts in. "We're in a good place now, but it took a lot of work. God, it still takes a lot of work."

"Have they always been disgustingly adorable?" Mia questions. "Yes, but it wasn't the healthiest relationship, and they both had a lot of growing up to do."

After giving Mia a look I can't read, Josie continues, "The point is, the two of us knew we wanted to make it work, so we decided to fight for it. And we know it'll always take work, so we continue to fight for it. That's what you do when you want it to last."

"It's actually quite simple. If you're wondering if you'd be better off without him, I think you already have your answer."

I blink at Mia, who just made it sound so simple, but it's never that simple.

"He's not the only guy out there," she continues, reading my thoughts. "I know what you're thinking, Kat. He's not the only man out there who can love you."

My jaw drops open again. "*How?*"

Josie shrugs. "Don't ask me. It's her superpower, and I've learned to stop questioning it."

Lips pursed, Mia pins me with a serious look. "You're sitting here with two women who get it. We know media and society can fuck with our self-image and confidence. Women like us don't get x, y, or z. For the most part, we know it's bullshit, but every once in a while, that insecurity creeps in, and we believe it. But that doesn't mean you have to stay with a shitty dude because he made you think he's the only one who'll want you."

"Whoa." I hold my hands up, trying to stop her. "He never said—"

She cuts off my lie before it can even leave my mouth, eyes narrowed into a glare. "Nope. No way. We are not making excuses for shitty men. I don't care what he did or did not say. I can see it written all over your face. I've known you for a couple hours but can already tell you're an intelligent, beautiful, badass woman. You don't need him to validate who you are."

I blink, an unexplainable surge of confidence welling up inside me. "Holy shit," I breathe, "you should be a motivational speaker."

She reaches for her margarita again, waving her hand as she takes a long drink. "Oh, absolutely not. I hate people far too much for that."

I look at Josie, who's smiling in amusement. "She's not exaggerating. I think we're two of maybe ten people she likes."

"Ten is generous." She peers at me again, looking calculating. "So, what are you going to do?"

I know better than to do anything about it right now. It'd be shitty of me to end a two-year relationship while I'm not in the same city as him. I need to use this time to think about it seriously, though. I need to figure out where I see us going. More importantly, I need to decide if I see him in my future, or if I even want to. If I'm using this time to prove myself—prove my worth and take charge of my life—that should be part of it, right?

"I guess I have a lot of thinking to do," I admit, playing with the straw in my drink. "Figure out what I want to do."

Sensing the shift in mood, Josie reaches over and squeezes my free hand. She's smiling softly when I look up at her. "We'll be here if you need to talk."

I realize this is one of those magical moments where a friendship starts. Where it becomes real and you start to get comfortable around each other, opening up about things you'd never talked about before. Most of the time, I keep people at arm's length, but I have the door open wide for these two. It's scary to be vulnerable, but it's freeing, too. Knowing I don't have to carry everything on my own and that there are people out there who get it and want to help.

Now I just needed to trust that I deserve this. Friends who care about me for who I am rather than for what I can get them or do for them. A friendship I deserve.

"I know we haven't gotten our food yet," Josie declares, breaking the silence, "but please tell me we're getting dessert."

I laugh as Mia groans happily. "I'm down if you guys are."

Mia reaches for the dessert menu. "If they don't have ice cream, we're going somewhere else."

I watch as Mia tugs Josie across the parking lot to her car, both still giggling at whatever idiotic thing set us off. A smile is still on my face, but I'm not sure where it came from. It'd been forever since I had a night like this—full of laughter and good memories. We'd all only had a single drink, which was hours ago, but we'd bonded over childhood celebrity crushes (Am I the only one who remembers the live action *Peter Pan* from 2003?), and shared experiences of being considered fat women by society, and how others seemed convinced that the only way a woman can be healthy is to be thin.

My phone vibrates in my cupholder as I start my car; another text message from Will.

Answering or calling him would mean potentially ruining my good mood, which isn't something I'm at all interested in. Ignoring him for long is also impossible. Which is why I'm dialing the number before I pull out of the parking spot, the sound of ringing overtaking the car.

Shockingly, he answers before the line can ring twice. "Why haven't you texted me back?" His tone is demanding, dampening my mood. "I've been texting you for hours! What if something happened to you?"

"You knew I was out with friends, Will." I roll my eyes, checking both directions as I pull out of the parking lot. The streets of Columbia are quiet at this late hour. "Why were you texting me that much when you knew I was busy? You've never texted me that much."

"That is not true."

"What?" I snort out a laugh. "Yes, it is."

Even when we first started talking, we never texted that much. His focus was on work, never on our budding relationship. I was the one who would start and lead conversations, and not much has changed since we've been together. At least now, I know what to expect from him.

"What do you need, Will?"

"Why do you think I need something?" He was being repetitive in a condescending way, trying to act like the victim in this moment, but I'm too tired and happy to lean into it. "Maybe I just want to talk to my girlfriend. Is that a crime now or something?"

"You knew I was at dinner." I stress my point, ignoring the acidic, nauseating way my stomach twists. A reminder of what I'd talked about only hours before. "You knew nothing was wrong."

"Let me get this straight. You ignore your boyfriend when you're with these friends?" I can see it unfolding—the way he's going to turn this until I look like the bad guy. "That's not like you. I'm not sure how I feel about you hanging out with people who make you think you have to choose."

"Well then, it's a good thing I don't ask for your permission on who I can be friends with."

I've never spoken back to him like that before, but it's kind of invigorating. It's not the first time I've thought about saying something like this to him, but it's the first time I let the words come tumbling out. I don't even care how mad it makes him; the strength I feel in this moment is empowering in a way I've never felt before.

"I don't like this, Katrina," Will warns, anger evident in his tone. "I don't like what these women seem to be doing to you. They're interfering in a relationship they know nothing about."

I rub at my brow, lips pursed into a thin line. "They had nothing to do with me not texting you, Will. I haven't told them much about you, if I'm being honest."

That was apparently the worst thing to say. "Oh, so you don't want to tell people we're together? And you're telling me to trust you?"

I groan, coming to a stop at a yellow light. "That's not—"

"I don't want to talk about it, Kat." I can't remember the last time he called me Kat. "I need to go. I'll talk to you later."

The car fills with silence for a second before music comes over the speakers to replace the call. Groaning, I laid my head down on the steering wheel, taking several deep breaths. Mia and Josie are right; I need to figure out what I want in life and whether it includes Will.

The light is barely green when someone behind me beeps their horn. I wave in apology as I accelerate, feeling more conflicted than I've felt in years.

The conversation with Mia and Josie rings in my ears, gently reminding me that I deserve to find someone who treats me right. Who doesn't make me feel guilty about friendships and having a life of my own outside of a relationship. The more physical distance I put between myself and Will, the easier it feels to breathe. And shouldn't that be the sign I've been looking for?

By the time I pull back into my rental, I've firmly made up my mind: the relationship has to end. Now I just have to figure out when that'll happen.

Chapter 12

Katrina

February 2024

One morning, as we're going over plans for the indoor pool, Bryce shocks me by randomly agreeing to add a solid wall of windows. I feel like I won a battle by default. It's not the main wall, but it is the one at the end of the pool. Liam's designs already call for quite a few windows, but still, it's a big ask, and I'm stunned when Bryce agrees.

He only let me show him one reference photo and I had ten ready.

I eye him warily. "That was way too easy. Did Josie or Mia tell you I was going to talk to you about this?"

I'd brought it up at dinner the other night, explaining how I still think we need more natural light. They both agreed and then proceeded to let me show them all ten of my reference photos before insisting on talking to Bryce again. If I can't have one huge wall of windows, why not compromise for a smaller one?

He shook his head. "No, I think it's a great solution. It's not that I hated the idea of the windows on the west wall; I just worried about the sun. You have a great eye for design, Kat."

I want to take the compliment and the win, but I know better than that. While I don't think he's lying to me, there's something more to it than that. "You want something, Bryce Clark. What is it?"

"Nothing!" he stresses, holding his hands up in defense.

Unconvinced, I cross my arms over my chest. "I'm not buying it. What do you want?"

He holds my gaze for two seconds before he folds. "All right, fine. Don't look so smug."

I try and fail to wipe the smirk off my face. "Okay, out with it."

"Do you have anything going on this weekend?" he asks. "From Thursday through Sunday afternoon."

Bryce has never once asked me something like that. "Um, no." I frown. "Not that I know of. Why?"

"Great!" He claps his hands together like he's forming some sort of evil plan and, I must admit, I'm a little afraid. Maybe I shouldn't have pushed him so hard. "That means you can come with us to the meet!"

"Meet?" My eyes are wide in surprise. "What meet? And where?"

"Josie, Mia, and I are all going up to Greensboro this weekend. There's a pro meet and Carter's competing, so we thought we'd go support him."

I'm still not sure how I fit into this whole plan, but my heartrate quickens at the idea of being in the same city as Carter. Am I ready for that? Either this man will live up to the crazy fantasy I've created, and we'll have an even bigger problem than we already have. Or he won't and things will go on like normal. Either way, I'll have to face him, eventually.

And where does this fantasy I've built up leave me with my current relationship? I'm not cheating, not even emotionally, but it feels like I'm doing something wrong. If Carter does live up to that fantasy, and this becomes something more real and harder to ignore, where do I go then?

"We'll head out on Thursday afternoon," Bryce continues, "and come back on Sunday afternoon. We figured you and Mia could bunk together. Does that work for you?"

"Sure." I nod along with the plans. "I'm not sure why you want me there, though."

"I think it'd be a great opportunity to see what a functioning natatorium looks like." He makes a good point, and I had been the one telling him that I was interested in learning more about the sport. "You can see what works and what doesn't work—ask us questions if you have them. Plus, you've been working here for a month and a half. Don't you think it's about time you meet Carter?"

If only he knew that was the part I was less unsure about than anything else.

"Does he know I'm coming?" I ask, not wanting to run the risk of Bryce somehow clueing in on what I'm thinking. "I don't want to catch him off guard. A swim meet is technically his place of work."

"I'll let him know," Bryce assures me, like it's no big deal. Which, to him, it's not. To me, I feel like I'm about to meet some mystical prince in a storybook. Isn't there some saying about not meeting your heroes because they never live up to your expectations? Is it true with men? "He'll be excited to meet you. So, what do you say? Are you in?"

"Sure." I grin because there's really no reason to say no. "Sounds like fun."

"Welcome to your first swim meet!" Josie's grinning at me, her arms spread wide before her like she's showing me the whole world.

But all that's in front of us is a pool. Granted, it's a packed pool, but still just a pool. I try to take in all the chaos happening in the water, the different voices fighting to be heard over the noise, and wonder how this isn't making anyone else anxious. Coaches are pacing the deck, swimmers are packed into the lanes like sardines, and there's so much whistling.

Then again, this is their world, so I'm sure they're used to it. I'm more out of my element than ever before.

"I'm not really sure what I'm supposed to be looking at," I finally admit.

Josie, Bryce, and Mia all have an ease about them that's different from anything I've ever seen before. They're in control here; they know what to do, who to speak to, and what's expected of them. Their confidence should be reassuring, but it's making my uncertainty worse.

"This isn't supposed to be a fun weekend away." Bryce is all business, as he turns his attention to me. "This is an opportunity for you to see a building like ours in use. The way we want it utilized. Figure out what's working and what's not. Maybe talk to some swimmers."

My eyes widen, cheeks flushing as a guy in a tiny speedo walks by. "You want me to talk to them?" Why has my voice gotten so much higher? "Why?"

His eyes narrow at me. "Because no one knows what a pool needs and doesn't need more than a swimmer. Is that going to be a problem?"

Another guy walks by. This one is in low-riding shorts but no shirt. Does anyone in this sport ever wear clothes?

Josie laughs. "Lighten up, Bryce. She's never been to a swim meet before."

Mia is also grinning at us in amusement. "Yeah, it took your girlfriend several before she could talk to anyone without blushing."

Josie gasps, turning to her best friend like some secret had just been revealed. "Mia!" she hisses her name under her breath, and I feel the smallest bit better.

"Wait, who else made you blush?" Bryce demands, looking between Mia and Josie. "It better not have been—"

Josie is quick to calm him down. "It wasn't! It was just everyone. It takes time to get used to talking to half-naked people."

So that answers my previous question about whether people wear clothes.

"Although she definitely blushed the first time we met Ronan O'Brien."

Bryce gawks at his girlfriend and Josie goes back to glaring at her best friend.

Mia is completely indifferent, though. "Can you blame her, Bryce? The man was beautiful."

I'm just lost. Completely and totally lost. I have no clue who they're talking about, but I don't miss the way Mia talks about him in the past tense. Which instantly pulls my focus from everything going on around me—clearly there's some kind of history there. I'm not privy to the information and something tells me Mia wouldn't give me any if I asked.

"He's still beautiful," Bryce relents with a sigh. "And I'm comfortable enough in my masculinity and sexuality to admit that."

Josie pats his arm as Mia scoffs.

"I'm glad at least one person knows what he looks like," she snarks. "He kind of fell off the face of the earth, didn't he?"

His brow furrows. "What are you talking about? Ronan—"

"I see some seats," Mia cuts him off. She doesn't wait for a reply before she walks off.

Bryce says something to Josie about going to talk to someone, while I follow the dark-haired woman who brought up a topic she doesn't want to talk about.

Josie catches up with me in a couple of strides, her arm linking with mine as she leans in. "Just so you know, that was Mia code for *we are not talking about this.*"

"I figured," I admit. "What happened between her and this Ronan guy?"

Josie frowns, looking ahead at her friend who is climbing the bleachers. "No one knows. Bryce has asked Ronan and I've tried talking to her about it. She won't budge."

Josie releases my arm as she climbs up behind Mia. I follow suit, stunned there's something these two inseparable friends have kept from one another. But I'm not going to ask Mia about it. If she doesn't want Josie to know, she won't tell someone who's practically a stranger. I take my seat next to Josie, who has a stapled stack of papers in her hand, skimming what looks to be a long list of names, and look at the new view I have.

As I scan the deck, I'm realizing several things about the design at once. First, Bryce is right about the amount of seating they'll need for spectators. We are early, but the benches are already crowded, some families basically in each other's laps. Hopefully, with the amount of seating we're installing, that won't be a problem during any meet they host. Another thing I notice is how the windows are going to massively help with natural light. Right now, everything feels hazy under the too harsh florescent lighting.

I should talk to Bryce about the kind of lighting we're putting in the pool.

As I type a note to myself, I feel a pair of eyes on me. When I look up, there are literally a hundred people around, but I keep looking until my eyes connect with someone else's. He's standing beside a starting block, looking directly at us with his mouth gaped open. He's tall, but not quite as tall as Bryce, and he's wearing the world's tiniest speedo. Now we're just staring at each other like two idiots who don't know what they're looking at.

Which makes sense because I'm not sure I do.

He's living up the fantasies I've created in my head.

"Who are you—Oh, that's Carter!" I can practically hear the smile in Josie's voice and see the shadow of her arm moving in a wave, but I can't look away. "The two of you haven't met yet, right?"

I shake my head, and then my heart sinks at the thought of her calling him over. I grab her arm and wrench it down in what is a completely obvious gesture. She looks at me, startled.

"I cannot talk to him while he's wearing a speedo," I exclaim, hoping the panic seems legit. She doesn't need to know I'm imagining watching water drops sliding down a well-toned, tanned chest. At this point, they both understand the relationship between Will and me is done. I'm just waiting to be back home to officially end it. I'd never act on my feelings toward Carter, but I also don't think it's smart to be that close to an attractive man when he's basically naked. "You said it yourself. It's weird talking to them when they're wearing nothing."

"He's not wearing a speedo." Josie laughs, shaking her head. I gawk at her, my eyes drifting back to where Carter stands, or stood. He's disappeared off the deck. I don't know what she calls a speedo, but that was it. "Speedo is a brand. What he was wearing is a brief."

I look at Mia, wondering if Josie has completely lost it, but the other woman just nods and leans closer to be heard over the crowd. "It's a common misconception that just kind of stuck. The suits they wear when they're racing are called Jammers. Carter's sponsorship is with another brand, so he's wearing their version of a brief."

I just blink, more confused now than I was ten minutes ago. Even the wardrobe needs translations and definitions. Could this sport get any more complicated?

"I was hoping he'd come say hello," Josie replies, looking a little sad. "I know it's weird seeing people like this, but it gets better, I promise."

"Plus, Carter is the easiest person to talk to," Mia adds. I want to tell her I already know that, but standing in front of him with all that skin on display and a brief that leaves nothing to the imagination would be dangerous to my heart and my sanity. "I don't know where he went, though."

I glance around the deck, noting that I don't see him either, and am suddenly thankful for small blessings.

"Oh, well." Josie shrugs. "He saw me wave. Maybe he went to find Bryce. I'm sure we'll see him soon."

Fucking hell, I internally groan. Hopefully, when he comes back, he'll have more clothes on.

Chapter 13

Carter

February 2024

I don't care that Bryce is talking to one of our old coaches when I find him; I grab his arm and drag him away from the conversation, flashing a smile at the coach as I do. My parents still raised me to be polite, even when I'm interrupting conversations.

"Hello to you, too." Bryce laughs, practically tripping over his own feet as I drag him to a mostly quiet corner.

Once we're away from anyone we know, I glare up at him. "Dude, what the hell? Did you kidnap our contractor or something?"

The smile drops from his face as he glances across the pool where we can see Josie and Mia. Beside Josie, looking confused and a little uncomfortable, is a strikingly beautiful blonde woman who I can only assume is Kat.

"No, she agreed to come. There was no kidnapping."

"What is she even doing here?" I snap. "And why didn't you warn me?"

"It's not that big of a deal, man." Bryce shrugs. "She's not sure what we need, but is willing to learn, so I figured this was a good chance for her to experience swimming firsthand. There's nothing she's needed for on-site today and wasn't going home for the week-end. It just worked. Why would I need to tell you she's coming?"

"Because it has to do with me and being professional." I fight the urge to look back to where the three women are sitting in the stands. "Some warning would have been nice."

A knowing smirk appears on my best friend's face as he crosses his arms. Internally, I groan. There's nothing worse than a smug Bryce Clark. "Oh, my god, you're flustered."

"What? No—no, I'm not!" My sputtering only makes him laugh. "Dude, shut up. Who the fuck says flustered anymore?"

He cackles. "No, you're totally flustered by this girl! Why?"

"Have you seen her?" I demand, vaguely motioning behind me. I silently pray they're not looking our way because Mia and Josie will know we're talking about them.

Bryce's smugness is back. "Yes, I have. I've been working with her for a month, but this is the first time you're seeing her."

"And I didn't expect her to look like that! You could have at least warned me about *that*."

Bryce knows my type, whether it's a man or a woman, and Katrina hits all my boxes.

"Oh, I'm sorry. I've been too busy pulling our business together to even think about playing cupid between you and our contractor. My bad."

I glare at him. "Stop being an ass."

His grin returns. "I'm not being an ass; I'm having an appropriate reaction to this new information!"

I want to walk away, pretend this conversation never happened, and spend the rest of the weekend pretending I have no idea who he is.

"She's got a boyfriend, man." The words—spoken in a sober tone—are like a bucket of ice water over my head, a reminder of something I'd so conveniently let slip from my conscious. "I don't want you to get your hopes up."

It is too late for that. "Yeah, I know. She told me."

He looks at me with such sympathy; I have to look away. "I know you guys talk, but I didn't know if you knew. From what she's told me and what she's told Josie, he's a bit of an asshole."

I know nothing about her relationship, but I'm instantly inclined to believe she deserves better. If Josie thinks this guy is a jerk, then he most certainly is.

"Apparently, she is considering dumping him." I feel like I've dropped into an alternate universe or something. I never thought I'd be standing on a pool deck gossiping with Bryce about someone else's love life. "If they do, you should talk to her about whatever this is."

That snaps me back to the present. "I'm not talking to her about this weird crush I have on her. I don't even know her. Besides, I thought you didn't like her."

"No," he corrects with the shake of his head. "I never said I didn't like her. I said I found her annoying."

"That's not much better, dude."

"I have a theory," he argues. This ought to be good. "If your best friend finds them annoying, maybe they'll end up being the one. Look at me and Josie!"

My brows arch as I fight back a laugh. "Have you run this theory by either Josie or Mia? Because I think they would tell you that you're an idiot. Besides, it doesn't matter, she has a boyfriend and I have an Olympic team to make. I'm not going to be a rebound."

Bryce sobers up and part of me feels guilty about saying something like that. Although the situations are completely different, I know it hits a nerve with him.

"Don't apologize," he insists before I can even say anything. "I get it. God, you know how much I get it, but don't make the same mistakes I made. I know there's a lot you still want to accomplish, but you've got a lot of life to live on the other side of the Olympics. And that includes things you don't get second chances at."

I swallow against the lump forming in my throat. I don't know how to tell him it's the things on the other side that have me scared shitless.

"Abrams! Get in the water!"

Both Bryce and I turn at the sound of my coach calling my name. He's standing at the edge of the pool, hands on his hips, looking less than impressed.

"You better go, man," Bryce warns. "I remember being on the other side of that look when he was still at Arizona."

Laughing, I nod.

"Just think about what I said!" he calls as I turn to head into the water.

I wave him off over my shoulder, already pulling my cap and goggles from where they were tucked into the edge of my brief at my hip. Coach raises a brow as I approach, ready to ask me if I'm good, but I just shake my head, pulling the cap on.

I can't think about this right now. I have a meet to focus on.

In the past, I've been distracted at meets by talking to my friends or signing autographs. There have been plenty of times I've used the excuse of not being able to avoid it or get away from people. It turns out, when I have the right motivation, it's easy to avoid people. I manage to avoid them until the end of finals, when Bryce basically ambushes me from behind, grabbing my backpack, and hauling me backward.

"What the hell, dude?" I question, turning to find him glaring at me. "I'm trying to get back to the hotel. I'm beat."

He scowls at me. "No, you're not. You're not tired. I've known you for twenty-five years; I know when you're tired. You're coming to dinner with us."

I scowl back like the petty asshole I am. "Why?"

"Because you need to eat." He levels me with a glare, knowing full well he's got a point. "And because my girlfriend is pouting—yes, pouting, because you haven't said hello to her yet. She's convinced she's done something wrong because why else would Carter ever wound her this way?"

My eyes widen in realization of how my behavior probably came off to Josie and Mia. Kat wouldn't know any difference, figuring this is normal for me during a meet like this, but the two of them would and it'd hurt them. Despite only being a couple of hours from Columbia, Josie and I haven't seen much of each other. Building a strong relationship with Josie was the one thing I promised myself I'd fix when she and Bryce got back together, and I would not shut her out again.

"The girls already went ahead to put our name in at the restaurant across the street; it's about a twenty-minute wait," Bryce continues, glancing around here. "Are you done here?"

Swallowing, I nod. He releases my backpack and starts leading me out of the natatorium. "You know I didn't mean to hurt her feelings, right? I was going to say hi. I just—"

"I know," he replies, barely looking at me. "It's just not like you to act like this over someone."

"What do you mean? I wasn't avoiding anyone! I was busy."

He glares at me again, and I deflate. It's hard lying to someone who knows you like the back of his hand. If I never believed Bryce when he told me he was over Josie, why should he believe me when I give him a pathetic excuse like this?

"All right, fine." I sigh. "I just . . . I don't know what to say to her or how to act around her."

"Are you seventeen again with a crush?" he asks. "I haven't seen you this nervous in literal years, not even when you were with the British dude."

"Ben," I stress, rolling my eyes. "His name is Ben, and you know that."

"Of course I do." Bryce smirks at me over his shoulder. "Josie and I got an invite to his wedding."

I roll my eyes, because even though Bryce pretends to dislike him, he and my ex are friends. "Me too. Are you going?"

"It's during the Olympics, so no. Are you planning on going?"

"Shut up." I shove him with a laugh. "Ben realized the mistake after he sent the invite and apologized to me. Which is so crazy to me; it's his wedding, but he wanted me to be a groomsman."

"The crazy part is you being able to be friends with your exes, like all of them," Bryce argues. "Who does that?"

"Step one is not being an asshole all the time," I tease back.

Bryce and I spend the walk over to the restaurant continuing to mess around. He teases me a little more about Katrina and I take the opportunity to turn the tables and focus on his own relationship. I wasn't about to miss the opportunity to give Mr. I-Don't-Want-Anything-Serious shit for buying a house with a woman he once kept at arm's length. By the time we reach the restaurant, I'd forgotten Katrina was even there as I relaxed into the easy familiarity of being around my friends.

I've done this countless times—dinner after a meet with Bryce, Josie, and Mia. This wasn't anything new. Until I saw the flash of blonde hair waiting outside as we approached.

My focus is soon pulled from her, as I see Josie Martin scowling at me, arms crossed in front of her chest. Bryce hadn't been lying when he told me she was pouting.

"Josie." I grin, ignoring Katrina and Mia in favor of wrapping one of my favorite people in a hug. Josie relaxed slightly as I came toward her with outstretched arms, and then she was crowding closer to me, returning the hug. "I didn't mean to ignore you."

She tilts her head to look at me. "You've never not said hi to us."

"I was distracted," I admit, hugging her tighter.

Sighing, she hugs me back just as tight before another set of arms wrap around us. Josie and I both laugh as Mia tackles us in a group hug.

"I'm here, too!" My arm moves to pull her in closer and the three of us stand there hugging for a second.

The two years these women were out of my life made things feel a little less full. It felt like something was missing, but I didn't understand what it was until they came back last spring. The fact we only saw each other a few times a year didn't matter; we'd woven ourselves into each other's lives and when things ended between Josie and Bryce, those threads were cut. I'd hated it. I'd hated not looking up in the stands and seeing them. Then Bryce retired, and the sport felt lonelier again.

Tonight was the first time in a long time I felt like things were back to normal.

Someone clears their throat behind us, and we all poke our heads out of the hug to see Katrina standing there, waving her phone in the air. "The table's ready."

The three of us separate from the hug while Bryce pulls open the door. Josie leads our group inside but, just as I'm about to walk through the door with Katrina trailing behind us, Bryce lets it go, sneaking in after Mia. Fighting the urge to yell at him, because I know exactly what he's doing, I snag the door, and step back to hold it open for Katrina.

She offers me a small smile as we step inside. "Thank you."

The other three are talking to each other as the host leads us on a winding path through the restaurant to our table. Neither of us has held eye contact with the other for longer than two seconds, but the awkward silence is starting to kill me.

Before I can break it, though, she does. "Bryce didn't tell you I was coming this weekend, did he?"

I bite the inside of my cheek, glaring at my best friend. I shake my head. "He did not."

"I figured based on how surprised you looked."

"You could have told me. We just talked yesterday."

"He told me he'd tell you!" she defends. "I had no reason not to believe him."

When we arrive at the table, we all take our seats after some shuffling. I'm not at all surprised to see the seat Bryce bullied me into is right across from Katrina. I kick his shin under the table, hard.

"*Shit*," he curses, reaching down to grab it as he glares at me. "What the hell, Carter?"

I give him my best innocent smile when I look up from my menu. "Oops?"

"Bryce, why didn't you tell Carter I was going to be here this weekend?" Kat doesn't even give him a second to get comfortable before the interrogation starts. I have to say, I'm kind of impressed. "You told me you'd tell him."

He gives her his innocent smile. "Must have slipped my mind. It's not like it's a big deal. Right, Carter?"

I position myself in a way that hides my glare from everyone except Bryce. He shrinks back under it, leaning closer to Josie like she'll save him.

"It's fine," I say in a tone I hope tells him to let it go. Not wanting to make Kat feel uncomfortable, I turn my focus back to her. "It's seriously fine, Kat. I'm happy you're here. What'd you think about your first meet?"

Between ordering and waiting for our food, Kat dives into all her questions. We all get a few laughs out of her slightly clueless understanding of the sport and what she thinks is happening. For the most part, the questions are legitimate, and I think she might have even had some fun. She talks about the feeling of excitement that overcame her as people cheered for their favorite swimmer, even if she wasn't sure what was going on.

I spent most of that time watching Katrina and struggled not to become completely captivated by this woman, but man, is it hard.

There's something about the way her eyes sparkle when she laughs, or the way she fiddles with the ends of her long, blonde hair when she's nervous or unsure. Her personality meshes easily with all of us, like she's been part of this group forever. Like she's the missing piece.

Except she's not, and she can't be. She's with someone else, not me, and any type of daydream I get wrapped up in is only going to result in me getting hurt.

When our dinner arrives, the conversation drifts to something calmer; not all of us talking over each other and fighting to be heard. I glance up from my pasta to see Katrina enjoying hers, but she's looking around like she's waiting for something to happen or looking for a conversation to join.

I can start a conversation with her, we've talked a hundred times in the last month or so. She's one of the easiest people to talk to, but I don't know where to start. She catches my eye and smiles before taking a bite of her food.

"So, you've never told me—what made you want to be a contractor?" She looks up at me in surprise. "I mean, I know your stepfather is one; did you want to follow in his footsteps or something?"

"God, no." She laughs, shaking her head. "I just liked the idea of being the one that got to build something that'll last. Architects can draw and design buildings, but I'm the one who oversees them as they become a reality. It's always been more interesting to me to focus on that side of things."

"So you're not much of a daydreamer, then?" I ask, ignoring Bryce listening in to our conversation from my right.

She gives me a coy smile, drawing my attention to her more. "Wrong again, Carter. I'm a huge daydreamer, but I like to see them come to life more. Building and interior design are also things I'm passionate about, but I decided not to let that be my focus."

"Which is why you're helping Josie and Bryce with the house," I point out, and she nods. "Josie's been telling me about some of the plans you've got and they all sound great."

She smiles softly. "The two of you are pretty close, aren't you?"

I shrug. "Next to Bryce, she's one of my best friends; Mia too. That's what you get with this group. Best to be honest with you about it up front."

She stares at me across the table in pure amazement. "What?"

My brow furrows as I look back at her. "You're part of this group now, Kat. Did you think you wouldn't be?"

"But . . . I'm just the contractor," she argues. "I'm not here permanently."

"You think distance bothers any of us? This is going to be the first time we'll all be in the same spot, ever. Charleston isn't that far away."

"What are the two of you talking about down there?"

I look down the table toward Mia, who is staring at us expectantly. "About how Kat is part of the group now."

"Without a doubt." With a brow furrowed, she turns to Kat. "Wait, did you not realize that?"

When I look back at Kat, she has that same mystified look in her eye, like she's grappling to understand the reality she's in. "I do now," she promises all of us, and the table goes back to different conversations effortlessly.

Throughout the night, Kat keeps looking at me like I've handed her the moon, but that can't be true, because I'm sure she handed it to me.

Chapter 14

Katrina

March 2024

"So I was thinking we could check out a couple furniture stores," I suggest, "that way I can start getting a sense of your style."

Josie and I are walking down the hall toward her apartment with a tray of coffees from a local café balanced in my hand while she carries a bag of pastries in hers. We'd just come from an early morning yoga session we'd started doing at least once a week together and we're now trying to figure out what to do for the weekend. I have no work to do on the pool, so I could start focusing on the house.

They're set to close on the house in the next couple of weeks, getting keys the same day. After that, it'll be full steam ahead. While design isn't necessarily my strongest area, I've been able to draw up some rough plans for them and Liam has agreed to help once they close, giving him time to finish up some other projects. In the meantime, I want to get to know what they're looking for, as I'll be the one authorizing most of the design choices and execute them on my own.

"Sounds great!" She pushed open the door, stepping aside to let me in. "As you know, we brought a weird mix of stuff from Omaha. I miss my couch."

I glance over toward the harsh, black leather couch, and laugh. I've only been at their place a handful of times but had always wondered about the story behind that thing. It's so different from her warm, natural tastes, and is a lot colder than even Bryce's tastes. Maybe he thought the industrial bachelor pad aesthetic was the only thing he could have.

"Don't blame that on me!" Bryce's voice calls from down the hall. He appears a moment later, dressed in gray sweatpants, and a loose black T-shirt, dark blond hair a mess of waves. "Your couch fell apart when the movers tried to load it. We had no choice. Plus, this couch followed me through several roommates."

That makes sense. It's a neutral, generic choice.

Bryce gives me a tired smile as his girlfriend rolls her eyes. When he moves into the kitchen and plants a kiss on her cheek, her smile is blinding. Even as he peers into the bag of pastries she'd just set on the counter.

"Are you free today?" I ask, turning my focus to him. "You could come with us. I want to get a sense of your combined tastes for the house."

He makes a face of disgust. "Spend the day furniture shopping with you, Dalton? I'd rather swim the mile."

Handing him his coffee, I stick my tongue out at him. "Jokes on you; I don't know what that means."

"It means he'd rather die."

The warm, deep voice joining the conversation causes my breath to catch in my throat and my spine to straighten. Carter Abrams yawns as he makes his way into the room, fingers combing through messy brown hair. My gaze scans over his shirtless chest, taking in the sculpted abs and broad shoulders leading down to his muscular arms. His sweats are resting low enough on his hips that I can see the faintest glimpse of his Olympic rings tattoo.

I swallow to keep myself from saying something mortifying, but my mouth feels like sandpaper. The man has been starring in some pretty detailed fantasies since we met at the meet a couple of weeks ago. The last thing I need to do is let something private slip out.

"Morning!" Josie grins brightly, oblivious to the fact that her contractor and friend are speechless in her kitchen. "Kat has your coffee!"

Carter glances my way, a slow, easy grin tugging at his lips. Which only made the sexy man look adorably sleepy and now I'm worried my knees are about to give out. "Good to see you again, Kat."

I hand over his coffee with a forced smile. "Here you go."

Amused, he takes it, instantly taking a sip. "Thanks."

"There are pastries, too." Josie pushes the bag toward him. "We got a variety because we weren't sure what you guys would be in the mood for."

Without wasting a second, he goes through the bag. I look at Josie, hoping to convey the panic I'm feeling, but she's already looking at me with a crease in her brow. Bryce, on the other hand, is looking at me with a smug smile as he sips on his own coffee.

What does he know that no one else knows? There's no way I've been that obvious to him.

I look away, terrified he'll be able to read something in my expression.

"What are your plans for the day?" Josie breaks the silence, directing her question toward the guys.

Bryce hoists himself up onto the counter, pulling Josie back between his legs. She goes willingly, leaning against him. "I'm taking Carter over to the pool to let him see the progress. Then we might get a workout in. Might even use the new pool. It's not bad out today."

There were still some small things to do on the deck and with the wiring, but the pool is usable now.

"Do you need me there?" I try to sound casual as I pick at the croissant I pulled from the bag. "Or you good to give him the update?"

The amused smile is back on his face. God, he can be cocky. "I think I can handle showing my business partner our business. Especially because I know our contractor has been keeping him updated on every little change. Is there a reason you want to come with us, Kat?"

Why did I let Bryce become my friend? Things were so much easier when we were at each other's throats.

Josie nudges his leg, shaking her head. "No, absolutely not. Kat is not working today. We're going shopping." She turns to me. "I already texted Mia; she wants to come. I figured after that we could all get dinner, giving Kat and Carter some time to get to know one another better."

When I look over at Carter, he's already looking at me. He winks when my gaze meets his. The simple, playful gesture has heat flooding my cheeks in a way I know will be hard to ignore. It was one thing when he was in Georgia, but now that he's standing before me, it's harder to ignore.

"Oh, yeah, they should absolutely get to know one another better." Bryce smirks around his coffee cup.

Carter glares at Bryce, and I realize I need to get the hell out of here.

"Wait, what?" Josie looks between the three of us with a furrowed brow. "Am I missing something here?"

"I'm going to run home and change!" I reach for my bag that I dropped by the counter. Carter seems interested in his second, or maybe third, pastry. "I'll pick you up in an hour, Josie?"

She looks from me to Carter and then back again before nodding. "Yeah, that sounds good. I'll have Mia meet us here."

"Perfect. Let me know if you need anything."

"We won't need anything," Bryce calls as I open the door. I turn to glare at him, but he just shrugs. "What? I'm serious. It's your weekend off."

"He's right, Kat," Carter adds. "Just enjoy the day with Mia and Josie. We'll be fine."

Nodding, I wave before stepping into the hall and closing the door behind me. Logically, I know they'll be fine, but I still wish I were there to answer even the dumbest question they could have. This is the first time Carter will see the pool in person since we broke ground, and I'm itching to know what his opinion is. I want to make sure he likes it, that he's happy with the direction it's going in, and how can I know that if I'm not there?

I'll just have to trust that one, or both, of them will tell me if there's something I need to know. They have to know I'll fix it; make any changes they need. Whatever it takes for them to both be happy with the result because I care about them more than I've ever cared about any client. I want their dream to happen.

"Oh, my god," Josie practically screeches as soon as she slides into the backseat of my car; Mia taking the front seat. "Why didn't you tell me?"

"Tell you what?" I demand, trying to calm my beating heart as I pick a playlist for us to listen to.

"Kat!" she screeches, reaching up to swat my arm. "Stop messing around!"

"I don't know what you're talking about, Josie!" I glance at Mia, who looks just as confused, before turning to look at the redhead. "Why are you acting like you've just met your favorite boy band?"

"Because you like him!" Dread fills me at her words. I figured she knew or had her suspicions confirmed by Bryce, because that man knows. I don't know how he knows, but he does. "You like Carter!"

"What?" Mia gasps from the passenger seat.

Okay, well, there's one person who doesn't know. Wait . . . does Carter know?

I look back at Mia to see her mouth agape in shock. "How am I just now finding this out? When did Josie find out?"

"I don't know!" I groan, and then quickly clamp my mouth shut after realizing what I just said. I'd literally just confirmed it.

"Mia." Josie leans up between the two seats. "Mia, you should have seen them this morning. There were so many sparks flying, I thought our apartment would catch on fire."

"Oh, shut up." I roll my eyes. "There were no sparks."

"No," Josie insists, "there totally were. Carter couldn't stop staring at her and she kept peeking glances at him. It was really cute."

"You forget I have a boyfriend," I remind them both. I straighten up in my seat, turning back to look ahead of me. If I drive, I'll be distracted from this conversation. At least, I hope that's what'll happen. "There's nothing happening between me and Carter."

Mia waves my comment off. "That relationship is over. You've been over him for a while. Answer me this: If you ended it right now, would you feel like you need time to move on?"

I stare down at the steering wheel, thinking the question over for just a second before I sigh and shake my head. "No."

It should bother me more that I wouldn't need to get over my boyfriend of two years, but I feel like I've spent the last six months doing that. Not only is the relationship at a dead end, but I've turned around and am actively trying to find a new road to take while he's still stuck where he is. I need to just end it.

"Then there's no harm in admitting that you have a crush on someone, or that you find them attractive," Mia comforts. "If anything, it might mean that you should end it sooner than you initially planned."

There's a charity event coming up that Will wants me to attend with him; I could end it that weekend. The only downside is we'll be under a microscope, both from his colleagues and my parents. Two weeks after that, I'm supposed to drive up so we can go on a date. There's nothing special surrounding it, just something Will feels like we should do once every couple of months. it's just a date. I can wait that long to end it.

But I will end it that day. It's not fair to me, or him, to keep pretending it's anything more or anything worth saving.

"I will. I'll end it," I promise them both. Speaking the words aloud makes it feel firmer, more concrete. Even though I don't give them a specific date, I have it in my head and I know I'll stick to it.

"And then you'll ask Carter out!"

Turning on my signal to exit the parking lot, I laugh, and look at Josie in the mirror. "Calm down, girlfriend, let's not jump ahead of ourselves. There are a lot of reasons that's a bad idea."

"Name three," Mia challenges.

"Okay, fine! First, he's a client that I'm working for. Second, he lives in another state. Third, he's not even interested in me."

"Okay, first of all, is there any rule that says you can't date a client?" I shake my head at Mia's question, because it's not something that has ever come up. "As long as you keep things professional, and I know you both will, then you should be good. Second, he's moving here in less than a year. That's a stupid excuse, and he's just as close to you as your current boyfriend is."

"And third," Josie pipes up from the backseat. "The idea that he's not interested is just ridiculous! We were all at dinner that night after the meet. We saw you two giving each other heart eyes."

I groan. "We were talking, not giving each other heart eyes." There's a momentary pause before I find myself weakly asking, "Wait, do you think he likes me?"

In answer to my question, I'm met with more piercing squeals from both Mia and Josie this time. They immediately start talking over one another, trying to fill me in on all the things I need to know about Carter, but I can only partially listen. I'm so wrapped up in this idea that there could be something more between the two of us, but I'm worried about what will happen if I pursue something like that.

The rest of the day is spent with the two of them feeding me little tidbits of information about Carter. His favorite color is jade green; he always puts the creamer in before his coffee and makes a big deal about it; he broke his leg when he was ten and claims it was Bryce's fault; his family is small but loud; his Olympic rings tattoo is low on his right hip. A bunch of information I don't need, but I find myself filing it away for future reference. These are all things that come from people who know someone well, and I crave to know more about him, but also want to discover those things myself.

Later that evening, everyone is scattered throughout my rental in comfortable clothes. Mia had just opened the second bottle of wine and we were discussing some of our favorite TV shows while the guys cooked dinner. It was going to be a simple spread of finger foods—things that I had an inkling Carter's coach wouldn't like so much. Apparently, he and Bryce had a solid workout, so he felt he could cheat a little.

With a wineglass in hand and comfy sweats on, I'm surprised by how easy it is for me to be myself among this group. There's no need to hide my dorky obsessions or present myself a certain way. Who I am is more than enough. The saying 'show up as you are' has never been true to me until this moment. My smile is wide and hasn't diminished in the hours since they got here. Bryce is making something that involves fried cheese and I'm excited about it. Mia is talking about a new yoga class she wants us all to try, and it's all just so easy.

These are the kinds of connections I've waited my whole life for. Even though they're fleeting, and I'll be gone in a couple of months, I long to hold on to them as long as I can. When Carter and Bryce start bringing food over to the large coffee table, I'm surrounded by foods I'd never be comfortable eating in front of Will or my parents, knowing comments about my "less than ideal" figure would be made.

Here, though, I reach for a mozzarella stick, sharing a grin with Carter because our hands brush as we go for the same one. Ever the gentleman, he hands it to me before reaching for another one. It's all so easy.

Chapter 15

Carter

March 2024

Pools have always been a calm place to me, a tool to help center myself as the world rages on around me. The shimmering blue tone, the reflections, the unstable way the lines seem to bend and arch beneath the depth of the water—a pool has always been home to me.

So, when I wake up early on Sunday morning, hours before I need to head back to Georgia, I know Bryce wouldn't be surprised to find out I left and sought out the comfort of the only pool I have access to in this state. My pool. Our pool.

"What are you doing here?"

The sun is barely peeking up over the horizon when I turn to see Katrina coming toward me, dressed in leggings, and a crew neck sweatshirt. There's not an ounce of makeup on her face and she's pulled her blonde hair into a messy ponytail. Most endearing of all, she's wearing glasses. Something tells me not too many people get to see her like this, and I instantly feel like one of the luckiest men in the world.

Even if it means nothing.

"Just getting caught up in my own thoughts," I tease. "What about you? As I recall, I'm the one who owns this place."

She sits next to me on the bench, so close our legs are practically touching. "Ah, yes, but I also have a key and free rein for the duration of the remodel."

I bite back a grin. "Seriously, the sun is not even up yet. Why are you here?"

"Couldn't sleep. I had a couple of things to check." She gives a casual shrug, like it's the easiest explanation in the world. "All right, your turn. What's got you up at dawn?"

I look back over the water, which is mostly still. "I told you, lost in my thoughts."

"That's not an answer." When she laughs, the sound seems to bounce all around me. "You're worried about this summer, aren't you?"

I fight not to let my jaw drop open. How did she possibly know that? "I've never done this without Bryce."

I can feel her gaze on the side of my face, but I keep staring straight ahead. "Never? I thought he retired a couple of years ago."

"The Olympics, I mean. I've gone to international meets since he retired, but I've never done Trials or the Games without him. I followed a coach out to Georgia after we graduated, and that was the first time we really separated."

"Because he's not there at all," she says in realization.

I nod and say, "People are still surprised that he retired while I didn't. They ask me all the time if he's going to make some kind of miraculous comeback or if I can even do this without him. There aren't a lot of people who think I can."

"Well, that's bullshit," she scoffed. "From my understanding, which I know is limited, you're doing well. The way Bryce talks, it sounds like you have a good shot at making the team."

The way she says it sounds so uncertain, and I can't help but chuckle. "Bryce wasn't kidding, was he? You really know nothing about this sport."

"I'm trying!" she protests, but her scowl only makes me laugh harder. "I'm attempting to learn. I know you mainly swim the 400-meter IM and the 200-meter freestyle. I don't know what any of that really means, though."

I fight the urge to recite my whole program, knowing it would literally mean nothing to her. "I appreciate your effort, Katrina."

"Going to the meet made me see how the sport can be fun, and it was exciting to watch the races, but I'm not sure I get all the work that goes into it. It seems like a lot of work for a few minutes of fun and a lot of staring at a black line."

Nodding, I let my gaze drift back over the mostly still water. "There's a lot of time to think. Which isn't always a good thing."

"Which brings us back to what you're doing here. You can talk to me about it if you want. I'm a good listener and it might help to talk to someone clueless about what you're going through."

She's got a point. Letting out a sigh, I lean forward, elbows resting on my knees. I keep my gaze locked straight ahead, unable to look at this woman as I rip open my chest and bare my heart to her. "I've had my eye on this goal my whole life—of being an Olympian. Everyone tried to keep me realistic, reminding me that hard work might not be enough, but I did it. I did it twice and am trying to do it a third time, but that's never been the part that's scary. I never let myself think about what would come next, and now it's coming quicker than I ever expected."

"I don't think that's true." Her tone is soft, barely audible despite the silence surrounding us. "If you didn't think about what would come next, I wouldn't have this job."

"I know Josie or Bryce told you how I bought this place. It was a panicked decision, and I didn't think it through until I signed the papers. This is the result of not knowing what I want and grabbing the first thing that sounded good."

"I don't agree with you. You saw the answer to a question and took a shot, just like you've been doing your whole life. The only reason you're unsteady now is because you can't imagine what it's going to look like yet, but you will. I promise you will."

My deep breath is shaky, her words settling around me. I want them to be true. More than anything, I want this future to unfold the same way everything else has. "I don't know what I'm doing."

"No one knows what they're doing, Carter. I can promise you that."

I scoff, turning to face her. She's watching the sunrise. "Says the girl who has a job she's building a career from."

She shakes her head but doesn't pull her gaze from the sunrise. "Says the girl who went after her dream and has spent every single day since graduation trying to prove herself to a room full of sexist assholes who'll never accept her as an equal. It's exhausting, Carter, and I'm not even sure I want it anymore."

I never would have guessed she was dealing with something like that. She seems so confident in her job and is always able to take control of a situation. Now that she's said it, though, things are making more sense. The way she was so determined to have Bryce take her seriously, the way she keeps stressing how badly she wants this project to be perfect—she's just trying to prove herself, just like me.

"Is that why you're here?" I wonder aloud. "Did you take the job to prove yourself?"

She doesn't look at me, even as she starts fiddling with a loose strand of hair. I want to reach out and tuck it behind her ear, but I can't. "Yeah, if my stepfather had it his way, he would have never hired me. It's all part of an image he and my mother put out there, two well-respected professionals in Charleston with a daughter following in his footsteps. It's a farce, but it was still my dream. It's just not working out the way I wanted it to."

Frowning, I shake my head slightly. "I still can't believe he's your stepfather."

"He never wanted kids," she tells me. "I was just collateral that came along with my mother. Still, she's determined to stick to an image. He would have preferred if I studied literally anything else. Now he's micromanaging every little aspect of this project because he doesn't trust me to do a good job."

"I'm sorry, that's some utter *Gilmore Girls* shit right there. What the fuck?"

Katrina lets out a surprised laugh that sounds like it's tripping over itself on the way out. It's a ridiculous sound that instantly makes me smile, wondering what else I can say to make her do it again. "You watch *Gilmore Girls*?"

Still smiling, I shrug one shoulder. "It might be one of my comfort shows. My mom worked nights; we'd watch reruns in the afternoons during the summer. Josie and Mia have gotten me hooked on it and we're all rewatching it."

Her jaw drops open. "Is that what they do on Monday nights? That's so rude! I don't have anyone to watch with."

I laugh at her pout. "We can fix that. Just remember, Bryce pretends he's not interested, but he has opinions."

Her grin is soft, her hazel eyes twinkling in the morning light. "I'm not at all surprised."

I don't know when the conversation shifted to focus on her, but I'm grateful for it. It's given me a rare chance to get to know her away from everything else. It's also helped my suspicions of her being someone who's not surrounded by a lot of people. Whether that's intentional or not, I find myself wanting to make sure she knows she's not alone in all of this. As long as she's here, she's got us, and if she wants us after this is done, we'll be here.

I bump her shoulder with mine. "You're not on your own out here, you realize that, right?"

Her cheeks flush, and she ducks her head. A second later, though, she's bumping her shoulder back into mine. "And you're not nearly as lost as you seem to think you are. Look around, Carter, you have something amazing waiting here for you and you're going to kick ass."

My instinct is to argue that there's no way she can know that for sure, that there's nothing wrong with preparing for the worst, but the words die on my tongue. When I look back at her, she's looking at the water again, a content smile on her features. The light breeze has the free strands of her hair whipping around her cheeks, and something in me twists. It's not like anything I've felt in years, but it's there, and I've missed it.

Bryce's words ring in my ear, reminding me she has a boyfriend. It doesn't matter that the relationship seems rocky, they're still together, and nothing can happen.

I push off the metal bench, stretching my arms over my head as I go, ignoring the way my joints move a little stiffer than they did ten years ago. "Come on." I nudge her knee with mine. "Let's go get breakfast. I'm starving."

She takes the hand I offer, allowing me to pull her up. "Are swimmers always hungry?"

Smirking, I climb down the bleachers before offering my hand once more, keeping her balanced. "Pretty much, yeah."

She jumps down onto the concrete and we're practically chest to chest. Our gazes locked on one another, and I want to reach out, pull her even closer, but I know I can't. She's not mine. Her hazel eyes drift around my face, never really settling anywhere. It feels like there's a current of something zipping between us, an imaginary line pulling us closer. I can take one step and—

My phone rings. The sound is loud in the otherwise empty space, causing us to practically stumble apart. I break eye contact long enough to dig it out of the pockets of my sweats. By the time I look up, she's heading back inside. Cursing under my breath, I answer the call and press the phone to my ear. "What's up, Bryce?"

"Hey, you're at the pool, right?" My point is instantly proven. We know one another too well. "Are you going to be much longer? Josie and I were going to go get breakfast."

"Why are you guys even up?" I ask, looking at my watch to find that it's barely six-thirty.

"Someone set the fire alarm off. There was no actual fire, but it woke us up."

I roll my eyes, wondering if this was fate's way of telling me to back off. Why else would something like that happen right as Katrina and I are having some sort of moment?

"Yeah, sure. Text me the place and I'll meet you there."

"Cool. Are you good?"

Absolutely not. "Yeah, of course. I'll see you in twenty."

By the time I end the call with Bryce and head back to my car, Katrina is gone.

Chapter 16

Katrina

March 2024

"Did you want to go shopping with Mia and me tomorrow?" Josie asks as Bryce locks the door behind us. "It's shopping for fun, nothing for the pool, or the house."

"But I find that kind of shopping fun," I tease, earning a laugh from Josie. "I'd love to, but I can't. I'm going home this weekend. My boyfriend needs me to accompany him to some charitable gathering for the hospital."

Bryce gives me a look of pure disgust. "That sounds boring as hell."

Josie swats his chest. "Don't pretend you didn't attend charity auctions and other events when you were swimming." She turns to look at me with a pout. "I was never invited because we were just friends." The who slept together was heavily implied by the way she put air quotes over the last two words.

"You would have been bored out of your mind," Bryce protests. I'm willing to bet money they've had this argument before.

"Probably, but I would have gotten to see you in a different kind of suit," she muses, pressing a thoughtful finger to her chin. I see the way her eyes rake over his form and suddenly become a bit uncomfortable. "Which would have made it worth it."

"You had three months of seeing me in a suit like that every day. I think I made up for the ten charity events you didn't attend with me."

Josie makes a face at the memory of Bryce's corporate job. I've yet to see any photographic proof of this job.

"Katrina!"

The deep, firm voice calling my name startles all of us. I'm shocked when I see Will's red, sleek sports car sitting at the curb. My boyfriend is striding toward us in dark jeans and a button-down, like he hadn't just driven two hours to get here.

"You've got to be fucking kidding me." Bryce's tone is low. I'm not sure he meant for anyone to hear him, but there's a darkness in it, too.

I don't have the chance to question what he means before Will is greeting me with an exaggerated kiss on my cheek. I turn my focus to him. "What are you doing here?"

"Picking you up, of course," he replies breezily, like it's obvious.

It's not, though. This wasn't part of the plan and Will always sticks to the plan. He doesn't even like it when I change a side dish for a planned dinner without talking to him. "I thought I was driving home to meet you."

He shrugs in such a casual way that I want to scream. Who is this man? Why is he acting like this? "Does it really matter? I thought I'd surprise you."

My suspicions are raised. Will doesn't do surprises, and he doesn't do romantic gestures. Most of the time, I'm lucky if I can get him to call me his girlfriend. He's up to something, or at least has a reason to be here.

Thankfully, I don't have to wait long for my answer.

"Bryce Clark!" Will pushes me away slightly as he puts on his best charming smile to shake Bryce's hand. Bryce looks down at the outstretched hand but doesn't shake it. Will drops it, undeterred. "It's great to see you, man."

Bryce glowers at my boyfriend. "Jacobson. Can't say the same about you." His gaze moves to me. "You're dating Will Jacobson?"

Something about his tone makes me want to say no and assure him I would never do something so utterly ridiculous, but it wouldn't do any good now. I've spent two months complaining about my crappy boyfriend, and now he's standing here. Even worse, I feel a prickling sensation up my spine that says I've been lied to. The way Bryce is watching his every move—the way his shoulders tense—indicates that there's more than just a casual rivalry between them.

"We've been together for two years!" Will brags, slinging his arm around my shoulder to wrench me into his side. "We make a wonderful team."

We're not a team. We're barely even a couple. There's also nothing all that wonderful about us.

Josie has her hand in Bryce's, trying to pull him away from the situation, but he remains firmly in place, glaring at Will, and then at me. I try to squirm away from Will's hold, but he just tightens it. A silent demand that I stay by his side and make him look good.

I don't know why, and I can be mad at myself later, but I cave.

"How long has this been going on?" He motions between Josie and Bryce. My brows arch at the realization that he doesn't just know Bryce, he knows them both. Which means he has to know about the blog she used to have with Mia. Their circles were more closely linked than he'd ever let on. Even when I flat out asked him. "Can't say I ever saw it coming. She doesn't seem like your type, man."

Bryce's lip curls with a snarl, but Josie is the one who speaks up. "Our relationship is none of your business. We don't really give a shit what you think."

Will's grin is amused as he looks her up and down, sizing her up. "Good. I don't want your opinion of mine, either."

"Kat's an adult, Jacobson," Bryce sneers. "She can speak for herself."

I stare at Bryce, stunned, not sure what to say. I know what that is meant to be. He's protecting me. Reminding me I don't have to let this man walk all over me. There's no way I'll get the upper hand now, though.

"Of course she can," Will jovially replies. This is nothing but a big game to him, a game to see who can piss the other off first. "Still, I don't want to hear whatever opinions you've formed about me from what she's said. It's been years and our relationship is our own business."

Does he know that I'm on the verge of ending things with him? Is he sensing that my being around them is some kind of threat to him? Of course, they've helped me see the truth, that I deserve better, but that's been something I've been thinking for months. It's not their fault.

"Time doesn't mean change," Bryce challenges, looking over at me. "You guys should go. You wouldn't want to hit traffic."

I look over at Josie, whose gaze tells me to listen to him. I'm not sure what issue they have with each other, but it must run deep, and is something Josie can see turning ugly. She's telling me to get him out of here before it gets that far, and she'll do the same with Bryce.

"Will," I say, slipping out from under his arm but keeping a grip on his hand to tug him toward the car, "let's go. I'll see you guys on Monday."

Josie's already leading Bryce away from us, toward her Jeep across the lot. At this point, there's nothing I can do with my car except leave it here. We have security drive through all night to keep people from stealing materials or breaking into the property. Still, I'll need to get my bag, but I'll wait for them to be gone before I do.

"Hey, Clark!" I can see the way Bryce stiffens at his name, but he doesn't turn toward Will. "Be sure to say hey to Abrams for me."

Bryce turns, like he's going to say something, but Josie is pulling him away. I quickly do the same, telling Will to get in the car while I grab my bag from mine. I'm hoping to have a moment with either Josie or Bryce to figure out what all this is about, but they're already in Josie's Jeep, pulling out of the parking lot.

With a sigh, I grab my bag from my trunk and head back to Will's car. He didn't bother to pull it up to where I was parked, despite doing so would give him a straight shot out of the lot. I wait until I'm buckled in and he's leaving the lot before I turn on him. "What the hell was that about?"

"It was nothing." He waves me off. "Just two friends catching up."

"Don't lie to me, Will." I glare at the side of his head, knowing full well trying to have this conversation with him is going to be pointless. "I saw the way Bryce looked at you. He never would have expected you to be the one standing there. What happened between you guys?"

"I'm surprised Clark didn't know I'm your boyfriend." Of course, he's going to blame this on me. I should have seen that coming. "Why didn't you tell him? I told you we knew each other."

"You told me you swam against one another and that's it," I argued. "Do not blame this on me. I didn't think I needed to bring up the fact that I was dating someone they occasionally swam against in college. I didn't even know if they'd remember you!"

Something flashes in his eyes, and I instantly recognize it as anger. What could he possibly be angry about? He'd told me countless times they swam against one another. Why would Bryce and Carter remember someone who quit after college? It's not like they were best friends with every person who had a lane in each race. That would be ridiculous. Unless there's more to Will's story than he's told me.

Which wouldn't be surprising, since he seems to enjoy lying about everything.

"Why does he hate you so much?" I ask, trying to get the answers I need.

Fiddling with the radio, Will shrugs. "Don't know, ask him."

The car fills with some medical podcast that I can't focus on, but it's enough of a sign from Will that I need to shut up. Instead, I take the opportunity to pull my phone out and start doing some research to find out just who I'm dating. If he lied about how well he knew Bryce and Carter, what else could he be lying about?

Chapter 17

Carter

March 2024

I can feel my phone vibrating in my pocket as I sign a cap for a kid who'd stopped me in the lobby of the hotel as I was checking in. I don't swim until tomorrow and was hoping to get some relaxation in before I had to head to the pool, but I'd been spotted by a bunch of age groupers as soon as I'd stepped through the door. Their parents had held them back while I checked in, but once I had my room key in hand, it was game on.

"Thank you," the young girl said, giving me a toothy grin as I handed her back the cap. "I can't wait to cheer for you at the Olympics."

I was hearing that more and more, even though we were still months away from the qualifying meet. My phone vibrated again. "Well, let's hope I make it then."

"We're sure you will!" The mom grinned as she placed a hand on her daughter's shoulder. "Thank you for taking the time to sign for them."

"Anytime," I assured her, and it's not a lie. Anytime a kid asks me to sign something or if they can get a picture, I do my best to accommodate them. I love hearing about their own races and goals for their life; it's a reminder I was in their shoes once. "I'll see you guys around."

My phone vibrates a third time when I step into the elevator. Sighing, I fish it out of my pocket and see it's Bryce calling. I answer it. "Hey, man, I just got to the hotel."

"Shit," he curses. "I forgot you have a meet this weekend. Forget I called. We can talk on Sunday."

"You called me three times; it's clearly something important," I reply, leaning against the wall. "What's going on?"

He hesitates for a minute and the doors slide open on my floor. "I need to tell you something."

"That's usually why people call." I make my way down the hall, keeping my voice low, and checking the numbers on the doors as I pass.

"Look, it's not my business, but I think you need to know this," he rattles, not making a whole lot of sense. I stop outside my door. "Just remember, I'm looking out for you."

I push the door open, ignoring the way my heart rate quickens at his nervous tone. "Dude, you're freaking me out here."

"Kat's boyfriend picked her up from the pool."

"Yeah, so?" I sat my bag down on the spare bed, then catapult myself on to other one, shoes be damned. "She told me she was going to Charleston this weekend for some charity event he wanted her to attend. I thought she was driving, though."

"He decided to surprise her."

That's surprisingly romantic of him, but I'm still not getting Bryce's point. "Is that all?"

"No." He takes a deep breath. "Dude, her boyfriend is Will Jacobson."

I sit up straighter, my blood running cold at the name. The one person I never thought I'd have to see again is suddenly back into my life in a matter of seconds. I haven't seen him since 2016, and that was only from a distance because Bryce made sure to keep us away from each other. After that, he left the sport, and went to med school. I was supposed to be free of him.

"Carter, you there?" Bryce asks, obvious worry in his tone.

"Y-yeah." I clear my throat. "Yeah, I'm here."

"Look, Carter, this doesn't have to mean anything." In typical Bryce fashion, he jumps right into protective mode. He has a plan, and he's going to do whatever it takes to keep me as far away from Jacobson as possible. "You never have to see him. We're working with Kat and her stepfather, not him. I can tell Kat he's not allowed on the premises."

"That's not fair to her."

"I don't give a shit, man," Bryce snaps back. "My priority is keeping us all sane, and we can only do that if Jacobson stays the fuck away from us all."

"She's going to want to know why." The idea of telling Kat about what happened back then was less than appealing. It was something I never wanted to rehash again. I'd handled it and moved on. "I can't do that, Bryce."

"She doesn't have to know anything," he insists. "I know you're friends with her, Carter, but for your own good, maybe you should back off a bit."

"What do Josie and Mia have to say about this?"

Bryce lets out a small sigh. "You know them. They're fiercely loyal." That's a trait that runs deep in our circle. "They know we want nothing to do with him and they're not fond of him either. They did say the trouble she's been having with her relationship makes a lot more sense."

I hadn't even realized it until he said it, but they're right. "Bryce, we need to tell her to leave him. He treats her like shit, and we know what he's capable of."

"Hey, that's her choice to make. The girls have both told her the relationship sounds toxic, but we can't make her leave him." I hate it when he's right. Besides, convincing her to leave him would mean telling her what happened, and I can't know if it would be enough. "You gotta stay out of her relationship, man."

Groaning, I lean back into the pillows. "How did someone like him get someone like her?"

"By being a charming, pompous asshole. "C'mon, Carter, you remember how he was able to wrap everyone else but us around his finger."

"Ronan," I remind him. "Ronan saw through him."

"That's because he's also a charming, pompous asshole." I laugh at the truth behind his statement. "The only difference is, he's also a good guy. Kat will eventually see him for who he is."

"If she doesn't?"

"Then that's on her, not you. Look, I know this might not be what you want to hear, but maybe some space would be good."

There's literally half a state between us, but I don't say that aloud because space is a good idea. Bryce had warned me back when he brought her to the meet that I was getting too caught up in someone who was taken, and my reaction to news of who her boyfriend is just proves he's right. "Space is probably a good idea."

It's going to suck, but what choice do I have?

"Don't let her, or him, get to you this weekend," Bryce continues. "There's no reason this news should have a negative impact on your performance. You've got races to swim, focus on that."

All swimmers have gotten good at it over the years, the way they can compartmentalize everything else going on in their lives and bring their focus to one thing. This, though, this has the power to knock me off my game. It's not even about Kat, it's about what happened between Will and me when we were kids and it's not something I've ever been able to just get over.

Knowing he's somewhat back in my life, existing just outside of it, makes me think back to all those years he did it on the blocks. When I couldn't quite shake him off, no matter what I did. He was always there.

"I'm serious, Carter. Don't let this prick get inside your head."

"I'll try," I promised my friend, despite already knowing it was too late. "But I'm serious, too, Bryce. He doesn't deserve Kat."

Bryce concedes with a sigh. "No, he doesn't, but we don't get to tell her that." There's a slight commotion on the other end of the phone. "I gotta go. Let me know how your swims go."

"Sure," I promise, rubbing at my temples to push off a headache. This weekend is going to suck. "Thanks for letting me know."

"No problem."

The line goes dead, and I pull the phone away from my ear, staring at it for a long moment. A text bubble pops up from Katrina.

> Why do you hate Will Jacobson so much?

Groaning, I toss the phone onto the other bed, needing it far away from me. Bryce is right, my focus needs to be on the meet, and I can't let something like this get in my way. Ignoring her, at least right now, is the only answer I have.

Ignoring her doesn't help. If anything, it distracts me through the whole rest of the meet and my swims are proof of it.

Friday night is an utter disappointment. I don't even make the medal stand in the 400-meter IM final, which is one of the few races I've remained consistent in and have been improving on. The race takes concentration, and there's a plan to it that's more involved than simply trying not to die. Everything is off beat for me in that race. I can feel the ache in my muscles in a way I never have before and every time I try to concentrate, I just picture her with him, and I want to be sick. Even more discouraging, I come in third in the 200-meter freestyle that night. I've been the top finisher in that race for at least the last ten meets. It's my other best shot at making the team.

That's the end of the meet for me.

When I get back to my hotel on Friday night, I have a bunch of missed calls from Bryce and a couple from Mia and Josie. Bryce texts me as many times as he tries calling me, if not more. Josie and Mia give me some space by sending one text each to let me know they're available if I want to talk. Bryce doesn't get the hint, though, because I don't want to talk.

I'm starting to understand why Bryce spent so many years refusing to give into his feelings for Josie, because this shit is hard. I've had plenty of relationships throughout my career, some that were even serious enough to talk about moving in together or marriage, but they all came naturally. There was nothing else complicating them; my partner had their career, and I had mine.

With Kat, there's not even a relationship to talk about. The two of us are just coexisting in the same place with no real chance of meeting in the middle. She's only here for as long as it takes to finish the remodel and then she's going back to her life with Will fucking Jacobson and I'll be stuck in Columbia, learning to get over someone I never had a chance of having.

This is why getting too close to someone is dangerous. Especially when you could see your future with them playing out. Which is exactly why Bryce never let Josie in.

I shouldn't have let her in.

Chapter 19

Katrina

March 2024

The weekend in Charleston is basically hell.

The charity event on Saturday is a night full of doctors kissing rich people's asses, and I hate every moment of it. No one was all that interested in the charity of the event, as they prefer to spend the night talking about their lives, trying to one up one another. In these moments, Will schmoozes with the best of them. Normally, I could brush it off as him doing what he needs to do, but I see it differently now. Now I can see that Will wants to be them. He wants to be able to brag about where he vacations and what kind of car he drives.

Deep down I know he'll be there one day, not because he works hard to take care of people but because he's power hungry. I don't want to be one of those wives on the arms of rich doctor husbands who are on the board of vague charities that can never talk about their cause. Spend the rest of my days brunching or getting a facial is not the life I want. I want a life that's my own.

I stay as long as I can handle it before begging Will to either let me leave or take me home. Unsurprisingly, he opted to stay behind and pretended I had a migraine that needed tending to. When people asked if he should be with me, he waved them off, assuring them I knew how to take care of myself. I order a car for the drive home; thankfully, the driver wasn't chatty, but it was a woman around my age who gave me a sad, commiserating smile. I hated it instantly.

By the time I walked back into my guest house, I was exhausted. Emotionally and mentally drained from a full day of being ignored by the people I've come to care about. Lamely, I check my phone once more after stripping out of my dress and pulling on a comfy pair of pants and tank top. When I see there are still no text messages, I collapse into bed. I knew I'd regret not taking my makeup off in the morning, or brushing out my hair, but that was a problem for Tomorrow Katrina.

Tonight, I just want to sleep and pretend the last thirty-six or so hours never happened.

The next morning, I wake angry with myself for not taking my makeup off the night before. The fact that tears are tracking down my cheeks by the time I brush out my thick, ever so slightly wavy hair is punishment enough. After I wash my face and pull my hair into a messy ponytail, I change into a comfy pair of jeans and a loose sweatshirt from my college days, then head into the house for lunch with Will and my parents. Normally, I'd do more to get ready to face them, but I can't be bothered to today.

No one says anything to me as I slip into the house. Mom just tries to hand me a mimosa. With a shake of my head, I grab a sweet tea before bypassing Thomas and Will, who are talking about setting up a day to go golfing, and head into the dining room. Lunch is already spread out, courtesy of the cook and housekeeper, but I know better than to start without everyone else.

"You know, Katrina has been making friends down in Columbia." I turn to glare at Will as he sets his beer down and takes his seat. He smirks back at me until I sink down in my chair across from him. "I'm not sure I like the influence they seem to be having on her."

"Are these the ones who are using her to fix a house?" Thomas gruffly questions, settling into his own seat. Will nods and he makes an irritated noise.

"Who are these people?" Mom frowns, looking around the table for answers no one really wants to give. "I thought you went out there for a job."

"That's exactly my point, Dr. Dalton," Will continues, ever the ass-kisser. "They're not her friends, they're her clients. Blurring this line is just going to derail her on her career path."

"What would you know about my career path?" I question, stunning everyone in the room.

Thomas sets his steady gaze on me. "Katrina, we just had a meeting about the project last week. You told me everything is on schedule, and you could handle it."

I shrink into myself at the reprimanding tone, but I don't back down. "I can handle it. Ignore Will, he's exaggerating. Everything is on schedule and under budget. It has my entire focus."

"Then why did you stop texting me that night?" Will presses. "You were out with Bryce's girlfriend, which I'm assuming is Josie. And Mia was the other friend you were with, right?"

"Who?" Mom's barely following the conversation, more interested in her third mimosa.

"Just Bryce Clark's girlfriend and her friend." Will waves the question off.

Mom's brow furrows. "Who?"

"You know, Tom, I never got the chance to tell you I know Bryce and Carter." Will is the only person besides my mother who can get away with calling him Tom.

"I always forget you were a swimmer!" Thomas laughs like being in the sport is laughable. "Got you through college, right?"

"Undergrad, at least," Will corrects with a shit-eating grin of his own. "I had enough sense to give up and pursue a more meaningful career path."

"You make it sound like they've done so horribly for themselves." I lean back in my chair, crossing my arms over my chest in the way I know Will hates. He says it accentuates my chest more than necessary. I say he needs to get used to the fact that his girlfriend has boobs. "They're both two-time Olympians, and Carter could be going for a third."

Plus, they have countless records, national titles, and other accolades I wasn't even going to attempt to name. While I was doing my best to learn more about the sport, I knew my limited knowledge would only add more fuel to Will's fire.

"That might be true, but that's all they'll ever have. I have a solid career that will provide for me and my wife forever. The two of them have a rundown pool."

I have the urge to gag at the word *wife*. I don't know who he's planning on marrying, but it sure as hell won't be me.

"Is that a lucrative business venture?" Mom is handed her fourth—or is it her fifth?—mimosa by our housekeeper, Betty. "It doesn't sound like it'll be successful. Who are these people again?"

"No one, Mom." My mother is dangerously smart and always the epitome of professional, except when she drinks, and she's well and truly on her way to sloshed. "Just the clients I'm doing the project for down in Columbia."

"Oh," she exhales, eyes wide as she takes a drink. "And they have a pool. Right."

Ignoring her, I turn my focus back to the men in the room. "It's not about being successful. Bryce and Carter want to provide kids the same opportunities they had growing up. The same opportunities you had, Will. You can't deny the sport opened doors for you; you literally just said it."

"Oh, sure, use the advantages the sport provides you, but they've made it their entire focus."

"He makes an excellent point, Katrina," Thomas says to join the conversation again. "They've had a moment or two in the spotlight, but they'll never have more than that. Look at yourself. You know your place."

Anger bubbles up inside of me, clawing its way to freedom. How could they not realize how damaging their words are? They'll never understand what it means to be dedicated to something like this. Something that matters. They can't see past their egos, and it's taken many therapy sessions for me to understand I can't make them change.

To realize that just because someone should love me doesn't mean they do, nor does it mean I deserve it any less.

I'm used to the biting, underhanded comments, but I'm not used to them being directed at people I care about. People who aren't here to defend themselves. I've always been better at standing up for others than I am at standing up for myself, so it's really no surprise to feel myself reacting this way.

"You're wrong," I bite out. "They are going to be part of history. Eventually, no one will know who any of us are. There's more than one way to have a legacy and they've found theirs."

Will scoffs. "That's not a legacy."

"Then why did you chase it?"

Silence falls around the room, even Betty stops refilling my sweet tea to see his reaction. Thomas and my mom stare at him curiously, but Will looks like he'd about to explode.

"I'm not sure I'm following what's happening here." Mom's frowning as she looks between me and Will, then to Thomas like he somehow has the answers.

I'm not backing down now. "Will was a talented swimmer in college. He had a couple of championship titles, even when to a couple professional meets—"

"I did what my coaches asked of me!" he argues, cheeks flushed. "I had scholarship requirements I had to keep up with."

"Then why did you have *Adair Swimming* interview you before the 2016 Trials?" I'm so tired of letting him make me look like an idiot. "You know, the meet that determines whether or not you made the Olympic team? The one that happened after graduation."

If we weren't in the presence of my family, I'm sure his clenched fists would have banged against the table. Instead, he just leans toward me, scowling. "How do you know about the article? Did Josie and Mia tell you about it?"

"They didn't have to. I know how to do an internet search, Will." I'm so tired of him talking down to me, making me feel small, especially in front of someone else. "You almost made the team. You got third in the 400-meter freestyle."

"What point are you trying to make here, Katrina?" He goes for casual, taking a sip of his beer. The way his glare becomes even harsher, though, gives him away.

"I'm just confused as to why you're giving Bryce and Carter so much shit for going after a dream you also chased." I'm pushing every button possible, but I don't care. Part of me wishes he'd explode just enough to give me a reason to end it here and now. I want to embarrass him the same way he's constantly embarrassing me. "Is it because you're bitter they made it, and you couldn't?"

He slams his beer on the table with so much force it echoes through the dining room; a small geyser of beer erupts all over the table. My mother flinches. "Let's step outside for a minute, Katrina."

I drop my arms, resting them in my lap as I shake my head. He doesn't want to have this conversation in front of anyone else, but I can't imagine a better situation. "I'm comfortable here, actually, and you're avoiding the question. You've never had a problem talking in front of them before. Why now?"

Will knows my parents usually take his side in any argument we have, ending with them telling me to be better and more understanding as his girlfriend. I know that wouldn't change this time, but he won't come out looking fantastic this time. Which is why he wants to hide the argument away—why he wants to pretend there's nothing he could do that would be seen negatively.

He grits his teeth. "I think this is a conversation that should be between you and me."

"But why?" I press. "You have never shied away from talking about your achievements before, so why start now?"

"I don't know why you're being so dramatic," Thomas interjects, confirming what I knew would happen. He's going to take Will's side and they'll team up to make me feel small, just like they always do. "Will was a talented and accomplished athlete, much like our clients. He made the choice to pursue something more substantial in the end, and that's nothing to be ashamed of."

Will looks smug at the idea of Thomas coming to his defense. "Exactly. You should listen to your stepfather, Katrina."

Thomas doesn't give me the chance to say anything, clearly having had enough of our argument. He breaks the conversation up by asking Will if he'd like to see the new car he'd just bought. Will eagerly agrees, and just like that, it's over. It's over and I still didn't get the last word. They're walking away and I am still dating this utter asshole. And I hate it.

Mom is handed her next mimosa, and I know Thomas is going to have to carry her to the couch soon. "You should be more sensible, Katrina. If you keep speaking to him like that, he's going to leave you."

"A girl can dream," I murmur, taking a sip of my sweet tea.

"What was that, dear?" Mom asks, brow arching.

"Nothing, Mom."

Chapter 19

Katrina

March 2024

The entire ride back to Columbia is silent.

Well, that's not entirely true. Will has a surgical podcast play-ing, which sounds exactly how a medical textbook would read to me—long, boring, and chock-full of scientific terminology I couldn't understand. Besides that, for almost two hours, neither one of us says a single word. The silence isn't even comfortable, it's tense.

By the time we pull up to my rental, I'm over it. This weekend didn't have to go down the way it did. He was the one who showed up to insult my friends. Will was also the one who continued to bad-mouth them when they weren't even present. He was the one who got all huffy when I called him out on his bullshit and then ignored me for the whole drive back.

"I think we need to talk," I say as he puts the car in park. "About everything that happened this weekend."

"Not today, Katrina," he insists. "I'm tired and still have to drive back to Charleston. I have a shift tomorrow morning."

"If you would have stuck to the plan, like you always do, you wouldn't have had to drive me back here."

"You're the one who's always telling me I should be more considerate and try to keep the romance alive." He raises his tone ever so slightly. "The first time I do it and I get my head bitten off. Not only that, but you humiliated me in front of your parents and then were short with my colleagues all night last night."

"Oh, I'm sorry, I can only give my opinion on the state of the country's healthcare system so many times before I die of boredom or piss off the wrong person," I shoot back. "You didn't need to make Bryce and Carter the target of your bad attitude with my parents."

"What is your deal with them? Why do you always feel the need to jump to their defense?"

"Why do you need to put them down?" I challenge back. "They weren't there to defend themselves and, even worse, they're clients of Thomas's. You shouldn't speak badly about them. I don't understand why you seem to hate them so much."

"They're the epitome of lazy, Katrina," he replies. "All they care about is swimming and getting medals. They could never hold down a career, even if they wanted to."

My eyebrows shoot up. "That's a bold thing to say about two men you haven't spoken to since college."

"I spoke to Bryce on Friday," he replies easily.

"You showed off to Bryce," I correct just as swiftly. "You did nothing but brag and degrade. Do you really think I told you to leave because I was worried about traffic? You were embarrassing me, Will."

Will scoffs. "I wasn't embarrassing you. If anything, Clark should be the one who's embarrassed."

"I don't think he has anything to be embarrassed about. He and Carter are doing what makes them happy. If more people could do that, maybe the world would be a happier place."

"You sound like a child." The way he says it is so patronizing, so diminishing of my contribution to the conversation. It infuriates me that he still thinks it's okay to talk to me like that. "Happiness comes from being productive and doing something worthwhile."

I want to scream at him, question why he seems to think what Bryce and Carter are doing isn't worthwhile. Dreams look different to everyone; happiness and success are different to everyone. Just because Will dedicated his life to a job that will get him prestige and money, which are his only priorities, doesn't mean everyone has to. In fact, a lot of his colleagues would argue they do the job to help people, but not Will.

"How long are you planning on sitting in here? I want to get back on the road."

There's no question about it. I'm being dismissed. Rolling my eyes, I grab the bag at my feet and wrench open the door. I don't say goodbye, don't tell him I love him—it'd be a lie anyway—I just slam the door shut behind me, knowing it would piss him off.

"Katrina!" I've barely turned toward my rental when his voice filters out the open window. With a deep, calming breath, I turn back to face him. "The only issue I ever had with Abrams was the fact he should have been more cautious with information he didn't want made public."

I can't get Will's comment out of my head.

I've known him long enough to know when something he says is supposed to be insulting. I'd been on the receiving end of those comments more than once, and this was one of them.

"The only issue I ever had with Abrams was the fact he should have been more cautious with information he didn't want made public."

That could mean a hundred different things, and very few of them would be painting Carter in a bad light. Drugs, cheating, lying—none of these seem plausible to me. Carter's a good person, Bryce is a good person, so are Mia and Josie. None of them would condone that kind of behavior. Plus, something like that would only stroke Will's self-righteous ego, and he'd brag about it.

It has to be something else.

Whatever happened, Will doesn't seem to regret his part in it, even if he's not ready to brag about it. Which tells me it's something he knows I wouldn't agree with. Something that could be a deal-breaker.

I reach for my laptop, logging on, and starting a new search. I start simple, typing: Carter Abrams. A bunch of results for an older businessman pop up. I narrow the search by tacking "swimmer" onto the end of his name. In seconds, I'm flooded with information.

The pictures showcased with the results mostly show him in a cap and goggles, so I only hesitate on them for a second. I wouldn't mind going down a rabbit hole of Carter pictures, but it has to wait. Right now, I need answers, and those answers can't be found looking at his stupid, perfect face.

I scroll away from the pictures.

The recent articles are about his accomplishments in the lead up to Trials this summer, and followed by highlights from World

Championships, and then the previous Olympics. It wasn't until the fourth page of results that a headline caught my eye:

Nashville University Freshman Carter Abrams Comes out as Bisexual.

I'm clicking into the article before I can even register how much this feels like an invasion of privacy. It's not something we've ever talked about and it's not something he needs to announce to me. I've always been a firm believer that no one owes anyone an explanation surrounding sexuality. We're all free to love who we love and be who we want to be.

And that's when it clicks. This must be it. Homophobia is a deal-breaker for me, and Will knows that. Plus, Nashville University is where Will went to school for his undergrad; no one told me Carter had attended there as well. I thought he graduated from Arizona with Bryce.

The photo that comes up with the article is of a much younger Carter and another guy I don't recognize. Carter has his arm strung over the other guy's shoulder, wide smiles stretched across their faces. They look like they're at Pride, as Carter has a bisexual flag painted on one cheek and the other guy has a sheen of glitter across his cheeks, rainbow sunglasses covering his eyes. I can't help but smile at how carefree they both look.

Skimming the article, I learn it's from his first year in college:

```
"Carter    Abrams,    freshman    at
Nashville  University,  starts  his
championship season off by coming
out  as  bisexual  across  all  his
social media accounts. Abrams, 18,
```

posted the photo below with the
following caption:
'As my collegiate career begins to
take off, I've been contemplating
how I want to tackle this aspect
of my personal life. This isn't
something new and it'll come as no
shock to those who know me, but
I feel the need to share it here:
I'm bi. I'm a bisexual athlete who
is proud of who I am, and I didn't
want to hide this anymore.
I want to take a moment to thank
my boyfriend, family, and friends
for being so supportive. I will
not be answering any questions,
but I want to share a piece of
advice with those wondering if
they should come out: You do not
owe an explanation to anyone. The
decision is your own, even if you
feel like it's being taken from
you. If you make the decision to
come out, please know there are
people and resources to support
you. Who you are is valid, who you
choose to love is beautiful, and
you're perfect the way you are.'
We were unable to get in contact

with Abrams or his coach about this
announcement, but we did catch up
with Bryce Clark at a meet in
Arizona the day Abrams made the
announcement:
'Like Carter said, this isn't new
information to anyone who knows
him. I'm proud of him for taking
a stand and opening up the dia-
logue for other queer athletes.
Especially when they feel they're
forced to make a decision based
on outside pressures. It changes
nothing. He's still my best friend
and a hell of a swimmer. This is
the only comment I'll be making on
this.'"

Any question I have is gone. This was Will's doing. I have no idea how he did it or what he had over Carter, but he was the one who took the choice away from him. This wasn't a moment of celebrating who he is, and who he loves. This was taken from him.

The rest of the article discusses what this could mean for his career, which was ludicrous to me. Why does it matter? What difference does someone's sexuality make to doing well in the sport? I read through their reasons, rolling my eyes at each one and then, my eye catches on one more quote.

The author was only able to get a comment from one person on the team, and it was Will. I read the comment once, then twice, and felt sick.

```
"I don't really care who he dates,
but I think everyone should be more
cautious about concealing informa-
tion they don't want to be public
knowledge."
```

I'm up and out my door before I even realize it.

Chapter 20

Katrina

March 2024

I pound on Josie and Bryce's door incessantly until it flings open to reveal an annoyed, shirtless Bryce. "Kat, what the fuck?"

Blinded by my need for answers, I push past him and make my way into the apartment. I barely notice Josie stumble out of the bedroom, half asleep, as she attempts to put on her glasses. I'm not even sure what time it is, I just know it's late. I turn to face Bryce, who takes a startled step back.

"Whoa!" He holds his hands up in surrender.

"Why do you hate Will, Bryce?" I clock the emotions as they move across his face—surprise, confusion, realization, and then defense. "The real reason."

Josie moves to stand beside her boyfriend. "What's going on, Kat? It's late."

"I'm sorry about that, Josie." I really am sorry for waking them up, but I need to know the truth. "I just need to talk to Bryce—get some answers."

"I don't know what you want me to tell you." He juts out his chin. "Will is an asshole who thinks he's better than everyone else, and from what I hear, you already know that."

"I know that Carter originally went to Nashville University with Will." His cocky bravado drops ever so slightly. "Will never told me that. He just said he knew you guys because you swam against each other, so I never told you who he is. When he showed up, I knew there was more to it than that. Especially because no one has texted me back all weekend. Tell me the truth, Bryce."

He doesn't flinch; he doesn't really give me much of anything to go off of. His loyalty to Carter is unwavering, and I'm clearly fraternizing with the enemy. "Why don't you tell me what you think you know?"

My gaze drifts to Josie, who looks more confused than I've ever felt, before I finally look at Bryce. I can't help but wonder how much of this she's been told and if I'll be betraying Carter by bringing it up in front of her.

"Seriously, Bryce, what's going on?" Josie demands, and that's his opening. It's his one chance to get me to not talk in front of her.

But he just stares at me, challenging me to be the one who says something. I remain just as quiet as him. Carter wasn't wrong when he said we're both ridiculously stubborn. "Katrina thinks she has us all figured out, that's all."

There's a bite to his words that I'm trying not to take too seriously. Right now, I don't feel like I'm part of this group at all. He's protecting Carter, though, and everyone else he cares about. Right now, all he knows is what Will is capable of and that I'm dating him. He doesn't trust me, and I'm not sure I blame him. The only way to get him back on my side is to tell him what I know and make sure he understands how not okay I am with it.

"I was at my parent's house for lunch today; Will and I got into a fight. Somehow, we got on the topic of you and Carter, and he has a lot of opinions about the two of you, specifically about what you're doing with your lives after swimming and your overall success. He wanted to pretend the sport was nothing more than a hobby, but I did some research after your confrontation, and I knew it wasn't true. Nothing he'd told me about his swimming career was true, so I called him out. As I'm sure you can imagine, he wasn't happy with me."

"So, he's a pretentious prick." Bryce shrugs. "None of this is new information to either one of us. You think I don't know he was pissed he never made a national team, let alone the Olympic one? Jacobson hates anyone who gets what he thinks he deserves."

I nod along with everything he says, completely agreeing. "Trust me, I know! But his reaction isn't what was surprising. It was something he said when he dropped me off after an extraordinarily long, silent drive. I tried to get him to tell me the truth about his issues with you, but all he told me was that Carter should have been more cautious with the information he didn't want to be public knowledge."

Bryce stiffens up. I keep going.

"I couldn't get it out of my head, you know? It was such a pointed thing to say, so I knew it had to mean something. I did more research. That's how I found out they started at the same school."

"So what?" Josie's question is confirmation that she doesn't know what he did. Not really. "Everyone knows Carter transferred out to

Arizona. It's not a secret. A lot of athletes do it. It usually means the team, or the school, wasn't a good fit."

"My question is, what made the team a bad fit?" I look back to Bryce, who's looking a little green. It's about to be worse. "I need the truth, Bryce. Did Will out Carter to their team without his permission?"

Beside him, Josie lets out a loud gasp. "What? No way! Bryce, you would have told me if that's what happened."

Bryce looks over at her, the pain evident in his eyes. "It was before we met."

Shocked, Josie immediately tries to rationalize the information she'd been given. "No, Carter came out on his own terms. I remember the social media post about it. Mia and I were so proud of him."

I don't look away from Bryce. "To the rest of the world, he came out on his own terms, but I think it happened because Will gave him no other choice. I found an article from some media outlet and saw the post. He ended the post by reminding everyone they don't owe an explanation to anyone, and they should do it on their own terms, even if it feels like the choice is being taken from them."

Her gaze drifts back to me. "I remember that article. The only person from Nashville University they could get a comment from was Will, and it basically was what he told you tonight."

I nod, but she's already staring up at her boyfriend. "Is she right, Bryce? Is this why you hate him? Why you've always hated him?"

Now we're both looking at Bryce, who's gone quiet. Part of me feels guilty. It's obvious there's pain in thinking back on this. And I get it. I know why he never told Josie; it isn't his story to tell. He wouldn't betray Carter the way other people have. He probably has a real fear that anyone who finds out he's bisexual might have a similar reaction, but that's not who I am.

"Bryce," Josie pleads, reaching for his hand. "What happened?"

He looks from her to me, conflicted, before he lets out a sigh. "It was a mess. I guess he saw Carter on a date with his boyfriend and took it upon himself to tell the team. Carter came into practice one morning and his locker was covered in homophobic memes and slurs. The coach did the bare minimum and Will got to be the smug bastard he is. Then he threatened to out him publicly to hold something over his head. Carter never did anything more than exist."

I feel sick, but there's a rage building up inside me, too. It's something I've only ever felt toward ignorant people who refuse to let other people, especially queer people, exist without being discriminated against. I never thought I'd feel that way toward someone I know—someone who I once thought I could build a future with.

Whatever deadline I set for myself flies out the window. I don't care.

Bryce looks helplessly at me, then at Josie. "That's why it happened the way it did. What choice did he have?"

"I need to go."

Bryce is blocking the door before I can even move, fierce protectiveness radiating from every piece of him. "Why? Where are you going?"

I sink back, realizing what he's thinking. He thinks I'm going to say something to Carter that will hurt him more or make things worse. Maybe he thinks I'm going to run to Will in a disgustingly commiserating way, but that's not the truth at all.

"Where do you think I'm going?" I stand up straighter, meeting his glare with a determined look of my own. "I'm going to do the thing I should have done a long time ago."

"Kat, no," Josie pleads. "You are not driving back to Charleston tonight."

Realization dawns on Bryce's face, and he relaxes against the door. In an instant, I know we're friends again. "She's right, Kat. You're too angry to deal with this now."

Josie nods. "You have every right to be angry, but don't go there tonight. Do it tomorrow. If you can't wait that long, then call him right now."

I shake my head. "I need to do this in person."

I know what they're trying to do, but nothing will stop me now. It might seem rash to some people, but to me, it's the final straw after a culmination of years of being treated like crap by Will and now knowing he's done it to other people, too.

He's fed me such bullshit over the last two years about how lucky I am to have him. How he's the only person who could ever love someone like me, but he's nothing more than a damn hypocrite. The superficial reasons I'm not worthy of love pales in comparison to all the aspects of his personality that make him toxic. Rather than pushing me down, he should be more concerned about what he'll do when I finally leave.

Because I'm leaving. I'm leaving him behind and I'm going to be fine. I know that now.

Tears well up in my eyes as I look at Josie, my heart breaking for Carter. "I . . . I . . . He . . ." I stumble over my words, not even sure where I want to start.

Josie's smile softens into something comforting and closes the short distance between us to pull me into a tight hug. "I know," she murmurs as I hug her back. I try to keep the tears at bay, but I can already feel them tracking down my cheeks. "You deserve someone better, Kat."

I hear Bryce excuse himself. Then he's gently moving past us and heading back down the hall. As soon as I hear the door to their bedroom click shut behind him, I allow myself to break down the rest of the way. I can't remember the last time I allowed myself to cry over this, but I know it's needed. For the briefest, fleeting second, I'm mad at myself for crying over him, but then I realize I'm not. Not really.

Instead, I'm crying over what I let him do to me. To my self-esteem. I'm crying over the fact I ever let someone else dictate how much love I deserve. Most of all, I'm crying because I know I'm not the only person he's done something like this to, and he's nothing but manipulative and toxic. He hurts people and pushes them down; it's what he does. For years, I told myself I could take it, but I won't let him do it to other people. Now I'm just done dealing with it. He doesn't get to call the shots anymore.

Instead, it's my turn to return the favor and make him realize what it means to lose someone. First thing tomorrow morning, I'm heading to Charleston to end it.

Chapter 21

Katrina

March 2024

Two and a half hours after leaving Bryce and Josie's, I'm pulling up to Will's apartment building, unsure he's even home. Since taking the job in Columbia, it's been harder to keep track of his schedule. He mostly just gives me a day that will work for a virtual date each week, and if there was a week we couldn't do one, he didn't seem to care. If I had called, we would have been done sooner, but I meant what I said to Josie. This needs to happen in person.

Not for him, but for me. I deserve to have my voice heard.

"Katrina?" I whirl around at the sound of Will's voice. He's walking from his building toward me, dressed in his work clothes with a bag slung over his shoulder. He's about to go to work, but I don't really care. "What are you doing here? I literally just saw you yesterday."

"So, I'm only allowed to see my boyfriend at scheduled times?"

He lets out a tired sigh, like my mere presence is too much for him to take right now. "We just spent the entire weekend together, Katrina. You know I don't like being caught by surprise."

"Then you're really about to hate this conversation." I cross my arms over my chest as he straightens. "I know about what you did to Carter."

He stays stoic, not a flash of regret or remorse. "I should have known they'd come crying to you as soon as they found out you and I are together."

"No one told me, Will. You tipped me off, and I did my research," I snap. "Stop blaming other people when you get called out for shitty behavior!"

"What do you mean, I tipped you off?" he demands, his own voice raising.

"When you dropped me off yesterday, you told me that Carter should have been more cautious with information he wanted kept private, and it stuck with me. So, I went looking, and it's the same comment you gave after he came out. I didn't want to believe you were capable of something so low, but what choice did I have when the evidence was right in front of me?"

"Because you know me, Katrina. I just did what I had to do. Every guy on that team deserved to know who they were sharing a locker—"

"You absolute prick!" I snarl, cutting him off. "That's such a cowardly, homophobic excuse. Did Carter ever try to hit on any of you?"

Will shifts, suddenly uncomfortable under my gaze. "It's the principle of the thing."

"Then you'll understand why this is over," I reply. His eyes widen. "I have no desire to be associated with someone like you. You have no regard for anyone but yourself, so good luck with the rest of your life, Will."

Before I can turn back to my car, he reaches out and grabs my arm. "You can't do this. Do you know what you're giving up? I chose you when I could have anyone."

I wrench my arm from his grasp, my cheeks flushing in anger. "Then go out and get anyone. Don't worry about me, I'll be fine. I might not be a size two, but you are not the only person who will ever want me, and I hate you for making me think otherwise.

"You took what you saw as a weakness and you preyed upon it, because that's what you do. You take other people down because that's the only way you'll ever get ahead. You did it to Carter and you're done doing it to me."

Anger flashes in Will's gaze as he takes a menacing step toward me. "You don't know what you're talking about."

"Back the fuck up, Will, and let me go." My heart beats wildly in my chest, but I stand up straighter, refusing to back down. "It's done."

He's not going without a fight. "What are your parents going to say about this? Your mom was so adamant I meet you, told me I'd be able to look past any flaw, and she was right. She picked me for you and she's going to be disappointed to know you're leaving me for someone like Carter fucking Abrams."

"First of all, thank you for finally admitting you only asked me out to please my mother."

He realizes his mistake as soon as the words leave my mouth, but I don't let him backtrack. It's liberating to know the truth, to know if it wasn't for my meddling mother, he would never have looked my way. It makes saying goodbye even easier.

"Second, I'm done giving a shit about what their opinion is. I deserve love, Will, real love, and this relationship benefited everyone but me. I'm done living my life for everyone but myself. Keep Carter out of it. I'm not leaving you for him. I'm leaving you because you're an ass."

"You have things in my apartment," Will sighs, going back to the exhausting manipulative tactic that's worked for years. "Come upstairs and you can calm down. You can spend the day there, and when I get home, we can talk, or you can gather your things."

I scoff, shaking my head. "I'm not going anywhere with you. Keep my shit, trash it, or give it away. I don't care." I open the door to my car. "Trust me, there's nothing here that I can't live without."

I slide into my driver's seat, slamming, and locking the door behind me. Will is still standing there as I back out of my spot and pull away. I don't look back. I have no desire to.

I want to see Carter's face when I tell him everything is over with Will. I want him to see my face, to understand how angry and hurt I am over what one person was capable of doing to both of us. I want him to know I don't share the same views. I'm never going to take something that's simply part of Carter, or anyone else, and use it against them, especially in such a cruel way.

I could drive to Georgia.

The thought retreats almost as soon as it enters my mind. It's ridiculous for me to even think about doing something like that. Mainly because I don't know where he lives. I can't just wander the city asking random strangers if they know the address of an Olympic swimmer. They'd think I was crazy and would more than likely call the cops on me.

No, the best thing I can do is try to get him on a video call. It's been hours since I've left Bryce and Josie's, so who knows if they've told him anything or if he'll even answer the call, but I have to try. I find a mostly empty parking lot and pull in.

I can see my reflection in the camera as I wait for the call to connect, and I look rough. I look like I spent the majority of the night crying. I did. And then drove two hours to end a relationship the next morning. I did. I should have waited until I look more presentable, but I don't want to. Plus, I can't hang up now.

The call connects and I'm greeted with a blurry Carter until the screen comes into focus. "Kat."

The way he says my name is breathless, like he's spent hours trying to reach me or waiting for me to call and almost can't believe it's happening. He looks almost as rough as I do with his soft brown hair a tangled mess and his usually bright, captivating green eyes are dull.

"Hey," I whisper.

"Where are you?" His brow furrows as he tries to make out the background. "Are you in your car?"

I nod, swallowing back tears that seem to be forming out of nowhere. I thought I'd run dry last night. "Yeah, I'm about to head back to Columbia."

"You're in Charleston," he realizes. I nod again, then wonder if Josie and Bryce didn't have a chance to catch him up. "Bryce told me you wanted to go last night; they figured that's where you went but weren't sure. Why weren't you answering anyone's calls or texts?"

Unlike the time Will asked me that weeks ago, there's no demand for an answer. Carter's asking purely out of concern for my safety. I can tell by the worried frown and tone of his voice. "I needed to do it, Carter, and I needed to do it in person."

"And how do you feel now that it's done?" he asks, focusing on the camera. "I'm assuming it's done if you're calling me."

I nod, smiling at him. "It's done and I feel so free. It sounds cliché, but I really do feel like I can breathe for the first time in years. I'm not waiting for a condescending comment or questioning whether he even cares. I feel relieved."

"I think that's a good sign that you made the right choice," he replies. "I just . . . I want to make sure you didn't make the choice because you found out what happened back in college. That was years ago, Katrina. I'm content with who I am in life and who I've loved and who I will love."

"It wasn't just you, Carter. He was such a jerk about everything over the weekend, and when I found out, everything made so much more sense. He's a cruel person who doesn't want other people to have what he can't have, and his tactic for getting that is to put people down. Knowing what he did to you made me realize just what he's done to me and that he's capable of doing more. I didn't want to be in that kind of relationship anymore. I was planning to end things in a couple of weeks because I wanted to do it in person. This just pushed the timeline up a bit."

I was up late last night, going back over every little detail of my relationship with Will and concluded that it was emotionally and verbally abusive, his manipulation taking control of how I saw myself. My therapist is going to be relieved when we have our next appointment. They've been hinting at me to end things for months, and I just never saw it the same way. Until now. Now that I've really let myself look at it, there's no other way to see it.

"Yeah, he is all those things," Carter admits. "I wish you would have told me his name; I would have told you as soon as I found out that he's not a good guy. A lot of what you've told me, and I've heard from the others, makes sense. I guess not everyone grows up, huh?"

"No, sometimes people just get worse."

He hums in agreement. "So, what are you going to do now?"

I stare at him through the camera, wondering if he's really asking me that or if he's simply being sarcastic. Or, maybe worse, he doesn't feel the same way as I do. He's not feeling whatever it is that's been brewing between us, and I'm about to have my heart broken. Or be utterly embarrassed. Even if that happens, though, I don't regret the decision I made today.

So, why not take a chance at something more developing between us?

"Look, Carter, I've never been the one to initiate this kind of conversation," I admit, suddenly feeling shy. "I just . . . I've felt something between us brewing for a couple weeks now and I know it's crazy, but—"

"Kat." My heart plummets to the pit of my stomach, where it'll probably stay forever. He's about to turn me down. "Don't do this now. I know what you're going to say, and I feel the same—"

And just like that, my heart's back where it's supposed to be and beating with foolish hope. "Then why aren't we doing anything about it? If you think it's too soon, I promise you it's not. I've had months to get over this relationship, and I want to move forward."

His smile is soft, gentle, and he licks his lips as he stares at me. "I know, and I don't think that's the problem."

"Then what is?"

"I want to do this in person," he admits, and my stomach swoops. Butterflies release within me, and I fight back a giddy laugh. "I want to be able to look you in the eye and hear what you're about to tell me in a place where I can react to it."

"React how?" I tease, wanting to keep talking to him about this. About the possibility of us.

His smile evolves into a smirk. "I don't know, maybe pull you close, and hold you? Or kiss you? You have a freckle on your temple; I noticed it that morning at the pool and have been wanting to kiss it since."

My hand moves to the freckle he's talking about. His smirk grows. "Okay, give me your address. I'll come to Georgia."

Carter's laugh is deep and wonderful, and I want to hear it next to me. In this car with me, where I can melt against him. "Let's not do that."

I pout, not wanting to wait the weeks it'll take before we can see one another again. "Well, how long are you going to make me wait, Carter? I'm not sure how patient I can be."

"I'll be there in the morning."

"What?" The word is breathless around a grin so wide my cheeks hurt. "Since when?"

"Since my best friend told me the girl I like is ending things with her dick boyfriend and might need a friend."

The giddy giggle escapes now. "You're making it sound so high school."

"That's not always a bad thing. Do you think you can wait? Tell me whatever you wanted to say tomorrow?"

"Yeah," I promise, unable to dampen my grin. "I can tell you tomorrow."

"You should get back to Columbia," he advises, not making a move to end the call. "Let me know when you get home safe?"

"Sure."

Neither of us makes a move to end the call, though. We both just sit there for a moment staring at each other. Eventually, my stomach lets out a growl that even he can hear. We both dissolve into a fit of laughter before I reluctantly agree I need to get food and head back, ending the call. If I drive back to Columbia with the cheesiest of love songs blaring through my speakers, that's no one's business but my own.

Chapter 22

Carter

March 2024

I was going to be patient.

I was going to wait until Kat and I could have a real moment together. Where we could talk about what's happening between us. I would not rush to her door as soon as I pulled into town. I was going to wait and do this right, maybe take her out to dinner or to get coffee or drinks.

I had a plan.

A plan that did not include showing up at her door instead of going straight to Bryce and Josie's; but what can I do? Sometimes life has a different plan than the ones we create, and you have to just go with it. See where the road takes you.

She must have seen me pull into the driveway because she's standing in the open doorway when I reach the porch. She's dressed casually in a gray T-shirt and black joggers that look soft. Her hair is down and she's staring at me shyly, biting the corner of her bottom lip. I want to free it and soothe any lingering pain with soft kisses.

"I thought you were going to Bryce and Josie's place first and we'd catch up later."

I shrug, coming to a stop at the porch. "I was, but there's this person I kind of can't stop thinking about."

Her cheeks flush a light pink as she leans against the doorframe. "Oh, yeah?"

I grin, stuffing my hands in my pockets to keep myself from reaching out to her. "Yeah. She said something yesterday about wanting to tell me how she feels. I didn't want to wait any longer, so I went straight to her."

"I don't know what to say, Carter."

My smile dampens slightly, worried she's changed her mind in such a short time. That's part of why I did it, though. Why I told her to wait until we could see one another in person. I know she's over him and ready to move on, but I want to give her the chance to make sure I'm what she wants. If she wants to be single for a while, that's fine. No matter what, this needs to be up to her.

"You don't have to say anything," I assure her. I'm fully ready to turn around and walk back to my car, pretending this never happened. "We can forget the call yesterday and just stay friends. No hard feelings."

She's frowning now. "Is that what you want? Are you having second thoughts?"

"No, of course not!" I'm more confused by her confusion. "You are, though. Right?"

"No!" She gapes up at me, pushing off the door to stand up straighter. "What would make you think that?"

"You said you don't know what to say! What am I supposed to think that means?"

"Not that I don't want to be with you!"

Sighing, I reach up to comb my fingers through my hair, probably making it more of a knotted mess than it already is, but I don't care. I take a deep breath before I turn back to Kat. "We're doing a horrible job at this. Should we start again?"

Smiling, she nods. I turn and walk to the edge of the porch, smiling as I hear her giggling. I turn to face her again and she straightens. I close the distance between us, standing a little closer than I was the first time, and take a moment to be captivated by hazel eyes. I can hear the moment her breath catches in her throat and the electricity between us thrums to life.

"Hey, Kat," I breathe out.

"Hey," she replies just as quietly. She clears her throat slightly. "Would you like to come in? So we can talk."

I nod, smirking down at her. "Yeah, I think that'd be a great idea."

I follow her inside, closing the door behind me. She leads me into the living room, motioning to the couch for me to sit. As I do, she picks up the remote to turn off whatever she was watching in order to focus on whatever comes next. She sits next to me, keeping enough distance that I can't really reach out for her, but not so far away this moment feels hopeless.

"I think the first thing we need to talk about is how you're feeling?" The look she gives me is so unamused that I can't help but chuckle. "I know, I know, but you were with him for two years. There's nothing wrong with not being okay with the way things ended or needing some space before we jump into something."

Her gaze locks on mine, wanting me to know she's being serious. "More than anything, I'm mad that I let it go on this long, Carter. He wasn't a good boyfriend, but he got in my head, and I let him do that. The final straw was finding out what he did to you, and it's not even because it's you. I just . . . I don't put up with that."

"But you were willing to put up with him doing it to you?" My heart broke a little as she shyly nodded. "Kat, that's . . . that's not fair to you. You don't deserve to be treated like that. What makes it okay for someone to do that to you, but not someone else?"

She reaches out, her fingers brushing over my hand. I intertwine our fingers. "I know that now. It's always been easier for me to accept it when it's directed at me because I grew up being treated like a second thought. I've gotten used to it."

I squeeze her hand a little tighter. "That doesn't make it better."

Her shoulders slump, and she pulls her hand away. "I know, Carter," she sighs, burying her face in her hands. "I know and I'm working on it, I promise. I have an appointment set up with my therapist tomorrow to go over all of this and really start focusing on what I want. If you want to wait until that's done before we really talk about this, I understand."

"Hey, no." I stand up, moving so I can kneel before her. I take her hands in mine, forcing her to look at me. Her eyes are glassy with unshed tears. She's not crying over the idea of being single for the first time in years. She's crying over the idea that her past relationship would somehow make me want her less. I need to make sure she knows that's the furthest thing from the truth. "I want this, Kat. I want you."

"I'm a mess, Carter," she says with a laugh, but her quivering lip betrays her.

"We're all a mess, and I'm working on myself, too. That's life. You don't have to reach some level or pass some test to be someone I want to spend time with. Spend my life with."

"Your life?" Her eyes widen, my words sinking in.

"I can't tell you what the future is going to bring, Katrina, but this chapter of my life, yeah, I want you with me."

She looks at me in awe, eyes wide, and mouth gaping open. It might be too much for some people to hear, but it's always been who I am. I've never shied away from my emotions; why would I start now? Especially when staying quiet could result in me losing her?

"This is all in your hands, though," I emphasize. "I know where I stand. I know what I want with you, but I'm not going to push you into something you're not ready for. If you need some time to be single, I get it. You know where I am, and I'm not going anywhere. I'll be ready when you are."

Her bottom lip disappears between her teeth. I track the movement with my gaze, but don't say anything else. Slowly, I stand, ready to move back to my side of the couch and fall back into the role of a friend who cares about her, but she stands with me. Gripping my hand, she won't let me move. We're standing chest to chest, and maybe this isn't about to be over before it starts.

Her eyes search my face, but I keep my gaze locked on her eyes., wanting her to understand I'm not going anywhere.

"Carter?" Her voice is a whisper, our joined hands dropping between us. "Will you kiss me?"

This isn't my first kiss, not by a long shot, but this is going to be one of those first kisses that always matter. One you'll never be able to forget, that will come with feelings you'll be chasing for the rest of your life.

Our eyes are lock together, anticipation shining in her gaze. I release one of her hands, trailing mine up her arm until I can place it on the back of her neck, my fingers diving into her thick blonde hair at the nape of her neck. She lets out a quiet gasp, her own hand coming up to grip my shoulder. Tilting my head ever so slightly, I tug her closer. Foreheads pressed together, noses brushing against each other; I take a second to breathe, letting her pull away if she wants to, before pressing my lips against hers.

Her lips are warm and soft, just as I always thought they'd be. She melts against me. Kissing back, her hand grips my shoulder tighter, pulling me closer. Her lips part, allowing my tongue to dip inside, but no matter how badly I want to, now isn't the time to deepen the kiss. I just want this moment to be as perfect as it is right now.

The rest can come later.

She seems to get my hint, allowing the kiss to be fairly chaste, but it doesn't stop the rampant feelings coursing through me. I want to pull her closer, want to know what it's like to hold her forever, and take whatever she's willing to give me.

I pull back before pressing back in for one more short kiss.

The awed look is still in her eyes when they flutter open to look at me once more, and I'm sure that same look is mirrored in my own gaze.

"Good?" I remove my hand from her hair, pushing a few strands away from her eyes.

"Perfect," she admits. "That's what a first kiss should feel like, right?"

I press my lips to her forehead, my eyes briefly closing. She lets go of my other hand to wrap me in a hug, and I pull her closer. "Yeah, Kat. That's what it should feel like."

Eventually, the two of us move back on to the couch, but this time there's no distance between us. Kat is snuggled against my side and my arm is around her, pulling her as close as possible without putting her in my lap. There's a lot we need to talk about, but that can wait. For now, I'm content to just be in the moment with her.

~

I never made it to Josie and Bryce's yesterday.

After just hanging out on the couch for a while, the two of us decide we do need to talk about where things are going to go from here. We both have busy schedules and being a couple of hours away from one another isn't ideal for the start of a new relationship, but if we're both willing to work at it, we could be great. In the end, Kat asks for a couple of days to be single and let the anticipation of a first date—something she's never really felt—build before we put a label on it.

I couldn't agree more. We pull up jam-packed schedules, playfully arguing over who's busier and we sift through date after date to find one that works. In the end, we settle on one two weeks away. Kat needs to be in Columbia to be on the job site that day, but I have nothing besides practice, so I decide to make the drive back down here. It gets added to both of our calendars, and we settle in to just hang out that night.

We order food and watch movies. There are a couple of kisses shared, but mostly we just take the time to be alone for the first time. Eventually, we somehow end up asleep on the couch.

It's late morning by the time I use my key to enter Josie and Bryce's apartment, stiff from falling asleep on a couch but with a smile on my face that I can't dim. I'm surprised to find both Josie and Bryce sitting at the kitchen island, facing the door as I walk in.

"Morning!" I greet, dropping my bag before going for the French press on the counter, a mug already waiting for me. "What are you doing?"

I'm surprised they're not at the pool, as that's where Kat was heading when I left. Instead, they're both sitting in front of their own laptops, with what looks like separate projects going on.

"I'm going over a budget for our first year," Bryce comments, eyebrow quirking up. "But I'll gladly put it on pause if you want to tell me what you were up to this morning."

"And last night." Josie's tone is teasing, but she doesn't look up from her laptop. "Did it involve our favorite contractor?"

"Not telling," I reply, downing the coffee a lot quicker than I should. I bend down to grab my bag, then head down the hall. "I'm taking a shower."

"Oh, come on," Bryce yells after me. "I've told you things!"

"You've what?" Josie's gasp follows me down the hall.

Opening the spare room, I laugh to myself as I hear her asking him how much I know. It's not much. Bryce would never disrespect Josie like that. Nor would I let him. Still, I know more than I am willing to tell either of them. Maybe in two weeks I'd be more willing to share, but right now I'm going to keep this between the two of us.

Chapter 23

Katrina

April 2024

"What are you doing there today?"

Carter's voice carries through the car as I turn down the street, heading toward Josie and Bryce's new house. They picked up the keys yesterday evening and are meeting me there to do a walk-through. Unsurprisingly, the inspection of the house came back with nothing major to be concerned about, but I warned them things could come up as we start tearing into things.

It's been just under a week since our first kiss and I'm counting down the days until this coming Friday when we'll finally have our first date. In those last few days, I've been living the single life as much as I can. I haven't been obsessively checking my phone to make sure I didn't miss an angry text from Will. Instead, I've been hanging out with my friends and exploring the city a bit more. Carter and I have also been texting and talking as often as we can, but there's no pressure.

We both know where this is going, we both are committed to it, so this gets to be the fun part. The part where we get to know one another and spend all our extra time flirting. Which is something

Carter Abrams is very good at, I've learned. I've blushed more in the last few days than I have in years.

"I am meeting Josie and Bryce at the house so we can talk about some of my plans and see what they're looking to do," I explain, glancing down at the GPS to make sure I don't miss the house. I've only driven by it once, when I initially offered to help, so I haven't gotten the directions down yet. "Then I think we're going to grab lunch or dinner, depending on how long it takes—talk things out."

"You know you're doing them a huge favor, right?" Carter questions. "If Bryce had to find people to help him do this, he'd lose his mind. He already knows he can trust you."

"You should have seen Josie's face the day she showed me the house, Carter. I could tell she really wanted it." I pull the car to a stop on the street in front of the house. "This place is so them. I can't wait to see what they do to it."

"I'm still trying to wrap my head around Bryce buying a house. You gotta remember, I lived through Bryce in college."

"Well, hopefully he's gotten better at household chores," I tease, checking my phone to see if I have any updates yet. "I'm the first one here."

Carter laughs. "Are you early or on time?"

"About five minutes early," I reply, leaning back in my seat. "What time do you have to be back at the pool?"

"In about . . . Ah, shit."

Amused, I glance at the time. "You need to be there right now, don't you?"

"Yeah, pretty much." I hear shuffling on the other end of the phone and the obvious sign of a door closing behind him. "At least it's just an extra practice. Hopefully, coach won't be too mad."

In the rearview mirror, I see Josie's Jeep coming down the street. "Hopefully! They're about to pull in, so I should let you go. Have a good practice."

"Send me updates and try to convince Bryce to paint a wall lime green."

"Absolutely not. That's not the aesthetic we're going for. I'll talk to you later?"

"You're no fun." I can practically picture him pouting. "Go, do your job, and uphold the dignity of the aesthetic. I'll call you tonight, beautiful."

Blushing, I tell him goodbye and end the call. Gathering my stuff, I cut the engine, and get out of the car, making my way up the drive as Josie parks. She jumps out of the car before Bryce even opens the door, a bright grin on her face as she waves the keys in the air. My laughter grows as she practically tackles me in a hug.

"Welcome home!" I beam at them. Reaching out to pull Bryce into a quick hug when Josie lets me go. "Are you ready for this?"

Bryce is looking between me, and the house, conflicted. "Kat, I can't let you do this for free. It's going to be a lot of work."

"Stop," I firmly reply. "We went over this. This is a challenge for myself, to see if I could do this on the side, and I'm doing it for friends who have been nothing but great to me. If you really want to pay me something, wait until the club is up and running, then we'll talk. Deal?"

He looks like he's about to argue with me again, so I link my arm with Josie's. "Please get the door unlocked before I fight with your boyfriend about money again."

Laughing, Josie leads us up the pathway to the house. It's a cute two-story brick house. On the left side, large bay windows accent both floors; from the listing, I know one of them is the main bedroom and already know Josie's going to want a window seat to read in. The porch is small but is highlighted by white steps leading to a door that I cannot see them keeping. It's a deep red with a muted stained-glass window.

As we walk up the porch, I release Josie to unlock the door and hang back a little. I want the two of them to have the moment of walking into their home for the first time. They weren't done with the closing until late last night, so Josie told me they hadn't gone over, too exhausted from a long day at the pool and with the realtor. Bryce rests his hand on the small of her back, both grinning as the door opens and they step inside. I follow, closing the door behind us.

"I hate that door."

I can't help but giggle at Bryce's declaration, Josie nodding along. I wave the notepad I have in my hand. "It's already on the list of things to go."

After stepping through the front door, we're greeted with the stairs to our right, and the living room to our left. We start in the living room, where there really isn't all that much to change. It's not a large space, but big enough to entertain their friends when they want to. There's a fireplace that adds a cozy vibe to the room, but we all decide the color of the brick needs to be changed and the carpet needs to go.

To get to the kitchen, we have to walk through the laundry area, which Bryce absolutely hates. I soon realize that the kitchen will be his domain more than Josie's as he starts talking me through what he wants and wondering how we can expand the space. The kitchen is small, the two of them would barely be able to cook together without constantly bumping into each other. I start walking them through all the ways we can change it. They have room to expand.

"I can take the laundry room out of the walkway," I tell them, flipping my notepad to a new page so I can sketch as I talk. "If you guys are still okay with only having two bathrooms, we can move the laundry into the one that's weirdly situated off the dining area, and then that'll be gone. That's giving you a ton of extra space without even needing to build on."

Josie's grinning at me, nodding along with what I'm saying. "I think that sounds great; we already knew the kitchen was going to be a total renovation."

With Bryce's nod of agreement, the three of us keep moving through the house.

A few hours later, the three of us are sitting at a booth in the back of Brick Tavern, waiting for Mia to arrive. Josie and I are already going over design elements after the successful walkthrough where I filled the notebook with pages and pages of notes. Most of them scrawled in my hasty handwriting, a couple in Bryce's choppy writing, and even a few in Josie's flowy script—it really was a group effort.

A couple of minutes after we get a table, Mia slides into the booth next to me. "How'd the walkthrough go?"

And that sets Josie off, telling her best friend all about the plans we'd come up with. I can't help but smile at the two of them talking, knowing that I had a small part of it. Of bringing Josie's dreams to life. It's why I decided to enter this field, after all. Bryce smiles fondly, adding his own opinions occasionally, but then his gaze drifts to me.

"What?" I ask, taking a sip of my water. "Why are you looking at me like that?"

"Back at the house, you said you were using this as a challenge for yourself," he reminds me. I feel my face flush. "A challenge for what? If Thomas won't let you do projects like this, do you think you're gonna prove something to him?"

"I don't know. Maybe I just want to know if I'm any good at the whole flipping thing or creating something better out of something that mostly exists."

"Are you thinking of branching out on your own?"

It's not a new idea, it's one I've had in the back of my mind for most of my adult life. It's just something I've never really let myself think too much about. Lately, though, those thoughts have been more prominent and now that I've ended things with Will, I can't shake them. Besides my job and a couple of work friends, there's not really anything for me back in Charleston, but Columbia has all the people I care most about. Mainly Carter. Will it suck to leave Nadine? Absolutely, but she'll also be the first person telling me to go.

Bryce is waiting for an answer I'm not sure I'm ready to give.

"It's good to keep your options open." I'm grateful that our conversation hasn't caught Josie or Mia's attention, because I'd hate for them to get their hopes up on something I can't deliver. "Don't you think?"

He nods, reaching for his beer. "You're good at it, just so you know." My phone buzzes on the table, where it's sitting facedown beside me. Bryce smirks, nodding at it. "Ten bucks says it's Carter."

I roll my eyes, grabbing the phone. "I'm absolutely not taking that bet."

Which is a good thing because he was right. Sitting on my screen is a new message from Carter. A message that makes my heart pound wildly in my chest.

> Bryce told me some of the plans you guys came up with. It all sounds great! If you ever find yourself needing a reason to stay in Columbia, I think you found one.

I look up at Bryce, waving my phone toward him. "Are you two sharing a brain cell or something?"

He shrugs, taking a drink of his beer.

Rolling my eyes at Bryce, I then text Carter back.

> Bryce told me some of the plans you guys came up with. It all sounds great! If you ever find yourself needing a reason to stay in Columbia, I think you found one.

> I thought the reason for me to stay would be you? Is that not enough of a reason?

> If you want to stay, you know how happy that'll make me. It's up to you, though. If you go back to Charleston, we'll make it work.

That's the thing, though. Eventually, I'd move my life here if things work out between us. Carter can't come to Charleston because of the club, but I can move. There's work for contractors everywhere, but would I really want to go from working for one company to another?

"All I'm saying," Bryce's low voice breaks into my thoughts, "is that there are a lot of reasons for you to stick around, Kat. If you want to. Plus, we're kind of big on chasing dreams, so you know you'll have support."

Josie and Mia are both being suspiciously quiet, but I can tell they heard him that time. Neither one says anything, but not in a way that makes me feel unwanted. No one in this group is going to force me to do anything I'm not ready to do, but they are going to make sure I know I have the support I need, and that means everything to me.

"No one knows what the future will bring," I say, a little louder to make sure the two eavesdroppers can hear me.

"Ain't that the truth." Bryce tips the neck of his beer bottle toward me before taking another drink.

Chapter 24

Katrina

April 2024

Friday comes quickly, which is aided by the massive to-do list I have for the club. I arrive even earlier than I normally do that morning, ready to tackle the day by prioritizing the tasks before us.

"I don't know what else needs to happen, but we need to get the wiring in the main pool done today." I'm standing on the deck talking to the electrician, Dave, while some of the other guys are making sure everything is ready for the installation of the new pool set for Monday morning. "This has been delayed long enough and it can't wait any longer. I refuse to let this be the reason we fall behind."

Dave nods, looking down at his phone. "That shouldn't be a problem. I think we can have it done by lunch, boss."

My phone buzzes on top of the clipboard in my hand. I glance down and frown at the screen. Why on earth is my mother calling me?

"Do you need to get that?" Dave asks.

"Yeah." I look back up at him. "Let me know if you guys need anything from me to make this happen, okay?"

Dave nods, waving me away as he yells out to one of his guys. Knowing I have a good crew who are more than capable of doing their jobs, I step off to the side to answer the call. "Mom? What's wrong?"

Her laugh echoes in my ear. "That's a strange way to answer the phone, Katrina. Why on earth would anything be wrong?"

I let out a shaky breath, allowing my fear to fade away. "You don't call me that often, Mom, so it worried me."

"Well, now you're just being dramatic. I call you all the time."

"What did you need, Mom?" I ask, deciding not to argue with her over this. We'll always see things like this differently. "I'm at work."

"They can live without you while you talk to your mother."

If I tried something like that with her, she'd go into a fit about how people die when she's distracted. Then again, what she does has always been more important than anything I have going on.

Bryce approaches me, seemingly about to ask me something. When he sees I'm on the phone, he hangs back. Wanting an excuse to end whatever this call will be as soon as I need to, I shake my head and wave him forward. I hold up two fingers, signaling this call will be over soon. "I'm really busy, Mom."

His eyes widen comically, but he doesn't run away. Instead, he patiently waits for me to finish and I'm grateful for the excuse his presence gives me if I need it.

"I just spoke with William," she says, tersely. I mentally curse. I should have known this conversation was coming. "What do you think you're doing, Katrina? How dare you end the relationship and break that boy's heart."

"Oh, please," I scoff. "I did not break his heart, and if he told you I did, he's just looking for attention."

"What he said is between me and him. I don't think you're understanding my point, Katrina. Why would you end things? I spent weeks talking about you, telling him how wonderful you are despite all your flaws, and he still asked you out. You shouldn't just throw something like that away."

"Despite all my flaws?" My shoulders tense at her words, wondering if this is the conversation we're finally about to have. "And what flaws would those be, Mom?"

The question catches her off guard, and she stumbles around for an answer. "Oh, well, you know. No one is perfect, Katrina, least of all you."

"Oh, I know that," I reply back. "I never pretended to be perfect. I'm just curious what flaws you'd deem something he needs to get past in order to date me?"

"Holy shit," Bryce groans beside me.

I wonder if he gets it, at least on some level. I hope no one has ever said anything cruel to him about Josie or their relationship, but I know what that is like. Bryce is still somewhat in the public eye, and people can be coldhearted and cruel. Sometimes even the people who are supposed to love us.

"Katrina, you know what flaws I'm talking about," she snaps. "I don't need to say them."

My mother is Hollywood perfection. She's tall with a slim, lithe figure that comes from years of working out and watching what she eats. Her metabolism must be through the roof, or something. Whatever it is that helps her be that way, I didn't seem to inherit the gene, and it's something she's constantly pointed out to me.

"Yeah, Mom, I do. I've always known," I bite out. "All those times my dessert plate got replaced with a salad and you'd make pointed remarks to seamstresses about needing to let something out. I've always known."

I'm half expecting Bryce to tear the phone out of my hands and throw it across the room based on the pure fury in his eyes. Honestly, I'm considering just handing it over to him.

"I'm an adult," I remind her. "I don't need to validate my choices to you. Will had real flaws—harmful flaws—but the ones you see in me are superficial. Thank you for finding a boyfriend for me, it's added a lot of great talking points with my therapist. I'm sure this conversation will come up next time I have an appointment with them."

"You're going to regret this, Katrina," she warns. "You're never going to find someone who will—"

"Hey, Katrina!" Bryce's voice is loud, surely can be heard on the other end of the phone. I don't know if he could hear what she was saying, or if he could just read it on my face, but I am grateful for him in that moment. "I need to talk to you."

"Mom, I really have to go." I can hear her starting to argue, but I just end the call, taking a deep breath before looking at Bryce. "Thank you for that."

"I could only hear your end, but your mother sounds like a piece of work."

He doesn't even know the half of it. "What did you need?"

"I was just coming over to see if you wanted some coffee. I'm going to run out and get some."

"Yes," I breathe out, smiling at him. "All the coffee, please. I'll need it to get through today."

"Nothing can be worse than that." He motions to my phone. "Just think, at least the end of the day has something that'll make you happy."

It's weird, talking to him about my date with Carter, but he has a point. It is going to make me happy. "Honestly, it's the thing that's keeping me going today."

Bryce laughs, turning to head back toward the entrance so he can go get the coffee. He's right, though, it really can't get worse after that.

I collapse into the chair in Bryce's office with a loud groan. Literally everything that could have gone wrong today did. I've been running around this entire property since eight o'clock this morning, putting out one fire after the other. I don't even know what time it is.

I reach up to wiggle the mouse, bringing Bryce's computer to life. With tired eyes, I squint at the screen until my eyes can focus on the numbers and—

"Fuck!"

In a second, I'm standing and scrambling to grab my phone to dial Carter's number. It rings as I scramble to gather my things, praying he won't be too mad at me. It's taken almost two weeks to get our schedules lined up for our first official date. He even drove out here, and now I've worked straight past fashionably late and am dangerously edging toward standing him up.

The ringing cuts off. "Ah, so you are alive."

He's teasing. I can tell by the lilt in his tone, but the words still hit me hard. "I am so sorry, Carter. I've had the day from hell, starting with a phone call from my mother, but I'm leaving right now. I'll be there as soon as I can."

"Well, that'll be awkward for you," he replies, "because I'm not at the restaurant."

The hope that's been fluttering around in my stomach for the last ten days comes to a screeching halt. I've blown it by getting too caught up in work, and now he's about to let me down. I'm sure he'll tell me it's a timing issue, and it's not my fault. Or the god awful, It's me, not you. I don't want to hear any of that.

"Bryce called me earlier." Carter's deep, soothing voice continues, and maybe I'm not getting dumped. "We'll get back to the phone call from your mother, but he told me that everything was going wrong today. He wanted to give me a heads up that you might not get out of there on time."

It's not Bryce's place to do that, but I can't help but feel grateful for my friend. It makes sense; it's what this group does—all look out for one another. "I kept meaning to text or call you, but something kept coming up. I didn't even know it was this late until a minute ago."

"You don't need to apologize. Things happen. I'm a flexible guy who's willing to adjust plans when I need to."

That's not something I'm sure I'll get used to, at least not fully. Will needed a plan and when someone deviated from the original plan, everything was ruined. Everything we did together came with a calculated reason and, in the rare moments it didn't, Will was usually more focused on something else.

But Carter is more than willing to meet me halfway. Not only meet me there, but completely change directions to be what I need him to be. I've never been someone's priority before. Never been with someone who wants to spend time with me simply because I'm me.

"Kat?" He sounds worried as he pulls me out of my thoughts. There's no reason to be focusing on what I had, especially when something so wonderful is standing before me. Or, at least, on the other side of a phone. "Are you still there?"

"Yeah," I assure him. "Sorry, I just got caught up in my own head for a second, but I'm here."

He hums, a comforting sound of understanding. "If you're still up for that date, I'd love it if you could meet me on the pool deck."

I glance down into the pool through the window in Bryce's office; it's pitch-black in there and there is no movement. "Carter, I can see the pool and you're not out there."

"It has been a long day," he teases. "We have two, remember?"

"Well, you didn't specify," I tease back with a grumble.

He laughs. "I have a surprise for you."

"I'll be right out," I promise, not waiting for a response before I hang up the phone.

I take a second to fix my reflection in my camera, wishing I'd taken even a moment to put on some tinted moisturizer. The bare-faced look would have to do since he was waiting.

I don't know what I was expecting to find when I stepped through the doors onto the deck, but it wasn't what I found.

It was like a scene out of a movie. Battery-operated candles spread across the deck, casting a warm glow that reflects across the water. There's a massive pile of blankets on the edge of the deck, and a picnic is laid across the blanket.

Carter stands off to the side, smiling at me. His green eyes sparkle in the dim light. "I figured if you can't make it to the restaurant, I'd bring the restaurant to you."

Grinning, I close the distance between us, greeting him with a kiss on his cheek. His hands find my hips, pulling me closer as I take in the scene around me. "How did you pull this together so quickly? When did you have time to cook?"

"Oh, no, I definitely didn't cook," he immediately replies. "That's a skill I have never mastered. I'm good at ordering takeout, though, and the restaurant we were going to offers takeout. Josie had some recommendations for the things she thought you'd like, so I got a bit of everything."

My gaze turns back to the spread he'd laid out, my palms turning sweaty at the obvious sign of how badly he wanted to make this happen. He didn't get mad when the plans changed; he adapted and came up with something I love more than a typical dinner at a fancy restaurant.

I don't know what Carter and I will look like together, but I have a feeling this is it.

"I know it's not a beautiful restaurant," Carter says, motioning to the blanket, "but I hope you'll be okay with a compromise."

Unable to hide my wide smile, I press it against his in a simple kiss. A dumbfounded look takes over his features as I pull back. "This is better than a fancy dinner."

His surprise is replaced with the grin that always makes me weak in the knees. "Then what are we waiting for?"

I allow Carter to take my hand and lead me into the middle of the blanket, the two of us getting comfortable. There's a cool breeze coming off the water, but it feels good after running around all day.

As Carter opens the food containers, I inhale a deep breath, looking up at the sky. I can't see stars in the middle of the city, but the smell of chlorine, even as it mixes with the food, and the gentle lapping of the water brings a sense of relaxation to me.

This is going to be the most perfect date I've ever been on.

Chapter 25

Carter

April 2024

"Do you have any idea how special tonight has been for me?" When I look over at Katrina, she's looking down at her hands instead of at me. Throughout our date, she has kept shyly glancing up at me through her lashes. "No one has ever done anything like this for me before."

There are so many reasons I want to punch Jacobson in the face, and this is becoming the number one. The way he's made Kat retreat in on herself, and believe she's not worth being treated with love and consideration. She's so unsure what to do now, and I hate that he diminished her confidence, but it's also something I've experienced.

What he did to me sucked, but it has allowed me to use my platform in ways I could have only dreamed about. I've had so many young, queer athletes tell me I've made an impact on their lives and helped pave the way for making the sport more inclusive. He cannot take that from me; I've never let him have that power. Now I'm also going to right every wrong he did to Kat, and hopefully, get her to see she deserves a great love.

"It's a good thing you decided to go out with me then." I grin at her. "This is my style. I'm sure some people think it's too much."

"That's impossible."

Silence settles between us again, but it's not the kind I feel the need to fill. Most first dates are doomed when the silence settles in, but not this one. I'm content to just sit here all night, even if neither one of us says another word. I'd still get to spend the night with her.

She's looking back at the pool now. The way the lights reflect off the surface, catching on something in her eye. Normally, I can get lost looking at her, but there's something else in her gaze, something different this time. There's a longing I've never seen from her before.

My eyes drift to the surface of the pool before sliding back to her. "When was the last time you went swimming for fun?"

The question must startle her, because she looks up at me with wide eyes. "What?"

I nod toward the pool. "When was the last time you went swimming?"

"I don't know," she admits with a laugh. "Probably high school."

"What?" I stare at her, jaw slacked. "No way. That's not possible. I don't believe you."

"That's your choice, doesn't make it any less true." She shrugs, looking back at the pool. "I wasn't the girl who got invited to pool parties, nor did I have much desire to leave the house in a swimsuit."

I could make a comment about how I hate knowing she's ever felt that way, but it wouldn't matter. I can't take those memories away. I can't stop people from being assholes or preying on people's insecurities, but I can help her make new memories. Maybe new memories will also help chase away lingering insecurities. I can show her, and constantly remind her, just how beautiful she is to me.

I stand, pulling my shirt over my head in a fluid motion I've perfected over the years. I can feel Kat's eyes tracking my every movement. When I look down at her, she's staring up at me, desperately trying to keep her eyes from roving over my chest. When I reach for the buckle of my belt, her eyes widen even more.

"What are you doing?" She laughs, but it's a strained sound and she's looking everywhere but at me.

"What?" I cheekily reply, toeing off my socks and shoes so I can pull my jeans off. They end up in a pile with the shirt, leaving me in just my black boxer briefs. "I can't remember the last time I swam for fun, especially with someone I was into."

She stares up at me, wide eyed. I'm sure if we had better lighting, I'd see a pink flush to her cheeks. "Carter, we cannot go swimming right now! Are you crazy?"

"Why not? I'm pretty sure I own this pool and my contractor said it's good to go, so I say we can go swimming."

To emphasize my point, I say nothing more, and take a few quick steps toward the edge to dive in. When I surface, she's still sitting there, staring at me in utter shock. This isn't how she expected our night to go. I push my hair back out of my face to focus on her better.

"Aren't you cold?" She moves to her knees but doesn't move to get up.

I shake my head. "Not at all!"

The weather in Columbia has already reached the upper eighties, with several days being sunny without a cloud in sight. So, the water is the perfect temperature, not too cold, and not too warm.

I'm just about to tell her she doesn't need to come in if it's not something she's comfortable with, but then she's standing and shimmying out of her shorts to reveal a pair of dark gray boyshorts.

Nothing too fancy, more practical, but my gaze can't help but linger on her smooth thighs. She hesitates for just a moment before pulling her tank top off to reveal a matching sports bra.

I bite my lip, taking her in as she pulls her hair into a loose ponytail. I knew she was beautiful, but now that she's standing before me like this, I can't look away. The lights scattered around the pool deck and floating in the water seem to dance off her pale skin, highlighting new areas to draw my attention to.

She flashes me a grin that stirs something deep within me. I know I'm in trouble. This woman is going to be the death of me, and I don't even care. I watch as she hesitates for only a second before she gets a jogging start to cannonball into the pool. I move toward her as she goes under, ready to pull her close as soon as she surfaces.

When she does, she's grinning from ear to ear. My arms wind around her waist, feeling the glide of skin against skin as I pull her in close. Her legs wrap around my waist, and I use my legs to keep us afloat in the deeper water. I move toward the wall in case we need some leverage. I guess I hadn't even asked if she can swim.

"Is it cold?" I ask, searching her face for any sign of discomfort. Whether it's from the way I'm holding her or the temperature of the water, I want to know what she's thinking.

She shakes her head, leaning down to kiss me. I'm caught by surprise, so she's able to deepen the kiss. It's the first one she initiates. I press her back against the wall, allowing my grip on the edge of the pool and my legs to keep us afloat as I kiss back.

The movement of the water keeps pressing us closer and closer together, the limited amount of clothing between us leaving nothing to the imagination. I let a hand trail down her shoulder, running my fingers over the strap of her bra before going lower to grip her waist.

"Carter," she breathes, throwing her head back as soon as she pulls away to catch her breath. I waste no time, moving my lips down her neck toward her collarbone, where I suck, and nip gently. I'm rewarded with a gasp, her legs tightening around me.

More than anything, I want her to keep making those sounds, to keep moving her hips against me, but I know we can't go further. Not here. I can't sleep with her for the first time here. I want it to be special, and I don't think that's what Bryce meant when he advised me to go for a romantic night by the pool. He can forgive a lot of things, but not that.

We're both breathing deeply when I pull away from her neck. I reach up to push the wet hair from her eyes, which earns me a grin. She's leaning back against the edge in a way I can't see as being all that comfortable, but doesn't complain.

"I should have asked; you can swim right?"

Her answer is to reach out and push the top of my head until I'm under the water. I feel the movement as she uses the wall to push off and swim away from me. When I surface, her laughter is across the pool. Grinning to myself, I chase after her. Despite nothing going the way we planned, this might be the best date I've ever had in my life.

We mess around in the pool for a little while longer, just swimming, and being playful. It's interrupted with a few more kisses and light make out sessions, but nothing that's as heated as the first one, before we decide to get out of the water. We collapse on the blanket, and I'm instantly regretting not having any towels. We make it work with some blankets, and then cuddle in close to fight off the chill.

"Why'd your mom call?" I feel her stiffen under the movement of my fingers on her shoulder blade before she relaxes again. "You don't have to tell me if you don't want to."

"It's not that. We just have a messy relationship and I'm not sure it's something that can ever be fixed." She tilts her head back to look at me. "I've told you my family is chaotic at best."

From what she's told me, they sound like assholes, but we're too new in our relationship for me to say that right now. "Do you want to talk about it?"

She moves until she's sitting up; her legs crossed beneath her. Something in the air shifts, telling me we're about to have a serious conversation, so I follow her lead and sit up a little straighter. She picks at the edge of the blanket but doesn't say anything. Reaching for the glass of wine I'd just poured her, I offer it to her and watch as she takes it with shaky hands. She takes a small sip before setting it back down.

"I'm a disappointment to my mother and Thomas in so many ways," she begins, and I hate her parents even more than I did two seconds ago. "Thomas never really wanted kids; he's not wired for them. He and my mom are perfect for each other, though. Two emotionally unavailable people who were able to find love and physical attraction with one another. All the emotional currency they have, they use on each other."

She continues, "It took me a long time to be okay with knowing I'll never measure up to what they want me to be. I didn't think Thomas would ever hire me, but my mom was worried about how embarrassing it would be for me not to have a job in the field my stepfather monopolizes."

"So that's why you got hired?"

Her eyes lift to meet mine. "Carter, this place is the biggest project he has ever trusted me to lead. Normally I'm assigned small businesses or family homes. Anything he doesn't think is worth the company's time—that's where I go and it's always in Charleston, so he can keep an eye on me."

My gaze sweeps across the amazing pool deck surrounding us, taking in all the hard work and painstaking detail Kat put into it. The way she brought a dream of mine to life. My gaze drifts back to her. "But you're amazing at your job."

She laughs, bitterly. "I know! He just refuses to see it and my mom refuses to see me as anything other than someone who should be on the arm of an important man."

"I'm sorry, what? Why would that be what she wants for you?"

"Because it's all I'm good enough for." She throws her arms out in the air, the anger at her mother coming out. "She's mad at me because I ended things with Will. She's the one who set us up. Apparently, she basically told him I'd make a good wife despite my many flaws. All the flaws she meant are superficial."

"Kat," I groan, closing my eyes, and counting to three in my head. "I want to be with you, but I never want to meet your parents."

"There's the family you're born into, right?" I nod, urging her to go on. "And then there's the family you get to create. I never really thought I'd be lucky enough to find one that I get to create, until I came here, and met all of you. You're the family I'm choosing to create and, to be honest, I'm not sure the family I was born into is necessary in my life."

I can't imagine not having my family on my side or never seeing them again. They mean everything to me, but they've never treated me the way Kat's parents have treated her. They've never made me question my worth. If Kat were to ask my opinion, I would tell her that people who make her feel small aren't worth the effort, but I know it's harder with family, and I'm grateful to know that she's found something better to hold on to. Something that will empower her.

"I don't know what the future holds for me or us," she says, "but I really don't think my future is in Charleston or at Dalton Enterprises. To be honest, I'm not sure they'd even care if I left. I think they'd be relieved to know they no longer had to babysit me."

"You're a thirty-year-old woman, Katrina; you don't need babysitting." I hope she knows the anger in my tone is directed at them, not her.

She nods, reaching out to take my hand. I unclench my fist, flexing my fingers before tangling them with hers, my thumb rubbing over her knuckles soothingly. "I know that now. I feel like the future is mine again, you know? Like I get to have control over where my life goes and if that means cutting out toxic people, even my parents, I have to do it. Right?"

I reach my free hand up to cup her cheek, tenderly wiping away one of the few tears that escaped the corner of her eye. She blinks in surprise.

"I'll never tell you what to do, Kat. That's not my style. I'll just stand here and support you—whatever you want to do. I'm on your side, no one else's. If they make you feel bad about yourself, screw them. If you want to give them another chance to make things right, I'm there. Whatever you need, that's my priority."

She blinks up at me, like I'd just offered to pull the moon down for her. Taking a deep breath, she grabs the hand I have on her cheek. "I'm worried I don't deserve you."

I've never felt my heart hurt like it just did, the pain shooting down into my chest. I lean forward until I can brush my lips against hers. "You deserve more."

I don't go back to Georgia until Sunday afternoon, which means Kat and I can have date number two and three in one weekend. By the time Bryce comes over to Kat's rental on Sunday morning, she and I have officially decided to be together, cute titles and all. Which I think Bryce can tell the second I open the door after he knocks.

"Say nothing," I warn, turning to go back to the living room where Kat's waiting for us.

"What would I even say?" he asks, closing the door behind him and following me. "Kat, your boyfriend is being mean to me."

"Nope." Kat's shaking her head, not even looking up at him. "We're not doing this, Clark. I don't know what he's told you, but I'm not looking at your weird, knowing smirk."

I haven't told him much of anything, just that we're officially together and I'm happy. Which I know, in turn, makes him happy.

"You're dating my best friend, Kat. Do you really expect him not to tell me things about the two of you?" I glare at Bryce as he sits down in the armchair.

Closing her laptop, she places it on the coffee table before moving to cuddle against my side, and my arm wounds around her shoulders, Bryce's gaze tracking every movement. "Of course, I know he's going to tell you things. Just don't make it weird around me or I'll return the favor. You think Josie hasn't told me things?"

I laugh at the look that crosses Bryce's face, the way his brow crinkles in discomfort. Turning my head to hide my laugh, I end up pressing a kiss against Kat's forehead, which earns me a soft look from her. Bryce gags in mock disgust.

She turns a glare back at him. "Why did you need to come over here to talk to both of us on a Sunday, Bryce? Why couldn't I come to your place?"

"Actually, it's more like Carter and I need to talk to you about something," he replies. "You could have come to my place, but I don't want Josie to hear this conversation. Plus, you kind of kidnapped my best friend for the weekend."

"Play nice," I warn. "There's plenty of me for both of you."

"Oh god," Bryce shakes his head, and Kat looks up at me with a grimace. "That's weird. Please don't say that."

"Ever again," Kat pleads. "No one's fighting over you."

"I mean, honestly, Kat, you can have him," Bryce replies. "I've had him for almost thirty years, kinda sick of him."

"But what do I do when I get sick of him?" She pouts.

I pull my arm from around her shoulder, moving so there's some space between us, and give them a mock pout. "I can go back to Georgia!"

"You know we're just kidding, right?" Kat replies, reaching out to grab my hand and tug me back. I go willingly, unable to resist her. Once we're both comfortable again, she looks over at Bryce. "So, what's going on, and why isn't Josie involved?"

He straightens up, looking more serious. "You told us you had a guy who can do the sign for the side of the building with the logo Mia decided, right?"

She nods. "Yeah, he said it'll only take a couple of weeks once you nail down the name and get it to Mia."

"Does he need the name if he already knows the font and everything Mia will use? Or can you add the name to the logo?"

She turns to me with a slight frown. "Why is Bryce being so secretive? And why don't you seem at all surprised?"

"Because it's a surprise," Bryce answers. "For Mia and Josie."

I can see the moment she realizes what Bryce is getting at because a tightlipped, playful smile spreads across her lips. "We can work something out. Tell me everything."

Chapter 26

Katrina

May 2024

"Kat!" Nadine grins brightly at me as I approach her desk. She stands to greet me with a hug. "I didn't know you were coming in today. I thought the meeting was going to be virtual."

I shrug, not knowing what else to say. "He emailed me last night asking me to come in for it. I had to get up ridiculously early to make it on time, because of course he isn't going to push back his next meeting."

She rolls her eyes. "Of course not. That meeting is his weekly chance to gossip and get drunk on a golf course." ☐

I stifle my laughter behind my hand, smiling at Liam as he passes by on his phone. I note the way their eyes track each other's movements, clearly aware of where each other is in a room. "Have things not gotten better between you?"

She sighs, sitting back down as I lean against her desk. "You know when people make a joke that's stupid, and then they apologize for it but can't seem to get over it themselves?"

"And end up making a bigger deal out of nothing because they're so worried about messing up again?" She nods in confirmation, and I groan. "No, I thought Liam was better than that."

Her gaze drifts in the direction he just went, even though he's long gone. "He is. I just don't know if he knows what he's doing. I've tried talking to him about it, but that's a conversation he's avoiding like the plague."

It's surprising to know that Liam doesn't seem receptive to the conversation Nadine wants to have with him. Maybe he's worried he'll end up sticking his foot in his mouth, but he's already doing it. I'd had the same conversation with Will when we first started the whole *I know I'm fat, so stop acting like I'm not*, but he'd taken it the complete opposite direction, making pointed, negative comments about my curves. Liam, I think, is strictly in the world where he thinks the word "fat" is bad and should be avoided.

Which isn't his decision to make.

"So, tell me how Columbia's treating you!" Nadine leans toward me on her desk. "I can't believe you're dating an Olympic swimmer. I looked him up; he's cute!"

Unable to hide my grin, my cheeks flush, and I duck my head. "Yeah, he's something special. A lot different from my previous relationship."

"Oh, Kat," she breathes out. When I look up at her, she's beaming back at me like I'd just told her something amazing. "I'm so happy you've found someone like that. I could tell the moment you walked in, you are in love."

"Whoa." I laugh, shaking my head. "We've been together a couple of weeks. No one said anything about love. Calm down."

Her grin is knowing. "But you're falling, aren't you?" Her phone rings before I can answer, and she rolls her eyes, reaching for it. "Yes, Mr. Dalton?"

I stand a little straighter, glancing at the clock on the wall behind her. I'm still five minutes early, and as I listen to Nadine's side of the conversation, I know Thomas wants me to come in as soon as I get here. I'm already heading toward his closed office when Nadine waves me away.

I knock on Thomas's door once before pushing it open. He waves me in without looking up, so I move into the room before closing the door behind me. He hasn't said a single word or even looked up by the time I settle into a chair across from him.

I clear my throat. "So, you wanted to see me?"

He holds a hand up before the sentence fully leaves my mouth. Chastised, and confused as to why I needed to come right in, I sink back in my chair and wait for him to finish whatever it is he's working on. I try to distract myself by looking around his office, a room I've barely ever been in, but there's nothing to focus on. It's completely void of life and looks staged right down to the dusty fake Ficus in the corner.

When I was a kid, I wondered if my mom had married a robot. As a fully grown, rational adult woman, the thought passes through my mind again.

"Thank you for coming in, Katrina," Thomas finally says about ten minutes later. He closes the laptop, steepling his fingers together on top of his desk. "We need to discuss the project you've been working on."

My brows furrow. "Sure, of course," I reply, trying to recall the details from my last email. "The pool installation is on track to be done this week—that's for the inside pool. We ran into some issues with the wiring—"

His hand goes back up again, silencing me. "I've been receiving your email updates, Katrina. This meeting is not one for you to talk in. You need to sit and listen. Do you understand?"

He raises a brow as though he's ready for me to challenge him, but I'm too stunned to say anything. If he's happy with my reports, why am I here? So, I just wait for this to make sense.

"I'm taking you off the project."

Immediately, I'm sitting up straight again. "I'm sorry, you're what?"

"Taking you off the project," he calmly repeats. "You'll finish this week out and have the weekend to clear out your rental. I expect you back in the office by Monday morning."

"But that doesn't make any sense! I'm on track, under budget, and the clients are happy with my work. You even said you were pleased with my reports. Why would you take me off the project now? It's halfway done!"

"Stop getting emotional. This is just business."

"No, it's personal," I shoot back. "This is you refusing to take me seriously. What's going to happen? I did half the work and now you can hand it over to Brent or Chad, and they'll take the credit?"

Thomas rolls his eyes, leaning back in his chair. "This isn't about credit. You've grown too close and, unsurprisingly, you've become too emotionally invested in this place and these people."

My frown deepens. "What do you mean by that?"

"You've always been too emotional." He peers at me over his glasses. "Now you're helping a client's girlfriend fix up a house for free—"

"I am doing that in my free time as a favor to a friend. I don't understand what that has to do with anything."

Thomas glares at me, peeved over being interrupted. "You're not acting like yourself, Katrina. Arguing with Will, spending all your free time with clients, refusing to answer your boyfriend's calls."

"Will and I broke up, Thomas." I keep my tone even, not letting my anger bubble over any more than it already has. Not only that, but Will hasn't reached out to me once. "I'm dating someone else now and am under no obligation to answer any attempted communication from Will."

"That's just ridiculous." Thomas waves me off. "Why would you end a perfectly healthy relationship?"

"Because it wasn't healthy." He scoffs, but I keep going. "I ended things because he did something horrible and he has no regrets about it. I ended it because he spent two years treating me like shit and has no regrets about it. He doesn't care who he hurts to get where he wants to be. I don't want to be with someone like that."

"Will has goals, ambition. You should want someone like that," he stresses. "Someone who can pick up your slack when you fall short, which you often do."

The words ring in my ear, the meaning behind it more evident than ever: I will never be good enough for him. For most of my life, that's really bothered me, but lately, I've found myself caring less and less. I don't need to stick around people who make me feel like shit about myself.

"I don't feel like doing this, Thomas," I admit. "I've spent my whole life justifying who I am to you, and I'm sick of it. Why don't we just acknowledge the truth you never wanted to own up to? You never wanted to be a father, and I'm nothing but a disappointment to you."

Thomas stares back blankly but doesn't argue. The words settle around us before he speaks again. "Now that you've gotten that out of your system, let's move on to the reason you're here."

It's the only answer I'll ever need, and it tells me everything I need to know.

Nodding, I cross one leg over the other and lean forward. "Sure. You'll need to find someone else to finish the project for Bryce and Carter, because it's not going to be me."

"At least you see sense on that. I'll assign it to one of the guys, and I'll see you in the office on Monday morning."

"No, I think I'll just do it now." I stand, bag in hand. "No use delaying it."

Thomas peers at me over his glasses again. "Do what now, Katrina?"

"Get a file on the project ready and clean out my desk." I'm amazed that I don't hear a single waver in my voice. "Have everything squared away so I can quit in peace."

I've never seen Thomas look so shocked before. I almost want to grab my phone and take a picture.

"What are you talking about?"

"I quit," I explain patiently. "When I leave today, I'm not coming back."

"You can't quit," he scoffs. "I hired you because your mother wanted me to."

"And I'm quitting because I want to. You no longer need to feel any sense of loyalty to me. I'm not an idiot, Thomas; I know you never wanted me. Here or in general."

"Now that is not true. I gave you everything you could have needed. You wanted for nothing."

"Except acceptance and love. All the things you gave me, they never came out of the kindness of your heart or because you cared. You did them because they were expected of you."

He pinches the bridge of his nose, a sure sign I'm driving him up the wall. "That's the way life works. You meet the expectations placed in front of you."

A part of me feels sorry for him because I know that's all his life has been. He inherited this business and the legacy of a major corporation responsible for building the state. That's his whole life. The only time he ever looked for more was with my mom, and they're two emotionally absent people who deserve one another. But I don't want that kind of life for myself. I want more.

"I've spent my whole life being told who I am and who I should be, but not anymore. I'm not feeling like I need to justify my choices to anyone, so I quit."

His frown causes a crease across his forehead. "Your mother is going to be so disappointed."

I grin. "Wouldn't be the first time."

For the first time in my life, I have the last word with my stepfather and step out of his office; the door swinging shut behind me. I take a few deep breaths, letting my new reality settle in before I head back to Nadine's desk.

"What's going on?" she questions, looking up at me from her computer with wide eyes. "Thomas just told me to collect your badge on your way out."

"I need to put together a file for whoever takes over the project in Columbia, because I just quit." Panic crosses her face, and I know what's she's worried about. She's worried about being left alone in this place without another woman to lean on and, if I could, I'd take her with me in a heartbeat, but this is where she needs to be right now. "Are you following me to my desk so I can get everything sorted?"

"I mean, technically, I'm supposed to." She waves over one of the interns, instructing them to manage the desk while she makes sure I don't do anything questionable, which gets a snort out of me.

Honestly, what questionable thing could I really do? Especially since I didn't feel like arson was the best answer.

About twenty minutes later, I'm almost done putting the folder together for whoever is going to take the project over. I knew it wouldn't take long, my notes are meticulous, and I like to stay organized during a job. Still, I wanted to make sure everything was as clear as possible. More for Carter and Bryce than whoever gets to take credit for most of my hard work.

"Okay, I was able to make to some arrangements for you."

I glance over at Nadine, who has been busy typing away at her phone and spinning in an office chair, before I look back at my computer. "What kind of arrangements?"

"With the rental you're staying in." My stomach drops as I turn to face her again. I hadn't even thought about needing a place to stay. "Obviously, there's no way Thomas will continue to let you stay on company funds, but it's also not our property. I talked to the landlord, who has had zero issues with you as a tenant, and she's willing to let you take over the remainder of the agreement."

"And how much is it?"

"Sixteen hundred a month with everything included," Nadine replies, scrolling on her phone. "This month has already been paid for, which Thomas will not be getting back, so she says you're covered. The remaining balance through September is about sixty-five hundred. She said you can terminate anytime."

It's less than what I'm paying Thomas and my mother a month for the guest house, which I'm surely vacating now. It's not ideal since I don't have a job, but I have enough in savings to manage the difference. "Tell her I'll take it."

Nadine nods, her fingers flying across the screen again as I wrap up the project file and send it off to Liam to hand over to whoever needs it. About five minutes after the email goes through, Liam is at my desk, his eyes practically bugging out of his head when he sees me packing things into the boxes Nadine has found.

"I can't believe you actually quit," he admits, pulling me into a quick hug. He and Nadine exchange a tight smile, confirming further that whatever tension they had is still there.

"She's a badass." Nadine smirks, handing me a stack of books I kept in my desk for when my days got boring. Like I told Carter, Thomas didn't trust me to do much. "What's your boyfriend going to think about all this?"

I stop, books held in midair at her question. I hadn't really thought about that, yet. "Honestly, I wouldn't be surprised if he threw me a party."

"I'm considering throwing you a party," Liam says, leaning against my desk. "What's next?"

◻I shoot off a message to the whole group:

I know I should text Carter separately, but I need to get a move on before I get kicked out. I'm officially unemployed. I'll explain when I get back to Columbia. Carter, call me when you land.

When I look up, both Nadine and Liam are patiently waiting for an answer. An answer I don't have.

"I don't know." I dump an entire drawer of pens into the box, anxious to get out of here. Word has spread and people are starting to stare at me. "I'll finish Josie and Bryce's house and then decide what I want to do from there."

"You could do that, Kat," Liam presses. "Those design ideas you sent me are solid. You didn't even need me to look at them."

The idea has been tugging at the back of my mind since I made up my mind to quit. Now Liam's brought it to the forefront, where I'll be harder to shake off. I glance around my desk. The last eight years at this job fit into a box and a half. I'm not even sad to walk away.

"I'm going to take some time, figure things out," I explain, hoisting the heavier box into my arms. "I'll figure it out after the Olympics. Nadine, are you walking me to my car?"

She nods, grabbing the last box. I give Liam another quick hug before I walk away from my now-empty desk. The only proof that I was ever there is an overly posed photo of me, my mother, Thomas, and Will. It's all fake smiles and picture-perfect family. I hated that picture with every fiber of my being, but it felt like something that needed to be there. Like I should have a personal memento. I'm happy to leave it behind.

Chapter 27

Katrina

May 2024

"Carter!" I gasp out, surprised to find my boyfriend standing on the other side of my door. He'd been in Texas for another meet and was supposed to be flying back to Georgia. "What are you—"

I don't get a chance to finish before he swoops down and kisses me. I let out a surprised gasp, which he uses to his advantage as his tongue slides in, tangling with mine. Sighing against the kiss, my hands scramble to find something to hold on to—his biceps, hips, hair, shoulders, anything. Everything. □

Hands on my hips, he's moving us further into the house, swinging the door closed behind him. I stay lost in the moment, lost in him, and the way he makes me feel. When he backs me into the wall, though, I pull back for a breath. Carter wastes no time, tilting my head so he can move his lips down to my neck.

"Carter," I breathe between kisses, licks, and bites. "What's going on?" I swallow back a moan as he sucks at my pulse point, not hard enough to leave a mark but hard enough to have warmth pooling in my stomach. "H-h-how are you here?"

"Changed my flight." I see a flash of his green eyes before he's leaning down to kiss me again. I melt against him. Eventually, I focus on what he said and have more questions. Questions I, unfortunately, need answers to. Tugging at his hair, I pull back until he focuses on me. Forehead against forehead, we both try to catch our breath. Which would be easier if Carter didn't keep pressing quick, sweet kisses against my lips.

"Why did you change your flight?" The question is breathless when I finally manage to get it out.

"You quit your job," he reminds me, squeezing my hips gently. "I'm so proud of you, Kat. I obviously wanted to be here for you."

I arch a brow. "And this is your idea of being here for me?"

Grinning, he presses even closer, which I didn't think was possible. "Being here for you." He presses a kiss to the corner of my mouth. "Celebrating what you did." Another kiss to the underside of my jaw. "Helping you forget." A kiss to my pulse point. "It's multilayered. Covering all my bases."

He finally brings his lips back to mine, allowing me to melt against him once more. As soon as I sink into the kiss, we're moving again. As he pushes me toward the stairs leading up to the bedrooms, he pulls away enough to lock eyes with me. There's a question in his eyes, one neither of us is ready to ask aloud, but I already know my answer.

"Take me to bed, Carter."

Groaning, he pulls away from me enough to give me space to take his hands and lead him up the stairs. He's practically running up them behind me. I let out a squeal of laughter when I'm suddenly picked up and slung over his shoulder in a fireman's carry.

"Carter!" I gasp, reaching out to place a smack on the easy target that is his ass. His laughter is more than enough to make my grin widen.

We're about to have sex, but we're laughing. I guess I never really understood that this can be fun.

"Put me down."

"Gimme a second," he calls back. A moment later, we're walking into a room that is unfamiliar.

"Carter, this is the guest bedroom!" The only time I've used this room is for yoga and other workouts. "We can't do it here."

"Why? It has a bed."

"But no condoms," I reply with a laugh.

Groaning, he steps back out of the room in search of mine, with me still slung over him. Seconds later, I'm tossed on the bed. Breathing heavily from my laughter, my eyes track his every movement as he tugs his shirt over his head and tosses it aside. He doesn't bother with his sweatpants just yet as he crawls onto the bed, hovering over me for just a moment before connecting our lips in a deep, dirty kiss.

After that, things kind of happen in a blur and we're both down to our underwear. I gasp, eyes rolling back as his lips trace the line of my bra. I arch my back as his hands reach behind me to remove it. He pulls it out of the way before he cups my left breast, tweaking the nipple as his lips close around the other one. I gasp his name, arching into him.

The air in the room is heavy, but I'm only focused on the way I keep trying to pull him in deeper and press closer to him. I feel the weight of him on top of me, so strong and broad, and I know I can get lost in this. In the way his hands feel against my skin, the way his hair feels running through my fingers, the way the faintest smell of chlorine will always linger on him. I want so much. I want everything and I don't even know how to ask for it.

His fingers trail down my stomach, then move to my hips to pull my underwear down my legs. I kick them off as soon as I'm able. He's switched his attention to the other breast by the time my hand drifts between us to cup the bulge in his boxer briefs.

"Fuck," he groans against my skin as my fingers skate down the hard length. "Condom?"

"Nightstand."

He shuffles off me, and I whimper at the loss of heat from his body. He's back as quickly as he goes, though. One hand holding the condom and the other pushing down his own underwear. I take the condom from him, opening the packet so I can roll it on as soon as he's naked. He groans as I pump my hand along him once, then twice.

"Love," he moans, pulling me in closer by the hips. I melt at the pet name. "You're perfect."

Every piece of me ignites with a fire I've never felt before, my legs tightening against his hips to pull him closer to me. I whimper his name followed by a please that sounds desperate to even my own ears. His fingers find my clit, circling in a way that makes my toes curl. I need him, all of him, now.

"Carter," I gasp, nails scratching down his back.

His fingers slip inside, causing my mouth to drop open in a silent scream as his lips trail kisses down my stomach. I know where this is going and any other night, I'd be all for it, but not now. Not tonight. Tonight, I'm too pent up, too ready for him to take me. My fingers grip his hair, tugging until he looks up at me through his lashes. He groans when I tug his hair again, but he seems to get the message because he moves back up to claim my lips in another kiss.

I take control of the kiss, and he lets me. Willingly melts against me. When we part for the briefest breath, I catch his top lip between my teeth before murmuring, "Fuck me."

"Shit, Kat," he moans. "I got you, love."

I arch against him at the name, which earns a faint smirk from him. He repositions us for a better angle, which results in me feeling him brush against where I want him the most. My eyes flutter shut as he sinks into me, giving me plenty of time to adjust. When my eyes open again, he's looking at me with such love and adoration I want to stay here forever, but then he moves, and stars explode behind my eyes.

It's never felt like this before and I'm not sure it'll ever feel like this again, but it's everything I've ever wished for. The rest of the room is still as we sink into this bliss together. The sounds we make are drowned out by the feeling of having all of Carter to myself. He tangles our fingers together, gripping my hand as he pulls me closer and closer to the edge. I finally tip over the edge I've been teetering on when he whispers, "let go," in my ear, tone low, and breath warm. He follows right behind me.

⸺

Later, Carter and I are just relaxing in bed. I'm on my side and he's sprawled out on his stomach beside me. My fingers trace over a faded tattoo inked into his shoulder blade. Despite meeting him shirtless for the first time, I've never noticed this one.

"I didn't know you had more than one tattoo." My voice is barely a whisper, not wanting to break the mood in the room. Goosebumps prickling his skin, and he turns his head to look up at me. "It looks older."

"It was my first tattoo. I got it when I was almost twenty." A smile tugs at his lips, the memory clearly coming to life in his mind. I want to understand the happiness. "It was a good night."

"Well, now you have to tell me," I tease, poking his shoulder until he laughs. "Come on, out with it. Why a wave?"

Carter turns, sitting up until he can rest against the headboard, hiding the tattoo from my view. His arm winds around my waist, fingers sneaking beneath the loose shirt I'd thrown on to rub gently against my side.

"I tried to stick it out in Nashville, after everything with Will went down, and at first, I could handle it. But the second year was hell. The more I started winning and breaking records, the more pissed off Jacobson and some of the other guys got. All because the queer kid can't have what they want. They all started making rude comments and wouldn't stop messing with me. The coaches did nothing, nor did any of the other guys. My grades were suffering, and my mental health was at an all-time low."

I frown, trying to picture Carter in that situation. This man is the literal definition of a cinnamon roll; he's sweet and comforting, so full of life, and love I can't even imagine someone being able to zap that out of him. I know it happened, though. I know what the person who did it can do and my heart aches.

"I finished my last final and flew out to Arizona to visit Bryce," he continues. "He still had a couple of days left and was planning on staying in Arizona for the summer to train, but it didn't matter.

I needed out of there and I wasn't ready to go back home to my parents."

"You weren't staying in Nashville to train with your team like Bryce was staying in Arizona?"

He shakes his head. "Nah, my coach in Nashville didn't see a whole lot of potential in me, so I was released to go back home for the summer. I was going to train at the club Bry and I grew up in back in Flagstaff. I don't want to say there's a reason he liked Will better, but it's kind of hard not to draw those conclusions."

The same conclusions I'm drawing just by hearing the story. Bryce had told me that none of Carter's coaches or the school did anything but the bare minimum. Whatever was needed to keep them from getting a negative reputation and Carter never pinpointed what was happening publicly. I wonder how that coach feels now, knowing Carter is still going strong and his star swimmer from that group doesn't even want to own up to his past career.

"I'd basically been lying to Bryce for months, not telling him how bad it had gotten, but I think he knew. He's always been able to tell when I'm not being honest with him. I basically crashed my first day there and Bryce let me get away with it. That night, we got drunk, and he took it as the opportunity it was and got me talking. I unloaded everything on him: how unhappy I was and how much I hated school. At that point, I was considering quitting the team just to make myself a little happier, but that'd mean giving up on the dream."

He takes a deep breath before continuing, seemingly needing to gather his emotions. "Bryce reminded me I didn't have to stay at the school. That leaving Nashville wasn't quitting or giving in to whatever was happening by leaving. When I decided what school I wanted to go to, I made the choice based on what campus would provide me with the best opportunity to reach my dream, and it ended up not being Nashville."

"Those are extremely solid points for a drunk Bryce Clark." I grin at him, hoping to ease some of the tension. It must have worked, because he gives me a small smile. "Especially at almost twenty."

"Hold on, he doesn't stay so eloquent," Carter laughs. "We made the decision to talk to his coach the next morning to see about getting me transferred to Arizona, which had been my second choice. The rest of the night resulted in us getting drunker and drunker."

"Unless you're about to tell me Bryce has a secret talent as a tattoo artist, I don't understand how this results in you getting a wave tattoo." His laugh brings a smile to my face.

Even the picture of Bryce being a secret tattoo artist was also more than I could bear, and my giggle sputtered out of me.

It took the two of us a second to calm down before Carter could continue his story.

"We were really drunk, and Bryce started talking about how important our friendship is to him and I was agreeing with him because I knew, even back then, he'd do anything for me, and I'd do the same for him. He decided we needed something permanent, a reminder of what it means. It wasn't hard to find a tattoo shop in a college town that would ink two drunk idiots, clearly under twenty-one."

I had to bite back a laugh. "Okay, but why a wave?"

"I actually don't remember," he admits with a sheepish smile. "All I remember lying on the table as the artist got to work on mine while Bryce was in the next bed. One of them asked why we wanted waves; Bryce drunkenly declared our friendship is like the water, always flowing."

I clap my hand over my mouth, trying to hold in the laugh, but it comes out sounding like a snort. "Oh, my god."

He's red now, blushing at the memory. "We were pretty wasted. One of the artists asked for clarification and all Bryce could say was, 'water, man,' and I nodded in agreement like it made total sense."

I bite at the corner of my lip, tears stinging the corner of my eyes. "I mean, at least it's something that's relevant to your friendship."

"True," he agrees with a laugh. "Now you know the story of the wave tattoo."

I'm barely able to contain my giggles. "I do, but does this mean Bryce has a matching one?" His cheeks turn redder. "Oh, my god, that's so cute! Where's his at?"

Carter is shaking his head before I can even get the question out. "I'm not telling you that. He will kill me if he finds out I told you. I'm not kidding, Kat, your boyfriend will be dead. Is that what you want?"

I pout, but he remains adamant about not telling me. "Fine. I'll just ask Josie about it."

If anyone knows where his secret bestie tattoo with Carter is, it'll be Josie. Josie will absolutely be willing to give me something else to tease her boyfriend about.

"Do what you have to do," Carter replies. "Just keep me out of it. Now, if you don't mind, I'd rather not talk about my best friend anymore."

I look up to see him staring down at me, heat in his eyes. Warmth stirs in my stomach. "Oh, yeah, what do you want to talk about then?"

Carter doesn't answer, and instead moves in a fluid motion until I'm lying on my back, staring up at him. He grins at me, my legs moving around his waist to pull him in closer as he leans down to kiss me. At first, it's not much of a kiss since we're both smiling too big for it to be more than grins pressing against grins. A few seconds later, we melt into something slow, languid, and deep.

I relax against it, content to stay in his arms for the rest of the night.

Chapter 28

Carter

May 2024

Groaning, I reach out a hand in search of the phone that's being extra obnoxious. Before I reach it, though, the ringing stops. Both Kat and I sigh in relief. She snuggles closer, her palm resting flat on my bare chest as we both start to drift back to sleep.

The phone starts ringing again.

Groaning, Kat rolls away from me to bury her face in the pillow. "Who is it, and why do they hate me?"

"It's Bryce," I tell her, sitting up a bit to grab my phone from my nightstand. Sure enough, the name on the screen confirms it. "He's the only one who will keep calling me until I answer."

She whines in anger, or disgust, I'm not sure. "Why can't he leave a voicemail like a normal fucking person?"

I laugh at the mere idea of Bryce being normal, but still answer the call. The quicker I get this over with, the quicker I can spoon my girlfriend. My girlfriend who's only wearing my shirt and a pair of lacy boyshorts. "This better be good, man."

"So, I might have done something drastic without talking to you."

I sit up straighter, ignoring Kat's protests at being jostled. "What did you do?" He remains suspiciously quiet. "Bryce?"

"Thomas called me this morning," Bryce explains. "He informed me that he'd given the project to Chad, who would be down over the weekend to touch base with us both before he starts overseeing the project remotely."

"He's overseeing the project remotely?" My question seems to get Katrina's attention because she's sitting up, motioning for me to put the phone on speaker. I hesitate for just a second before I do as she asks. "You're on speaker; Kat's here."

Bryce is quiet for a moment. "Hey, Kat."

"Bryce," she greets. "Who's taking over the project?"

"Chad." She drops her head on my shoulder. We'd gone through her whole team, deciding who the best-case scenario would be. He was not at the top of our list. "That's not the reason I'm calling, though."

"Yeah, you said you did something drastic," I remind him, which only makes Kat's frown deepen. "What'd you do, man?"

Bryce lets out a disgruntled sounding groan, which usually means he let his mouth get ahead of his head. Which could mean many, many things. "He started talking shit about Katrina. Apologizing for the overdramatic, emotional mess of a contractor he provided us with the first time. He was being a misogynistic asshole and was trying to get me to join in, making jokes about my girlfriend and relationship he knows nothing about."

Commiserating with toxic masculinity was something I was more than aware of. I also knew how much Bryce hated it.

"That's Thomas, that's just the way he is," Kat says, but I can tell by the way she's looking up she knows it doesn't make it better. "Please tell me you didn't do something stupid, Bryce."

"He did something stupid," I reply. "I'm just not sure what."

Bryce's silence is just further proof of what I already know.

"Dude," I warn, "we already know you did something, so just tell us."

"I fired Thomas and Dalton Enterprises."

Katrina gasps beside me and I can feel my eyes widening, my lips pressed in a firm line, unsure how to process this. It's not that I'm necessarily mad about the decision, but it's something we probably should have talked about before he fired them. Plus, the pool is over halfway done. It's going to be harder to find someone to take over the project with the remaining balance we have set aside for it.

"You signed a contract," Katrina argues. "When I quit, I didn't want this to happen. I made sure everything was in place to hand things over to someone else. This is supposed to be a simple trade. I can't believe you would just—"

"I know we signed a contract." Bryce raises his voice ever so slightly, making sure he'll be heard over Kat. "We signed a contract that Dalton Enterprises is technically in breach of, as we signed it with you as the contractor. Yes, you left the company, but that doesn't mean he can just assign someone new without our approval. It falls into our rights to withhold payments, should we find the work lackluster. He had ample opportunity to inform us of your exit yesterday and he chose to make decisions for his clients instead of with. There's a reason we didn't sign a contract until we spoke to him about who we'd be working with, Katrina. I read the whole thing, multiple times, and we're well within our rights to dissolve the agreement."

My eyes are still focused on Kat as jaw drops in surprise. I can't help but laugh. "You wanted proof that Corporate Bryce Clark existed."

Her jaw snaps shut, and she glares playfully up at me. Before she has the chance to say anything else, Bryce continues on.

"He didn't seem too happy with the idea of dissolving the contract based on those reasons alone, so then I made it a bit more personal. I told him how pleased we were with the work Kat has been doing on the club and that she's become such a close, personal friend that integrated herself into our little group."

"Oh, my god, Bryce," I groan, knowing where this is going.

"I think he thought she was lying about that part to them," he says. "Anyway, I told him we knew all about her relationship with Will and the sexism she experienced on a day-to-day basis at Dalton Enterprises and would hate for word to get out that he took her off a project simply because she was happy and doing a good job."

The room is silent as the two of us just stare at one another. She looks completely stunned at the idea of Bryce standing up for her like that, but I'm not even a little surprised. This is what Bryce does for the people he cares about, and he's never one to back down from bullshit.

"As of an hour ago, we are no longer working with Dalton Enterprises and all work has been halted," Bryce says cheerfully. "Oh, and Kat, Thomas says you need to be out of your place by Friday."

"What?" Kat exclaims, looking at the phone with wide eyes before sighing. "I guess I'll text Nadine and see if she can help me."

"Goodbye, Bryce." I watch as Kat reaches over to her nightstand to grab her phone.

"Don't you think we should talk about what we're going to do now?" Bryce questions.

Kat is already typing away at her phone. "We'll talk when we're at your place later." Without giving him a chance to reply, I hang up, and turn all my focus onto my girlfriend. "What's Nadine saying?"

She's squinting at her phone. "She actually has my spare key, so she's going to get a head start on the packing this week, and I'll head down on Wednesday when you're back in Georgia."

"We can go today if you want to," I argue, wanting her to understand I'm on her side and willing to help her, whatever she needs. Especially because my idiotic best friend is the reason she needs to vacate so quickly. "I can also push it back a couple of days—train at the club."

"No, absolutely not. Carter, you're less than two months away from Trials. I'm not going to be the reason you're not training the way you should. Nadine and I can handle this. I honestly don't have that much stuff."

I relent, not because I like the plan, but because I want to make sure I give Katrina the space she needs. Her relationship with Will was stifling, he was always wanting to know where she was and to be the one fixing her problems, but that's not my style. Yes, I want to be there to support her and help her, but I can also recognize when she needs to do something for herself, by herself, and I respect that decision.

Which is how, a couple of hours later, I found myself in the empty living room of Bryce and Josie's house. Mia, Kat, and Josie were off adding sticky notes to things, marking what we need to get rid of and what was staying; Bryce and I were standing in the living room, waiting to be pointed in the right direction.

"We're going to need to find a new contractor." Neither one of us had brought the topic up since Kat and I arrived, but I know we can't put it off any longer. "What about the design? Do we have the right to the design anymore?"

Bryce nods. "Yeah, that was part of the stipulations I set forth."

"Wasn't that whole thing blackmail?"

Bryce shrugs casually, like the thought hadn't even occurred to him. "That's the world of business, Carter. It's full of black-mail." My brow arches because who was this man? Certainly not my kind-hearted best friend. He groans, busted. "It's more karma. He lives for making other people small. I thought he needed a taste of his own medicine."

Bryce is struggling with what he did, worried he caused some-one harm or alienated someone from their family. I know him well enough to know the thoughts running through his head, but he can't ruin what was already ruined, and I want to make sure he knows that. "So, we have the design. We'll have to talk to Kat and see if there's anyone she can recommend."

His eyes light up at the thought, which sets me a little on edge. That kind of look in his eye either means he has a great idea or he's about to do something stupid. Again. "I have a great idea for that."

My arms cross over my chest, eyes narrowed at him. "I'm listen-ing."

"So, you know how Kat quit her job and will be wanting money?"

"Obviously," I reply dryly.

"What if we hire her? She already knows the plans like the back of her hand. We'd be giving her the money instead of someone we don't know, and the subcontractors she hired aren't barred from working with us or her. I asked Carl."

It was a good plan. A great one, in fact. I'm kind of mad I wasn't the one to think of it first. I know it'd take a lot of stress off Kat's shoulders and Carl seemed loyal to her. If she got him to stay, I think he'd get the rest of the crew to sign on, too. "That's a great idea."

"Right?" he asks, grin brightening. "When we walked through the house a couple of weeks ago, I told her she's good enough to branch out on her own, whether it's working on houses or on businesses. I stand by that, and honestly, there's no one else I'd want to trust with the project."

"I agree." I nod. "We'll talk to her about it when she gets back down here."

"Talk to who about what?" We both turn to see the girls walking back into the room, Mia leading the group with a dark eyebrow arched. "What were you two talking about?"

"Kat, can we talk to you for a minute?" Bryce asks.

She looks at me, worry about what it could mean reflected in her eyes, so I give her a reassuring smile. "Sure, what's up?"

Part of me wants to suggest we go into another room. I don't want Kat to feel pressured to say yes to this if it's not something she wants. We haven't had much of a chance to talk about her plans for the rest of her life. Between the activities that transpired last night and her rapidly texting Nadine through breakfast, there just hasn't been time. Maybe she's not even sure she wants to do this anymore. Maybe she has a different career path she wants to go down. Of course I'll be there to support her, whatever decision she makes, but I don't want her to feel pressed into doing something simply because she feels like she owes us.

"Would you continue to be our contractor?"

Bryce asks the question so simply, no one is sure how to process it.

"What?" Kat questions, looking from him to me, face scrunched up in utter confusion. "I don't work for Dalton Enterprises anymore and you fired them."

"Right, but you still have all the licenses you need to be a professional contractor. Carl already told me he'd stick around to help you finish it. You know the plans like the back of your hand. We already have the money we were going to pay Dalton Enterprises for the rest of the project. We'd rather give it to you."

"That is such a great idea!" Josie squeals, clapping her hands together.

"I don't want you to feel like you owe me something," Kat explains, looking from Bryce to me. For the most part, Josie and Mia have stepped back from this conversation, allowing us to conduct the business we need to, because this conversation is business, not friends, or a couple making plans. "You don't owe me anything, either of you. I will understand if you want to find a bigger firm. I have some in the area I can recommend for you."

Bryce is already shaking his head. "That's the thing, though, Kat, we don't want to work with a bigger firm. We want to continue working with the kick-ass contractor we've been working with because we know she'll do the job right and do it well. It doesn't matter that she's not tied to a major firm anymore. We want her to finish what she started."

Kat's gaze drifts over to me. "What do you think about all of this?"

"I'm firmly with Bryce on it," I reply, trying not to let my emotions get ahead of me. It's not like I don't realize what this would mean for her, for us. She's staying, at least for a couple more months. "You've done a really incredible job, Kat. What do you say?"

She nods, eyes bright with joy. "Yes, of course I say yes!" Bryce relaxes, and I know I'm feeling the same way. "I'll want to do this properly. I think we should have an updated contract with the new terms outlined and everything. It has to be legitimate."

"Of course," I assure her, unable to hold back my own grin.

"Absolutely," Bryce agrees. "Besides, you'll want to make sure you do it properly, as we'll hopefully be the first clients after you branch out on your own."

"What?" Josie gasps, looking at Kat. "Are you serious?"

"Bryce, I never said I was going to do that!" Kat's shaking her head, but she's still smiling.

"I know." He grins back. "Now, are we going to beat the shit out of my house or what?"

We end up dividing into teams. The only person who's not part-nered up is Mia, but Kat seems confident in her ability to break things alone without getting in trouble. Apparently, Bryce needs to be supervised. I can't help but grin when Kat comes toward me with a sledgehammer in her hand.

Her brow arches. "Why are you looking at me like that?"

My gaze roams over her from head to toe, soaking in every inch of her. "Is this what I missed out on when we were doing demolition at the pool?"

She rolls her eyes. "Yes, because me in a pair of ratty shorts and a paint-splattered tank top is the epitome of sexy."

"I was talking more about the tool belt." Grinning, I latch my finger into it and pull her toward me.

Her cheeks flush a light shade of pink that only has my grin widening. "I have a lot of stuff to carry with me, Carter."

"Hmm," I murmur, pressing my lips against her temple. "If that's what you're going with."

"Hey!" We spring apart at the sound of Bryce's voice, both of us flushing when we see him standing in the doorway with his hands on his hips. Behind him, Josie looks gleeful. "There will be no canoodling in my house!"

The laugh escapes me before I can stop it, which only results in me partially choking on it. Kat pats my back until I can gain control over myself. Josie's biting both of her cheeks to hold back her laughter. Kat's eyes are shining with mirth.

"Don't say canoodling, Clark." The sound of Mia busting shelves down in a closet follows her groan from the hallway. "It's weird."

Bryce scowls, gray eyes drifting from me to Katrina. "That's it, we're changing partners. I'm working with Carter."

"Hey," Josie protests. "What did I do to deserve that?"

"Someone needs to watch them," Bryce warns, moving to stand next to me. "So, I'll take Carter and the two of you can work together."□

"Aw, man, if you want to spend more time together, all you gotta do is ask," I tease with a slight shove.

Kat's grinning as she makes her way over to Josie. "That's fine. We'll work together and get more done than the two of you combined."

He should know by now that we take competition seriously. Bryce and I exchange looks, nodding to each other in unspoken understanding, before looking back at our girlfriends. "You're on. Loser buys drinks."

"Deal." Then she and Kat are bounding out of the room.

Hours later, I'm sore in places I'm not sure I've ever been sore before.

"Aren't you the one who exercises eight hours a day?" Kat teases. She drops her keys on the table by the door as I collapse on the couch with a groan.

"That's different." They're not all that different, both extremely physically taxing, but I used different muscles today and in ways I haven't used them for years. I can't remember when I was last on my feet for that long.

Unsurprisingly, the girls won and, honestly, seeing the determination on their faces while holding sledgehammers was a little humbling for both Bryce and me. We parted ways to shower and change before meeting up at Brick Tavern for dinner. I've only been there a handful of times, but half the staff knows the rest of them. It's going to become our spot here in Columbia. Which is reassuring because it means we're all putting roots down.

Kat sits beside me, curling against me, and resting her head on my shoulder. I sling my hand around hers, tilting my head until it can rest on hers. We sit in total silence for what could be seconds, minutes, or even an hour. Still, I let us float in it for a little longer before breaking it.

"You said yes to staying and helping us."

"I did," she agrees, shifting to get more comfortable. "Are you okay with that?"

I brush my lips against her forehead. "I'm more than okay with it. I don't think it's a secret that I'd rather have you here with me. With us. What are you thinking about doing after the club's done?"

"I haven't really thought about that yet," she admits. "Everything happened so fast, but I couldn't pass up your offer. I want to finish this project, see what it's going to be, and spend more time with you."

My finger brushes against the soft fabric of her shirtsleeve. "Have you thought about staying?"

She's shifting to face me then, tucking both her legs beside her. When she's having a serious conversation with me, she always wants to make sure we're facing one another. That we're close enough to touch, should we need to, but the real focus is going to be on the words. Wanting to put her at ease, I shift to face her better.

She's fiddling with her hands as they rest in her lap, but says nothing for a couple more minutes.

"What are you thinking, Kat?"

"I'm thinking that I'm worried we're moving too fast," she begins, but I can tell this is going to be one of those moments where once she starts, she'll just keep gaining momentum. "I'm worried what leaving everything in Charleston behind will mean for me. I don't want to feel like I'm stepping into someone else's life, or their dream. I want to find my own thing."

"Which is exactly why I think staying will be a good idea." The last thing I want to do is make her feel like I'm taking options away from her, so I choose my words carefully. "We're not moving too fast. I'm not asking you to move in with me. I'm asking you to be in the same city with me, to give us a real chance. I know it'll still be months before I'm here full time, but that's not something that's changed."

She bites her lip. "I know. I know you're not trying to push us into anything we're not ready for, but after the disaster that came before, I can't help but worry. We dove into the serious end."

"Did you really just hit me with a swimming pun about a man I hate?"

She giggles, shaking her head while waving the comment off. "You know what I mean!"

I catch her hand mid-air, lacing my fingers with hers to lower our joint hands to the couch. She tracks the movement with her eyes. "I do, and you know what I mean, too. I won't let what happened then happen to us. There's too much at stake for both of us here. We're adults. I want this to be a real, adult relationship. Which means working at it. I'm ready to do that."

"So am I," she promises, quick to make sure I know where her intentions are. "I want that."

"Good, then we're on the same page about that." I give her hand a gentle squeeze. "I know I'm looking at things from the perspective of your boyfriend, but I don't really know if there's anything left for you in Charleston. You've lost your job, your place, and you're not exactly anxious to make amends with anyone there. Maybe starting off somewhere new is what you need, and don't you want to do it with people who care about you? I know what Bryce told you after the walkthrough, and he's right, you'll have such a great support system here."

She goes back to biting her lip. I can see the millions of questions running through her mind and I want to pluck each one out, answering them until the stressed-out look leaves her features. Until the slight worry line in her forehead fades into the tanned smoothness I'm used to. I don't want her to be freaking out about what comes next; I want her to know and believe that things will turn out okay. And, even if they don't, she's not facing it alone. I'll be there with her, every step of the way.

"You don't have to make a decision now," I promise her, which helps to ease her nerves. "Just promise me you'll think about it? And think about knowing I want you here. We all want you here, and whatever comes next, we'll be by your side."

She doesn't say anything, just turns back to face forward, sinking back against my side. Seamlessly, flawlessly, we're cuddled back up on the couch in the same position we were in previously, the silence washing over us once again. There's no place I'd rather be.

Chapter 29

Katrina

May 2024

Carter goes back to Georgia the next day. It's a weird feeling to be saying goodbye to someone you don't want to see go. I'm literally seeing him at a meet in less than two weeks, but watching him pull out of the driveway made me feel like he was leaving for years and to a destination much further than a couple of hours. Still, I was a mess of emotions—giddy from a new relationship, stressed about not having income after the club is done, and unsure about what I want to do with my life—and I'm handling it in one of the unhealthiest ways possible. By throwing myself into my work.

Just as Bryce has said, all the subcontractors I'd hired easily followed me, wanting to finish the job they'd started. Apparently, Bryce had a lawyer friend draw up new contracts for all of us, using the previous ones from Dalton Enterprises to make sure he had everything covered. Between the club and their house, I had plenty to keep me occupied rather than constantly wanting to distract Carter. He had more important things to focus on.

Things were moving forward at a rapid pace I didn't expect after I kind of imploded my life. I wasn't complaining, but I did feel like

I was on a hamster wheel, constantly running with no direction or progress.

Right now, for example, I'm at the house, overseeing the expansion of the kitchen, which is the first thing we're really focusing on. Liam had looked over the plans I'd come up with, made some slight adjustments, and strengthened them, but overall gave me the go-ahead to move forward. Thomas would have a fit if he knew Liam was helping me on the side, a fact my friend knew. It didn't stop him, though; he just shook his head and told me not to worry about him.

"Building up like this is going to give them more room upstairs, too." Carl and I are standing in the backyard, watching as his crew works. "But it's expanding the main bedroom, right?"

"Nope, it's going to give them more storage and an office space for Josie," I explain, hands in my back pocket, trying to ignore the prickling sensation of the sun on the back of my neck. "She doesn't really have that right now, but Bryce wants to make sure she has a space all her own."

"Smart man," Carl chuckles out.

One of the guys calls him over to check something, so he gives me a quick nod before heading over to assist them. I pull my phone out to take some pictures in case I need to use this project to help find another job, before heading around the front to check to see if Josie is here yet. I'm surprised to find her chatting with another woman, motioning to the house excitedly. When she sees me approaching, her smile widens, and she calls my name, waving me over.

I smile at the other woman as I approach, who just grins back at me like she was about to be overly polite in that totally patronizing way. I fight back the frown as I look over at Josie. "Is everything okay?"

We've been respectful of the neighbors as we work on the house, ensuring anything with loud noises didn't start too early or run too late. I've done my best to keep the site as clean as possible. Still, I've done enough home renovations to know that at least one neighbor is almost always annoyed when work is being done. I've gotten good at handling it, but I'd rather not deal with it today.

"Everything's fine." Josie grins at me, placing a hand on my arm before turning back to the woman. "This is our contractor, Katrina Dalton. She's been fabulous! She has tons of experience and is also the contractor for the swim club my boyfriend's opening. Kat, this is our new neighbor, Lucy."

Lucy's already sticking her hand out before I fully process what Josie's saying. "It's so nice to meet you, Katrina."

"Yeah, you, too." I shake her hand, but I'm still completely lost on what's happening.

"Do you have a card or something?" Her question surprises me, but I try not to let it show. "I was just telling Josie that my husband and I are looking to add an apartment above our garage. We've talked to a couple of big firms, but I don't like how cold they are. I'd much rather work with a local contractor and, if it's a woman-owned business, even better."

I glance at Josie, who's grinning with accomplishment. I can't believe this is happening. It's not at all what I expected, but maybe this is what Bryce and Carter really meant when they told me this group is big on chasing dreams. It's always been in the back of my mind and having another project would mean that I need to stay in Columbia, at least for a little longer.

Lucy is waiting patiently for an answer. "I don't have a card, no. I'm just starting out on my own, but I'd love the chance to talk more with you and your husband, figure out what your needs are. Do you have a design?"

Somehow, she gets even more excited. "Yes!"

As Lucy dives into the logistics of the project she has already planned out, Josie quietly slips away to let me handle the rest. As Lucy talks, she informs me she has several friends who are looking to hire someone as well, and with each potential project mentioned, something settles in me. I can do this. I can branch out on my own. We talk for about twenty minutes to go over the basic premise of the design. She doesn't even hesitate when I shyly admit that I'd want to wait until at least one of the projects I'm working on is done and that I wouldn't be able to start until after the Olympics.

When she learns that my boyfriend is one of the swimmers opening the new club, her gears change to how excited they are to have an alternative to the school team for their son to join. Apparently, his current team doesn't view swimming as a viable option for scholarship opportunities and would much rather put money toward football and baseball. The longer we talk, even when we bring Josie back into the fold, the more I see the future unfolding ahead of me.

Me running a business. Carter and Bryce running a business with Mia by their side. Josie finally having the space and time to write and publish the book she's been hiding from me. This little found family we've created for ourselves could have it all.

After meeting Lucy, everything falls into place over the next few days. I decide to take the leap and open a renovation and construction company. When I tell Carl and Dave, they both make me promise to always come to them first for any project, which makes me feel even more confident in my ability to lead a project. Bryce sets me up with their lawyer friend to help make sure everything is in place for my business and Mia offers to help with the marketing of the business, which I demand I pay her for because I'm going to do everything right.

Carter again surprises me by coming back up to Columbia for a night, despite the fact he has a meet in less than a week. He's too excited about the prospect of the business, and we stay up way later than we should to talk about the details. He comes up with the name Effervescent Renovations, knowing that Thomas always complained about me being too much. Carter argues that my "too much" will be the thing that helps me succeed. It's short, catchy, and flows. When I text Mia the official name, she's immediately firing off ideas of an iridescent color scheme, something that will catch the eye without being too overpowering.

By the next morning, Mia already has a bunch of social media posts created to market my new business endeavor. I know she's getting bored since the guys haven't told her the name of the business yet, but I'm still amazed by everything she's done in such a short time. When Carter comes bounding into the office, all grins, I realize I might not be the only reason he drove back to South Carolina on short notice.

"Hey! Can you two come with me for a second?"

He doesn't give us the chance to answer before he's happily going back the way he came. Mia and I exchange a look before she shrugs, sets her tablet down, and stands. I follow her lead, the two of us trailing my rambunctious boyfriend down the stairs, through the lobby, and out into the parking lot. It's an overcast, rainy, chilly day.

"What are we doing out here, Carter?" Mia asks, wrapping her arms around herself to keep warm. "It's freezing."

"Just wait a minute," he admonishes.

A second later, Bryce and Josie, who are bundled up in warm sweatshirts, exit the building, and head our way. I'm relieved to see two sweatshirts gripped in Bryce's hands.

"Oh, thank god," Mia grumbles, taking one. I take the other. "I never thought I'd see the day Bryce Clark is more considerate than you, Carter. You could have at least told us we were going outside."

He shrugs, a timid smile replacing the blinding one. "I didn't want to risk ruining the surprise."

"What surprise?" Josie asks, leaning against Bryce.

He clears his throat, his arm going around her shoulder. "You know how we've been quiet about the name?" Mia and Josie nod. "Well, we wanted it to be a surprise, and they just finished putting the sign up, so we thought now was a good time to reveal it."

Bryce motions behind us, and we all turn to look up at the sign on the side of the dark blue building. It turned out beautifully. The logo is a swimmer, done in a beautiful mosaic of blues, coming up for a breath while doing the fly. Coming off the end of the wave in beautiful, but legible, script is the name of the club:

Adair Swim Club

Josie lets out a gasp, her hand shooting up to cover her mouth in surprise. "Oh, my god, you guys!"

Mia is staring up at the sign, looking a little teary-eyed. "Are . . . are you serious?"

"Hell yeah!" Carter wraps an arm around Mia's shoulder; his other reaches out to tug Josie into his other side. They both go willingly. "You guys are part of this, too!"

"Besides," Bryce adds with a smile, "I don't think either one of you will ever understand how much your support has meant to us over the years. How much it means to us now. Just because the blog is done, it doesn't mean Adair has to be."

Mia leans her head against his shoulder, squeezing his side tight. In a second, the three of them have moved into a group hug that has me pulling my phone out to take pictures. It only takes some mild convincing to get Bryce to join in. It lasts all of three seconds before Mia complains her boobs are being smushed. All of us dissolve into a fit of laughter.

Chapter 30

Katrina

May 2024

Walking into the pool that was supposed to be the home of Carter's college swimming career is a weird feeling.

The whole time we were walking up to the entrance, Bryce was curling his lip like the natatorium had personally offended him. In a way, it had. This is the first time either of them have been back for a meet since college.

Most of Carter's events didn't even come up until the third day of competition, where he had both the 200-meter freestyle and the 400-meter IM. According to Bryce, these two events are the ones he's most likely to make the team in and the ones he's already represented Team USA in during the Games, earning a silver last year in the IM but not making the final in the freestyle, which also resulted in him being passed over for the final in the relay.

I swear, every time I talk to Bryce, I realize the world of professional swimming is far more complicated than I'd ever guessed it to be.

Mia and I are lingering off to the side of the line while Josie grabs enough heat sheets for all of us. Mia's looking down at her phone and asking me questions about some of the feedback I already have from social media posts. I have a meeting set up with Lucy and her husband after we get back from the meet next week to go over the details and sign the contracts to start on their garage apartment. The pieces are falling together, which means I can sit back and enjoy this part.

I don't have to be anything more than the supportive girlfriend here to cheer on her boyfriend.

"Should we go grab some seats?" Josie's beaming as she comes bounding back to us, heat sheets in hands. "Bryce said he'll come find us."

Just like in Greensboro, Bryce disappeared almost as soon as we walked through the door. I'm not exactly sure where he goes, but I'm sure he's got more people to say hello to than we do.

"Yeah, let's go." Mia nods, already leading the group toward the stands.

Once we're settled in our seats, a couple of people I've never met, or even heard of, come up to say hi to Josie and Mia. They do their best to pull me into the conversation, but it's always clear that I'm the odd one out. The only thing linking us all together is my relationship with Carter. It's not a bad thing, and I don't feel left out, but it is a little weird to be on the outskirts.

This is the first time I've been at an outdoor pool, so I look around, taking note of things to bring up to the guys later and things I'm grateful we didn't do. My eyes scan over where the coaches and officials are standing, barely taking in the faces of the people, but focusing on the venue.

And then my eyes land on a familiar figure with short, dark red hair, and my blood runs cold. My elbow is digging into Mia's side before I can even stop it.

"Ow," she hisses, pushing it away from her. "What the hell, Kat?"

"Will's here." And he's staring across the pool at me.

There's a small commotion as they both gasp and try to locate him in the crowd. I look away, hating the way he's glaring at me, scrutinizing everything about me. A million questions run through my head. If it weren't for the people beside me, I would want to cower and hide, but my main concern right now is Carter. I've already had the chance to say everything I need to say to him. There's nothing left. Carter, though, hasn't faced him since 2016 and I know there's more he'd like to say to him.

Knowing Will, he'll find a time and place to interrogate him.

"I'm texting Carter," I declare, reaching into my bag to grab my phone.

"He probably won't even look at it," Mia argues. "Text Bryce; I'm sure he's around Carter."

Nodding, I pull up my thread with Bryce and type out the message. "What is he even doing here? I thought he had nothing to do with the sport anymore?"

"He's an alum," Josie says. "More than likely they invited him back to present a medal or be the face of the sport for the college."

"But why did he say yes this time?" If what Josie says is true, I'm sure this isn't the first time he's been asked, but he's never accepted before. For a man who claims he hates everything about this sport, he's making a public appearance that suggests otherwise. Unless . . .

"Wait." I gape, looking between Mia and Josie. "You don't think he's doing this because he knows Carter's going to be here?"

"I think that's exactly what's going on." Mia frowns at me. "If there's one thing we all know about Will, it's that he likes to have the last word. In his mind, Carter got the last word because he got you. Which is a disgusting way to look at things, and one Carter doesn't agree with, but it's right on brand for Will Jacobson."

I feel like I've been sucker punched in my gut. "He's going to target Carter instead of me."

Josie's fingers are flying across the phone as she relays all this information to Bryce. Her phone is chiming quietly almost just as quickly, which means he's replying. It only helps me relax a teeny, tiny bit.

"He's probably embarrassed by how things ended." Mia's glaring at him across the pool. When I glance back toward him, I'm not at all surprised to see him glaring back like an immature child. That's Mia, though. Meet her with a challenge means she'll rise to it and make you regret it. "He's a fragile, sexist pig who doesn't like being told off by a woman. My instinct tells me he'll aim for another target, especially if it's one he thinks he can already hit."

"Whatever happens, we need to keep Carter away from him," I decide.

Mia hums in confirmation but doesn't break eye contact with Will. "Come on, asshole. Give up."

"You know you could just look away?" Josie suggests from her other side. "Be the bigger person."

"No way," Mia snaps. "If he gets to be a petty asshole, then I do, too. What's Bryce saying?"

Josie looks back down at her phone. "He's with Carter now and has already told him. They're asking some of the coaches to figure out what he's doing here. No one seems to know, which is a little concerning. Carter's not letting it get to him, though. He's determined to focus on the race and leave the past where it belongs."

Across the pool, Will is forced to break the staring contest with Mia when someone approaches him. Mia lets out a triumphant cheer that earns a few strange looks from the people surrounding us. She flips her dark hair over her shoulder and pays them no mind.

After all, we have bigger things to worry about.

Bryce joins us in the stands about ten minutes later, his shoulders tense as he sits ramrod-straight on the bleacher beside Josie. The stance immediately takes me back to Will showing up at Adair all those weeks ago. In reality, not that much time has passed, but I feel like we're all completely different people now. So much has changed, so much has happened, and I'm happy where we are. So much so that I'm scared something's going to set us back. Which is why I don't bring up my ex's presence with Bryce. We have a meet to focus on and Carter's final is up first.

Despite everything else going on, Carter has a great night. He places first in both his finals with times that are well within his personal bests for the year and on track with some of the predicted times for Trials. He and Bryce both seem happy with his swims, and I get a whole new vantage point as I watch my boyfriend do his thing. He chats easily with the interviewer, despite always claiming he's horrible with the media side of the sport. The moment he really shines, though, is whenever there are over-eager kids dying for an autograph and photo.

He takes his time with them, smiling, and chatting. It all seems so effortless for him that I can't help but snap a couple of photos for myself. I want to remember this moment. Eventually he has to get pulled away by his coach and other officials as he needs to be ready for the medal ceremony or to swim the 200-meter freestyle.

It's not until after he's won that race that things take a turn.

Since it's the last meet of the series before they head to Olympic Trials, they're presenting the swimmers with awards. Apparently, Carter has the most first place finishes on the men's side for this entire series, a fact I should have known, but I barely knew him when it started. We're all cheering along as everyone else receiving an award is mentioned.

Then our cheers fall silent not a second later.

"Presenting the awards," the announcer says, voice rings over the crowd, "is Nashville University's own Will Jacobson!"

Even from far away, I can see the way Carter stiffens up. Bryce whispers a quiet "fuck" under his breath that I somehow hear without being anywhere near him. My hands drop to my side.

"They seriously couldn't get anyone else? He did nothing!" Mia grumbles.

"Will had a decorated career here in Nashville," the announcer continues. "He has gone on to pursue a career in medicine."

My eyes track the movement of Will as he goes down the line, handing out the medals, and flowers to each swimmer. When he reaches Carter, he hesitates for a second before smirking slightly. Carter lowers his head to have the medal placed around his neck. He stiffly accepts the flowers before standing up straight. Will doesn't say a single thing to him and moves down the line.

I feel like this isn't going to be the end of it, though.

Bryce stands abruptly. "I'm going to head back there. Just in case."

Out of all of us, he's the only one who can walk back to the athlete area. While I know Carter is more than capable of handling himself, I don't want him to be alone.

"We'll head to the restaurant," Josie tells him.

I grab Bryce's arm as he passes by, causing him to turn to look down at me. I level him with a gaze. "Step in if you have to."

He nods before I let go of his arm and he heads back to meet Carter. When I look back at my boyfriend, he's staring straight ahead, but the slight flicker of his eye tells me he's tracking Bryce's movements, too.

Chapter 31

Carter

May 2024

As soon as I'm off the podium, any niceties I feel compelled to display vanish. I bypass the media without a single comment and, for the first time in my career, the kids asking for photos and autographs. The sound of their disappointment follows me, and it breaks my heart, but I need to get away from here. Away from him.

"Carter Abrams, fleeing the scene!" Will's voice is taunting as it echoes behind me. Thankfully, we're out of the public eye, but there are still plenty of people around to witness this. "Why am I not surprised?"

Taking a deep breath, I turn to face him, standing tall, and staring him head on. "What do you want, Jacobson?"

Ever casual, he shrugs. "Just want the chance to catch up with an old friend. Where's the harm in that?"

I cross my arms over my chest, glaring at him. "We're not friends and no one thinks we are. Now please, do me a favor, and fuck off."

I turn, ready to get away from him and leave him in the past for good this time. I can see Bryce weaving through the crowd toward us, still able to get back to where the athletes are with no problem.

Several other people are lingering around us, clearly pretending not to listen, but I know they are.

"She's going to leave."

I freeze at his words, which are said with a slightly raised voice.

He's trying to get people's attention. "When the project is done, she's going to leave. She'll move back to Charleston, keep working for Thomas, and will eventually see that I'm the best option for her."

He doesn't know; I realize. He doesn't have a clue about what's happening in Kat's life, despite the apparently close relationship he has with Thomas and her mother. Two people I'm not sure I'll ever meet, but have an opinion of already.

I turn to face him, knowing Bryce is coming to stand by my side. "What are you talking about, man?"

He's smug—so fucking smug I want to smack the smirk off his stupid face. "Katrina, obviously. What else would I be talking about? I can tell by the way she talked about you that you have a little crush on her, but she's going to realize I'm what she needs, and she can't have her career without me."

"What?" Bryce asks, confusion evident in his voice.

I stop him from saying anything else, taking a step closer to Will with a glare. "I hate to break it to you, Jacobson, but you lost. Again. You lost the best—and only good—thing that will ever happen to you. She's not going to take you back because you blew it. You refused to see the great thing you had before you and screwed it up. I'd feel sorry for you, but it's typical behavior for you, isn't it? So unable to get your head out of your own ass that you lose things."

With clenched fists and a flushed face, he takes a step toward me. Bryce steps closer, but I do not back down. "You don't know what you're talking—"

"But I do," I cut him off. It's not my place to tell him what happened with Katrina, but I'll make damn sure he knows he doesn't have control over her anymore. "Katrina has nothing left in Charleston; she's not going back. To you or to that life. Listen to the words I'm saying, Jacobson, you lost."

He jerks toward me, hands shoving at my shoulders until I stumble back. Everyone around us is suddenly moving. Bryce steps between us, takes the next shove, but stays standing. A couple of the coaches run over, asking whether things are good. My coach is one of them, lingering after we all assure them we're good. We're all adults; it shouldn't come to this.

"Let's go, Carter." Bryce grabs the sleeve of my shirt to tug me away. "He's not worth it."

Will, who always has to have the last fucking word, laughs. It's a cruel, humorless sound. "Yeah, Abrams, do what Clark says. We already know who the man is in the relationship."

I wrench my arm out of Bryce's grasp, but don't get back in Will's face. "What the fuck does that mean?"

If I turn to look at Bryce right now, I know he'll be tense beside me. I can practically feel the anger radiating off him, but he doesn't say anything.

"I'm bi, but that doesn't mean I get with every person with a dick," I snap. "Bryce and I have never dated. We will never date. He's straight and not my type."

"I'm too high maintenance," Bryce says so casually I know he's shrugging. "And Carter snores."

I *do not* snore, but that's beside the point.

"Look, I don't get what your problem with me is besides the fact I'm queer, but this is ridiculous. Let it go, man, you almost ruined my life ten years ago. How is that not enough? It didn't ruin me then and it won't ruin me now."

"Everything came easy to you," Will shoots back.

"That's your perspective, man," I tell him. "I put in the work, every goddamn day. You didn't make the team, I did. Bryce did. That's being willing to put in the hard work and the fact you don't do that is no one's fault but your own."

He snorts. "I'm a doctor, Abrams, not chasing a kid's dream."

"Then why are you here? Why can't you let it go? Why did you show up at my business to start shit with two people who don't care about your shitty opinions?" He opens his mouth to say something stupid, but I don't let him. "The choices you've made in your life are your own. You're mad at me because I'm the way I am, and you think I deserve less, but I got more. I'm sorry you feel that way, but don't you dare tell me I got it handed to me. You walked away."

"Okay, Abrams," Coach calls, clearly worried it's getting heated. My voice is rising, and people are watching. "Wrap it up."

He's not telling me to walk away. He's telling me to get my points across and let it go. I'll take it.

"You walk away when things aren't handed to you because you don't want to put in the work. Don't pretend. You retired when you didn't make the team. You kissed ass to the one doctor who could elevate your career and then you started dating her daughter. For two years, you destroyed her, and never once put in any effort. Your choices have led to the life you have and if you're bitter about it, dude, that's on you. No one else."

I take a small step back, mainly because I'm afraid he's about to throw a punch. He's so red, hands clenched into fists, I think he might explode. Maybe there's one more thing I can say to him.

"And Kat's not choosing me over you. She's choosing herself, and if I get to be part of that, then I consider myself damn lucky. You lost because you didn't want to work for it. Never forget that."

I turn to Bryce, pushing his shoulder. "Let's go. I'm done here."

Bryce follows me as we walk away from Will, hopefully for the last time. Bryce waits until we're an appropriate distance before bending over his knees to laugh hysterically.

"Holy shit, dude!" Amazement glimmers in his eyes, but he can't stop laughing. "Where the fuck did that come from?"

"A long time coming." I shrug, reaching down for my stuff. "And I do not snore."

"Whatever you say." He cackles, following me out to the stands to watch the rest of the meet with the girls. "But I get to tell everyone about what happened."

"Whatever you want, Bryce," I say with a chuckle. When we walk toward the stands, I can see Will arguing with my coach and a couple of officials. It looks like they're trying to kick him out. Apparently, the status of this being his home pool isn't nearly enough to make up for what just happened.

Which is fine because I'm not sure I'll be asked to come back to this pool either.

⌒

"I don't want to talk about it, Kat," I warn. She shuts the door behind us as I tug my sweatshirt over my head. I'm a ball of anxious energy, adrenaline pumping through me. The last thing I want to do is talk about the run-in I had with my girlfriend's ex. Who also happened to try to ruin my life. "Please leave it alone for now."

"I'm not going to make you talk about it," she promises.

In a couple of short steps, she closes the distance between us, her hand reaching up to cup the back of my neck. After a few shaky breaths, I'm able to meet her gaze. Her eyes search my face, worry evident in them, but she doesn't push.

"I want to make sure you're okay, that's all," she whispers, her voice low, and her breath fanning across my face.

I want to assure her I'm okay. That I'm here and I'm not going anywhere. That I will not shut her out or pretend what happened didn't take a lot of energy out of me. I refuse to pretend around her. Open, honest communication is the goal I'm striving for, even if I can't produce it in words.

I hum, hoping she'll take it as confirmation I'm okay, before lowering my head so I can capture her lips in a light, lingering kiss.

She lets me get away with it for a few glorious moments. Lips gliding together, hands pulling each other closer, but all too soon, it's over. She's back to staring up at me with a slight frown, but her cheeks are flushed and her breathing just slightly erratic.

She places a hand on my chest, firmly keeping the distance between us when I try to pull her in again.

"Kat," I whine, not even caring how ridiculously desperate I sound.

"You're avoiding the question, Carter," she scolds, but she's giving me a playful look.

"I'm not avoiding the question." I grip her hips in my hands, stepping backward until I feel the bed at the back of my knees. I drop down onto it, pulling her between my legs. I lean my head back until I can gaze up at her. "I'm choosing to answer it with actions instead of words."

She rolls her eyes, but still her fingers find my hair to comb through it. I let out a groan as her short nails scratch against my scalp, my head dropping forward to rest against her chest. Any other time, I could just stay in this moment for hours, being close to her, and slowly relaxing, but it's not enough right now. Right now, I want her in whatever way she's willing to give me.

Lifting my head, I crane my neck to look at her, but she's already leaning down for a kiss. This one is deeper than the previous ones. One hand tangles in her loose blonde waves, the other draws her in closer until she's straddling my lap, her thighs on either side of mine. I can't help but groan as she settles in my lap.

She sighs against my lips, briefly parting just to change the angle before she dives back in. I let her take control this time, following where she leads. My hand moves to the small of her back, fingers dipping beneath the hem of her shirt, which is a loose-fitting coral top that highlights her tan and brings her eyes to life. She had my attention from the moment I spotted her in the stands today. When the tips of my fingers ghost along her spine, she shivers in my lap. Fighting back a grin, as I'd rather not end the kiss, I trace the pattern once more.

"Carter." She squirms, laughing softly as she catches her breath. Her lips are still brushing against mine. "Stop it!"

"Why?" I tease, tracing her spine one more time. It has her arching against me in an enticing way. "Are you ticklish?"

"Yes!" She squirms against me and, this time, I relent.

Flattening my hand against the small of her back, I use the hand in her hair to pull her back down for a kiss. Instantly, her mouth opens, granting me entrance to deepen it further. Everything moves syrupy slow from there. We stay in that position for God only knows how long, just making out before I pull her in closer and move us until she's laying beneath me, more fully on the bed.

She blinks up at me, eyes hazy, and a little breathless. "That was very smooth."

Chuckling, I capture her bottom lip between mine for just a moment. "You sound surprised."

"Not surprised." Her leg hooks around my hip and she just as fluidly flips us, settling against me. Now it's my turn to stare up at her, stunned, her hands flat against my pecs. "But I was rather enjoying being on top."

Groaning, I push myself up until I can kiss her again, my hands already pushing her T-shirt up. When we part, I pull it off the rest of the way, my fingers dipping down to toy with the front-clasp of her bra. "I rather like you being on top of me too, love."

Her hips grind down against my rapidly hardening dick, her gasp mingling with a grunt of my own. As we strip one another and ourselves, we only part when we absolutely must. I move my kisses down her neck as my fingers dip into the front of her panties. She tips her head back, letting out a gasp before squirming in my lap in a completely different way.

This woman is going to be the death of me. She's so responsive to every touch, every breath against her skin, and everything feels so much stronger because I know I'm falling in love with her. I know she's the one I want by my side as this all comes to an end. She's the one I want to start the next chapter with, and, hopefully, who I'll have with me for the rest of this life.

I'm lost in every small feeling as we move together. Every time we do this, it gets better and better, but this might go down as some of the best sex of my life. Even the logistical side of safe, comfortable sex with a partner you care about and trust feels exhilarating in a way I've never felt before. When she slowly sinks down on me, I throw my head back and I swear I'm seeing stars.

Her moan echoes through the otherwise still and empty room. Her fingers squeeze against my pecs, and I want this moment to last. Every urge in my body is telling me to roll us over and take control, but it's not what I want. Not really, I'm fine letting her lead this and as her hips start on a slow grind, those urges are silenced. Hands gripping her hips, I help guide her, but don't take an ounce of control, allowing myself to be fully at her mercy. □

The curtain of her blonde hair falls against the side of my head as she bends down to kiss me. The kiss turns from sweet and languid, to one that's just as dirty as the grind of her hips. When both our orgasms have ripped through us and we've started to come down from the high, she lays down beside me, hand resting against her stomach.

We both stare up at the ceiling, our labored breaths trying to catch up with what we just did, but I feel my body melting against the plush mattress. Turning my head, I take in Kat's profile and the small, content smile she has on her lips. Unable to resist the gorgeous woman beside me, I roll onto my side and lean over to kiss her.

I love you. It's on the tip of my tongue, but I don't let myself say it. I'm worried it's too soon, and it's definitely too cliché to say it right after intense sex, but it's there. I can feel it hanging above us like the sun behind a cloud, just waiting for the barrier to move so we can both bask in the light.

Eventually, we get up to shower and change into clothes more comfortable for sleeping in before we climb back into bed. The meet is over, and tomorrow I'll head to one last training camp in Colorado

Springs while they go back to Columbia. This is the last time we'll see one another before we're getting ready to head to Omaha. If there was any moment to tell her, it'd be now.

Still, I can't bring myself to say the words.

She's practically asleep in my arms by the time I finally switch off the TV, bathing the hotel room in darkness. Just as I'm about to drift off to sleep myself, she shuffles closer, and kisses the underside of my jaw.

"You okay?" The words are barely a whisper, just wanting to check in on her.

"I'm so good," she promises, sleep heavy in her voice. Her eyes flutter open to meet mine in the dark. "I love you, Carter."

Just as I expected, the cloud hanging over us moves and we're basked in warmth. I know my smile's big, but hers mirrors it. I brush the lightest of kisses against her lips. "I love you, too. Now get to sleep."□

"M'kay," she agrees, settling back down against me and almost instantly drifting off.

Still smiling to myself, I quickly followed her lead.

Chapter 32

Carter

June 2024

Rather than flying out to Omaha with the team I train with, I decided to fly out with Kat and everyone else. Unsurprisingly, Bryce has been asked to do some interviews and signings during the meet, so he needs to be there almost as early as I do. Those extra few days will give him and Josie a chance to see her parents, who are stopping off at home for a couple of days before heading down south to do more exploring.

It's not what my coach would necessarily recommend for me, but he doesn't really argue either. It's my last Olympics and I'm nearly thirty; I can make the choice not to travel with a bunch of college kids. Especially since I'm one of the few pros who train with them.

Omaha is just how I remember it, but there's also something different about it this time around. It's not just another city I travel to for a meet or another city a friend of mine has lived in. Instead, this place has a small piece of Bryce and Josie that it didn't have before. No matter how fleeting it is, they built a life here, and it's one of the few aspects of my best friend's life I never had a part in.

After getting loaded into the rental car Bryce secured, we start the somewhat familiar drive into the heart of downtown from the airport. It's changed a bit, but most of it feels eerily the same. Bryce and Josie point out Hunt & Sloan, the building on the river they both worked out, the place they reconnected. I stare at the imposing brick building, trying to picture him working there. It's almost impossible.

"Hey." Kat leans in, nudging me slightly. I turn my attention from the window to her. "Are you sure you don't have photographic proof of Corporate Bryce? I mean, I know it happened, but I'm not sure I believe it."

Bryce must hear her, because he's talking before I can give her anything more than a cheeky grin. "It's not like the first day of school. I didn't send him a picture of my outfit. It happened. I can drop you off so you can go in and ask them yourself if you want me to?"

"How about no one ever steps foot back in that building and we call it a day?" Josie offers.

While I'm sure people would be happy to see Bryce, I'm not sure if Josie would receive the same hospitality. Despite working there for longer, when she finally had enough and tried to put in a proper notice, they were so angry they told her she could go. Which should have been confirmation she was making the right decision, as they obviously didn't care enough to fight for a valued member of their team.

Besides, do we really need photographic proof when we've seen that side of Bryce in action as he dissolved the partnership with Dalton Enterprises? He knew exactly what to say to make our case from both a legal and moral standpoint, ensuring the man understood we owe him nothing. I know how capable he is. It's one of the reasons I asked him to run the club with me. My degree in sports management will help us as we become more well known, but the day-to-day operations of a place like this are over my head.

Still, I don't think I'll ever be able to come to terms with the idea of Bryce sitting at a desk eight to ten hours a day, wearing some rendition of a suit. It's not his style.

Kat squeezes my knee, once again trying to get my attention. When I look at her, she's got a soft smile on her lips. "You're quiet. You okay?"

I lean in, pressing a kiss to her forehead, my fingers intertwining with hers on my knee. "I'm good, just in my head."

"That's okay, just checking in with you and reminding you I'm here."

I doubt Kat realizes how much those words mean to me, but they're grounding in a way I've never experienced before.

This isn't even the first time I've been in a relationship during Trials, but something about sharing this moment with her is different. During the last one, Ben spent his time trying to distract me. He wanted to make sure I didn't slip too far into my head, not understanding where a meet like this takes swimmers mentally. He didn't like it when I got quiet; he didn't like when I didn't offer more to an outing than simply existing. He wasn't a bad guy, and one of the few I saw a forever with at one point, but he fought too hard to understand something he likely never will. Instead of trusting me to handle it, he tried to fix something unfixable.

It wasn't long after we split up. I'd gained more notoriety after my silver medal in Tokyo, and he wasn't sure he wanted to be the partner of a professional athlete anymore. I got it then and I get it now.

We both were looking for something the other couldn't provide, so we stayed friends and parted ways. Now he has his almost-husband and I have a good friend, who texts me well wishes, and an amazing girlfriend, who is sitting beside me now.

Kat might not get it. She might not understand the sport, or the way it can consume a person's life, but she gets someone needing space. She never tries to force me to talk about things I'm not ready to talk about, nor does she try to get me out of my head. She reminds me she's here for me, a gentle but formidable force at my side. With her there, I feel steadier than I have in years.

"And here it is!" At Josie's words, my gaze drifts back to the passing scenery. She's motioning to Riverview Convention Center as Bryce turns the corner to pass by it. This is one place that hasn't changed. "Our home away from home for the next week. Your ass will be numb by the end of the week."

Mia laughs, but is nodding in agreement. As we pull up parallel to it, I take in all the decorations adorning the building. Suddenly, I feel a little nauseous as we come to a stop at a red light and I'm staring at a massive photo of myself plastered above one set of doors. I didn't know it was happening, nor would I have been expecting it, but there it was. The photo was taken during Worlds when I'd won a gold medal in the 400 IM.

"Oh, my god, Carter!" Kat already has her phone out, taking about a hundred pictures.

My cheeks are flushed pink, but I focus on the rest of the decorations. Every year it feels like they take up more room to help hype the meetup. Omaha's always turned up for US Olympic Trials and the athletes are always grateful for the fantastic meet they put on.

Bryce is making a face as he looks up at the photo. "That's going to be weird. Do we have to go through that door? I'm going to feel weird walking under Carter."

"You're just pissed they never put your pretty face up on a window," I tease, reaching forward to swat him across the head before the light changes. "All you got was a door back in 2021."

"You're right," he comments, flipping on his turn signal to turn into the hotel. "My face is pretty. Thanks, man."

Rolling my eyes, I turn back to the window, watching the remainder of the building pass us by before Bryce is pulling into the drive of the hotel so we can all get checked in.

"This is going to be great," Kat promises, her arms winding around my neck as soon as we get out of the car. "I'm excited to be here with you."

Placing my hand on the small of her back, I pull her in closer until I kiss the top of her head. "No one else I'd rather have here."

"Well, I take offense to that," Mia teases, hoisting her bag over her shoulder. "Come on, lovebirds! I want to take a nap."

Laughing, Kat and I each grab our carry-ons while the valet and bellhop take care of everything else. For the most part, the Riverview Convention Center is obscured from my view as we walk in, but I can see the corner of the picture. The picture that's making me realize how many people are paying attention—how many eyes are on me. If I'm named to the team, I'll be one of the oldest. They'll look to me as a veteran to show the others the ropes and be there to help with everything that goes into being an Olympian. I've been a team captain for an international meet before, but somehow this feels different.

A couple of hours later, we're all hanging out in the hotel lobby. Most swimmers are arriving tomorrow, but there are still a few people we know who are coaches, media personnel, or even swimmers themselves. After tonight, Kat will room with Mia for the remainder of the meet, giving me plenty of space to ensure I'm well rested and not getting distracted; it was the one thing my coach made me agree to when I told him I'd travel out here alone. Now, she's standing across the room with Bryce, chatting with one of our old coaches from Arizona, while I sit on one of the couches, lost in thought.

"Hey, buddy!" Josie is grinning as she plops down on the couch beside me. "How are you feeling?"

"Oh, I'm freaking out." My tone is casual as I wrap my arm around her shoulder, pulling her into my side. "Happy to know you'll be there cheering me on, though."

"Of course I am! I wouldn't miss this, and I'll be there to do it again in Paris."

It's never been difficult for me to understand what made Bryce fall for her—she's vibrant, open, and the type of person who always makes you feel seen. She's beautiful, inside, and out, and I'm lucky to have her as a friend.

"You're going to be there if I make the team?" I haven't had the chance to talk about it with Bryce, not knowing if they'd be able to get away with everything going on back home. They have the pool, the house, and it's expensive. Sure, our team is starting to develop with Bryce now utilizing at least one pool, but we're not rolling in money yet.

"Stop."

Startled, I glance down to see Josie glaring at me. I frown in confusion.

"Stop whatever is going on in that head of yours. Just stop it."

Busted. "You and Bryce don't have to come. That's all I was going to say."

"Yes, we do," she insists. "It won't just be us, either. Mia and Kat are going to be there, too."

I knew about Kat, spent many nights trying to convince her she doesn't have to come, but I didn't know about the rest of them. "You're kidding me."

"Um, no, absolutely not," she says. "Come on, Carter. Did you really think any of us would miss this?"

Warmth floods me as I glance over to where Bryce stands talking to Kat. He never said anything to me, but I know he'd have given just about anything to have that moment with Josie back in 2021. He knows he's the reason he didn't get it, and there's no dwelling on the past. If anything, I just want to acknowledge that I know how lucky I am, and I don't want to take it for granted.

"You know, I missed you when you and Bryce broke up, or whatever you call it," I admit, turning back to her. "It sucked I lost you, too."

Her smile dims ever so slightly. "I missed you, too. I thought about reaching out but never did because I didn't think you'd want to be friends with me after everything. I respected you and your friendship with Bryce too much to put it in jeopardy."

"He was an idiot for letting you go." I want her to understand how much I mean that. How many times I told Bryce that same thing after the breakup and before, knowing he'd regret it if he lost her. "I told him that so many times. He knew I was right, but I kept telling him losing you would end up being the thing he'd regret the most."

"I know." She bumps my shoulder with hers. "He told me. Thanks for having my back."

"But I should have been a better friend to you—"

She cuts me off. "Don't do that to yourself, Carter. He needed you more, and I had Mia. I don't blame you for how any of it went down."

"He pissed me off, seeing him treat you like that. It wasn't like him, and I was so angry."

"And he knows that." Her gaze drifts to him before looking back at me. "Can I tell you something?"

"Anything."

"The time apart did us all some good. We lived in this dream world where anything was possible, and nothing could touch us. We all had some growing up to do, reality to see, and we had to do it on our own."

I look over at my best friend, who's so at ease with himself and where he is in his life right now, and I know she's right. He's the one person who's been by my side my whole life, constantly proving he'll always be there. Bryce and everyone else in this room are the family I choose, and I'm pretty damn lucky.

"You two are good now, though, right? Because I don't—"

"Bryce Clark is the love of my life." There's not a flicker of doubt in her features, and I'm fighting the urge to smile. Maybe scream aloud, because my best friend found it. "He's it for me."

Bryce found something solid, real, and good. He's not going to freak out this time. I've always wanted him to find happiness—real and true happiness, but I never would have guessed it'd come in the form of a spunky, yet shy, curly-haired blog owner who saw the future impact he'd have on the sport of swimming. Yet here we are, and I got to be part of their story the same way they're part of mine.

"You know, I think you might have saved him." My tone is quiet as I lean closer to her. "He hated that job; he hated doing the responsible thing. You were the thing that kept him sane again and helped him see what else is out there."

Josie smiles back at me. "I think we saved each other. He's always been the one person who can make me be brave."

"Nah, Jos." I wave her off. "You've always been brave. He might shine a spotlight on it, but it's always been there."

A blush coats her cheeks. "That's sweet of you to say."

"It's true, Josie, and Bryce sees it, too. He's told me so many times how fearless and strong you are," I counter. She needs to hear it. "I know you always told me you're a big Bryce Clark Fan, but I think he's a bigger Josie Martin fan."

Chapter 33

Katrina

June 2024

"Is it normal to feel like you're going to throw up?"

"Absolutely," Mia confirms, barely glancing up from her phone. "It's also normal to throw up. There's a lot at stake here."

Her words offer little comfort. Instead, my stomach gives a sickening twist and I try to remember where the quickest restroom is. I don't know if I'll ever know how Josie and Mia managed to spend so many years in these seats, caring about people whose entire careers were about to be defined by something that'd be over in moments, if not seconds. I've been part of this world for six months, with Carter for three, and I'm a little relieved he's not going to keep going after this.

If he wanted to, of course I would support him. But Josie and Mia had a point: It hurts to care.

I'm feeling helpless. Over the last few months, I've learned how to be emotionally supportive and there for him when a meet goes well, or horrible, but this is different. Glancing down at my phone, I make sure I haven't missed a text I knew wouldn't be there. He's trying to get in the zone, focusing on the race in front of him, which means pretending nothing else exists.

Including, or maybe especially, his anxious girlfriend.

"He has a good chance," Bryce assures me, lowering himself into his seat. I assume he's talking to Mia or Josie, so I don't say anything. I'm shocked when he nudges my shoulder to get my attention. When I turn to him, he gives me a reassuring smile. "He's trained hard. His times have been solid, and his lane placement is good."

"But none of that guarantees him a spot on the team," I reply. "It doesn't matter that he's been training his ass off. Someone can still be faster than him."

He sighs with a nod. "Yeah, that's true, but he knows what he's doing, and we need to trust that he can pull this off."

I look over at Josie, who is pretending not to listen in. Bryce is the only person who can give me any sort of insight into what's going through my boyfriend's head right now, but he's never been one to open up about his feelings. Especially not with me, and especially not when it could mean speaking on behalf of his best friend.

"The only thing you can do right now is be there for him," he continues. "No matter what happens tonight or the rest of the week, what goes right or wrong, just be there for him. Even when Josie and I weren't together, I knew she was in my corner and that meant everything to me."

Josie reaches out to squeeze his knee, a sign of comfort which is strengthened by the way he reaches down to entangle their fingers. This is a first for him, too; the first time in years he's in the stands instead of getting ready to step behind the blocks. His career is over, he's moved on, but now he is supporting his best friend. I'm insanely grateful for him.

"Do you think he's going to make the team?"

Bryce hesitates at the question, not wanting to be overly confident, but still wanting to be supportive. It's a feeling I know well. "I
think he has a much better chance than he seems to think he has."

I frown. "So, he's having those same conversations with you?" He
nods. "Why doesn't he just trust in his own abilities?"

"Unlike this one," Mia joins, reaching past me to flick Bryce's arm.
Bryce winces, leaning away from her. "Carter has never been cocky."

Bryce laughs. The sound relaxes me slightly. If we can make jokes,
it's okay to be fine. Right? "It's not cocky if it's true, right, babe?"

Josie grins at the heat sheets in her lap. "You're a cocky asshole.
Always have been, always will be."

"Oh, whatever." He rolls his eyes.

"I love when I'm right," Mia gloats, before she pulls my attention
back to her. "Carter has always been the humble one, but the talent
is there, too. He's the most consistent swimmer we ever followed.
I'm confident he'll make the team."

"But it might not be tonight," Josie adds, "and he doesn't have to
come in first to make the team. He just needs a ticket to Paris, the
rest he can take care of when he gets there."

Between Bryce, Josie, and Mia, my anxiety slowly begins to ease.
They're confident in his abilities, and they've been following this
sport, and his career, for a lot longer than I have. They're the people
I should trust, and I do, but I'm still nervous as hell.

"The 400 IM is up first." Josie motions to the heat sheet in front
of her. "He has a solid chance, but there is no semifinal for this one.
Whoever wins tonight will go to Paris."

"Well, that just made things ten times more stressful."

"Strongest leg is the freestyle," Bryce reminds me, checking something on his phone. "He has a decent backstroke, too."

"That just means he needs to make sure he gets some distance in the fly," Josie continues. "He wants to make sure he doesn't have too much ground to make up on the last leg. There are some strong swimmers in both the front and back half of this race."

There are so many words and phrases related to the sport that I don't understand being bounced around right now that I feel the anxiety starting to creep back up my neck. I can't tell them they're making me more anxious, because I know they're just trying to help. And in their own way, they're easing their own panic. They know what those words mean, and the comfort they offer them isn't shared by me.

"Will the two of you shut up?" Mia cuts off their musings, allowing me to relax. "You're going to make this poor woman have a nervous breakdown."

Josie's gaze snaps up to me, instantly apologetic. "Sorry."

I don't get the chance to assure her it's okay because the lights dim, and an eerie hush goes over the crowd. Seconds later, loud, electric-sounding pop music starts pumping through the speakers, lights start flashing, and the crowd goes crazy. The sequence is doing its job of hyping people up, but it's making my anxiety skyrocket. On the other side of this moment is the beginning of the last chapter—my boyfriend's career is at the beginning of the end and, more than anything, I want this to go his way.

Everything leading up to the start of the actual final session passes in a blur—the calm before the storm, Bryce calls it. Then the music picks up and they're announcing the finalists for the men's 400 IM.

When they call Carter's name, our friends let out loud cheers, but I find I can't. The lump in my throat is so large, I can't speak around it. My heart has sunk so far into my stomach, I can't tell if I want to pass out or be sick. My eyes never leave him. Not as he changes, stripping down to the Jammers he's swimming in. Not as he shakes his muscles out, getting in another stretch before he gets on the block. Not as he steps up onto the block, the crowd instantly dying down.

"Take your mark."

Every swimmer moves in a fluid motion, taking their places on the block. There is a brief pause, a slight buzzer or whistle, and they're off.

My eyes follow every precise stroke as he pulls himself through the water at a steady pace. Beside me, Bryce yells out instructions I can barely understand and know Carter can't hear, but I get why he does it. Why he feels like he's doing something helpful. Mia and Josie are cheering him on, but my eyes just stay locked on him.

This is what people mean when they say everything fades away. Right now, the other swimmers don't exist, the crowd surrounding me blurs, and my only focus is on Carter and how insanely proud of him I am. No matter what happens tonight or this week, I'm so proud of him.

During the first 100 meters, Carter manages to get into a solid third place position. As they move into backstroke, he starts to pull ahead. His lead is narrow, but obvious, and I'd feel better about it if we didn't still have half the race in front of him. In the last forty or so meters of the breaststroke leg, everything starts to fall apart.

"Shit." Bryce's voice is tight, like he's finally feeling the anxiety I've been feeling this whole time. In the pool, they move into the last hundred meters, freestyle. "C'mon, Abrams!"

He's in fifth place as they move into the freestyle, and my heart is plummeting. Which is fine, really. What do I need a heart for right now?

I don't know enough to understand what's going wrong; all I know is Carter went from first place to fifth in a hundred or so meters. And now he's barely holding that position.

He pushes off the wall in fourth place, heading home, and I feel like it's over. I don't care how good of a freestyler he is; there's no way he can make up the ground he's lost.

But then, as he surfaces, it's like a switch is flipped as he pushes through the last fifty meters. Everyone around me is going crazy, and I find myself screaming along this time as he pushes into third place. I watch as he battles against the young swimmer from California as my boyfriend proves me wrong. No, he's not going to get first, but there's still a chance he can get second.

Carter and the kid touch the wall at what looks to be the exact same time. A lull goes over the crowd, and I can hear the blood pumping in my ears as my gaze snaps up to the screen hanging above the pool.

By one one-hundredth of a second, Carter came in third, failing to make the team in an event he felt confident in. Beside me, I see Bryce deflate. Tears sting the corner of my eyes. Down in the pool, Carter has torn his cap and goggles off, taking fast, shallow breaths. The look on his face is blank, but he offers a small smile to the kid who came in second. He laughs and says something to him, constantly being the good sport he is.

When the kid turns away, though, Carter's features crumble, and my heart crumbles with him.

—

"Okay, talk to me," I tell Josie as she takes her seat beside me. "What are his chances looking like tonight?"

Despite not really knowing what to expect, I'm hopeful we'll walk out of the Riverview Convention Center with Carter on his way to Paris tonight. I'm not sure I can take another night like the first one. Listening to him go over all the ways he could have swum the race differently and the ways it could've happened is heartbreaking. Logically, I know it's part of being the girlfriend of a professional athlete. There's going to be bad races and meets, but that doesn't mean I have to like it. I don't like listening to him beat himself up over something like this.

I knew he'd be hard on himself, everyone warned me, but I wasn't prepared for how much he'd blame himself. Or how crushed he'd look. The weight of the world is on his shoulders, and I don't know what I can do to lessen the load.

She gives me a sympathetic smile. "This is his last chance to make the team."

I appreciate her being honest with me, but it's not what I want to hear right now. It's something I already know, but I'm choosing to focus on the unknown of it all.

"You saw him in Nashville," Mia adds, leaning across her friend to talk to me better. "That time was within the top times of the year in the country. He has a great shot at this."

"And his lane placement is good."

I glare at Bryce. "That's what you said the other night."

He's looking at me over the top of Josie's head. "You know I can't predict what's going to happen, but I have a good feeling about this, Kat. I wouldn't lie to you about that."

This really is Carter's last chance to make the team, and Bryce is just as anxious about this as I am. Maybe more so. Obviously, I trust him, but what good does trust do in this situation? We all believe in Carter and trust his talent is good enough to pull him through, but what if someone else is quicker? Sure, up to six qualifiers can go to the Olympics in this event, but the field is out of eight. Of those six, only the top two will get spots in the actual event in Paris.

He doesn't have to come in first tonight, I remind myself. *He just needs to get a ticket to Paris.*

I'm gripping Josie and Mia's hands in mine as they announce the raise. I don't break my gaze from his as he steps up to the blocks, ready for this last chance.

Take your mark . . .

Chapter 34

Carter

Paris Olympics

July 2024

Everything I've worked on for the last dozen or so years has been leading up to this moment. Either I'm going to get an Olympic gold medal, or I'm not.

I, like so many other athletes, used to think the moment that mattered the most would be the first time I achieved my dream, but now I'm not so sure. My career, this sport, has allowed so many doors to open to me and has provided me with a stable foundation to step into who I want to be. I've achieved goals and dreams so far beyond my wildest imagination that even I have trouble reconciling them sometimes. I'd do it all again in a heartbeat.

But this—these last few seconds is what matters. The last few seconds that determine how it ends, the legacy that I'll leave behind in this sport will either be shadowed or highlighted by this moment. How it all ends, I've learned, is just as important as how it started.

I push off the wall, feeling the burning sensation in my arms, legs, and lungs as I drive into the last fifty meters. Fifty meters. That's all that's left and I'm ready to fight for it.

The rest of the field fades away. I don't check where any other swimmer is. I focus on my own race. I can hear the roar of the crowd in muffled bursts. Tomorrow, I know I'll be feeling every second of this race deep in my bones, and will feel it for weeks to come, but I still push harder. It doesn't matter because this is it. It's the last time I'll be doing this, the last time I will feel the burn in my lungs and the adrenaline pumping through me.

In just a few seconds, my life will be completely different.

I glide into the wall, hand punching against the touchpad to clock my final time. Back pressed up against the wall, the sound from the crowd is deafening. I turn to the screen, finding my name, and time—

My cheer mingles with the rest of the crowd, my hand coming down to slap against the water. My heart is pounding in my chest, the blood pumping so hard through my veins I can feel it pounding in my head. The reality of what this means sinks in faster than I expect. There's no need for a moment to take it in, no waiting to see if disqualified will appear beside my race. I swam a good race, and it paid off.

I'm an Olympic gold medalist.

"Presenting your Olympic gold medalist, Carter Abrams!"

My face aches from smiling as I step up onto the podium, arms raised in the air. This is the moment I've worked my whole career for and one I wasn't sure I'd ever get. I duck my head, accepting the medal, and shake the hand of the presenter, thanking him, and accepting his congratulations. Cameras flash in my face as I hold the medal up for photos. The crowd is cheering and screaming; the sound making my ears ring more than any concert ever has.

When the crowd quiets down, and the anthem begins to play, everything around me shifts.

I take the moment in, blinking back tears as I watch the flag raise. It's the culmination of every bit of hard work I've put into my career. It's the bisexual kid from Arizona who'd been told his dreams wouldn't come true countless times, seeing them realized before his eyes. When I decided to go for this, I didn't set out to change the game or to be a voice for athletes who've been pushed back, quieted for years. I did this for myself, because it's what I wanted to do with my life. Everything else is a bonus.

I have measured every high and every low of my life to this sport, as it is as much a part of me as my sexuality is. It's woven into the pieces that come together to create my story, and I know that kid from Arizona would be damn proud of the man standing here today.

As soon as I step off the podium, I follow the same path so many other athletes have made and climb the stands to greet my family, not caring about the cameras following close behind me. I'm not sure there's a single dry eye in the entire row. As my parents pull me into a hug, their tears mix with my own. When my mom finally releases me, I hand her the flowers, thanking them for everything they've done for me over the years.

When they release me, I move down the line, starting with Bryce and Josie, who give me a quick group hug, knowing I don't have much time. When I reach Bryce, his hand claps against my back, pulling me in close. We're both laughing, but there are tears mixed in there too as he tells me how fucking proud he is of me.

Kat's the last one I reach, and I instantly pull her in for a kiss. Her hands are shaking as they cup my cheeks. She presses a few more quick kisses to my lips once I pull away.

When I finally pull back, she's looking at me with wide, glossy eyes. I expect her to tell me how proud she is of me or how much she loves me, both things I already know. Instead, she swallows and says, "I'm so grateful to know you."

There's nothing terribly romantic about the words, but they're true. The truth behind them rings louder than the words themselves and I get it. I get what she means. How meeting her, getting to know her, changed everything for me, and for her.

Bryce and Josie might have saved each other, but Kat and I fought through hell to come together.

An official is telling me I need to go, so I don't have a chance to tell her anything else before I'm pulled away. As soon as I can pull my phone from my back pocket, I send her a text without knowing when she'll get it with this crowd, but I need her to know.

I love you, too.

Chapter 35

Katrina

July 2024

I fight my way through the crowds, trying to use what little height I have to my advantage. Why did everyone in this goddamn sport have to be so tall? And why were they all making some kind of mass exodus?

A couple of feet away, I spot a bench that's half unoccupied and make a beeline toward it. If I can't grow, I can stand on something taller. I can hear my friends amusement as they call my name behind me. I climb up to scan the crowd, ignoring the startled look from the lady occupying the other half.

It's been weeks since I've seen Carter, and I'm anxious to be back in his arms as we turn our attention to the rest of our lives. And whatever the future brings us.

"Kat, you're going to get in trouble," Josie warns, but she's smiling up at me. "Seriously, someone's going to come yell at you in angry French."

"I'm not bailing you out of Olympics jail, Katrina," Bryce warns.

I stick my tongue out at him. "That's not a thing!" He raises a brow, making my joy falter ever so slightly. "Is it?"

"That's where they put the athletes when they break their card-board beds after having too much sex." He shrugs and nods to his left. "Do you really want to join them?"

Turning, I can see a police officer weaving his way through the crowd, eyes focused on me. Which means I need to find my boyfriend before he reaches me. It can't be that hard to spot his messy brown hair.

"Mademoiselle—" The guard begins only a few paces away from me now, but it doesn't matter because Carter seemingly appears out of nowhere. He looks exhausted, but the smile on his face hasn't dimmed in days.

Before I can say anything, his arms are around my waist, effort-lessly picking me up from the bench. It takes my breath away, and I feel like I'm in a movie where it's only us and everyone—especially the police officer—melts away. I grew up wanting this kind of rela-tionship. Spent most of my adult years believing I'd have to settle. Now I have it, and I am not letting it go.

"Okay, let her down before she gets seasick," Mia jokes from somewhere.

She's not wrong. I am starting to feel a little dizzy, but I'm not sure if it's a result of the moment or Carter spinning me around. He lowers me to my feet, but he doesn't let me get far. Hands resting on my hips, he pulls me in close, still grinning brightly. "Hi, love."

Still a little breathless myself, I grin back with my hands tightening on his shoulders. "Hi. I'm so proud of you, Carter."

I've said those exact words at every opportunity I've had since we left Omaha all those months ago, and it always has the same effect on him. His grin drops slightly, like he can't believe what I'm saying, before the normal, brilliant smile is back.

"Okay, lovebirds." Bryce's voice breaks into our bubble. "We all want congratulations hugs. Break it up."

Reluctantly, we release one another, and I hand him over to his best friend, who immediately engulfs him in a huge hug. Standing back, witnessing how loved he is, makes my heart melt. His family let us handle this, and we're meeting them for dinner after this. Then we're heading home in a couple of days. Back to Columbia, and back to real life.

We all offer to stick around for a couple extra days, let him enjoy the city and the rest of the Olympics, but Carter is ready to go home. He still had some media requirements, but he'd only agreed to the bare minimum, and he'd be back in South Carolina within the week.

As he finishes hugging everyone, he finds his way back to me and pulls me into his arms. Everything about him is radiating happiness and I want to melt into this moment, live in it forever. "Hello again."

I throw my head back, laughing. His fingers tangle in my hair as my arms wind around his neck. When I meet his gaze again, the delight is gone, and it's been replaced with pure love. I know I'm staring at him the same way. "Hi yourself."

He leans in, closing the distance between us to press a soft kiss against my lips. It ends a second after it started, leaving us staring at one another. I can see how exhausted he is, but there's a glimmer of something else in his green eyes, adrenaline, and contentment.

I comb my fingers through his hair, and he leans into the touch. "Are you sure you're done?"

"Yes," he promises me, not a single sign of doubt on his handsome face. "That was amazing and I'm glad I did it, but I'm done."

I don't ask him again, trusting him to be honest with me. Bryce has pestered him for months, mostly out of regrets surrounding his own experience, and he's tired of answering the same questions. I don't ask again. Instead, I cup his cheek, and lead him into another kiss. This one is deeper, his tongue instantly seeking entrance as I sink back against him. Our friends are making all kinds of amused noises around us, certainly drawing attention our way, but I don't care.

When we separate, we're still in our own little world, but Bryce seems to have other ideas as he reminds us about dinner.

"We should go," I whisper against his lips before he steals another kiss.

"I also need to talk to you about something," Bryce calls to get us to move along. "I have someone I want to hire."

I almost groan because Bryce really does have the worst timing.

"Not now," Carter replies after another quick kiss. He glances at his best friend over his shoulder. "Can't you see I'm busy? Tell me tomorrow!"

At those three words, my mind instantly goes back to a quiet morning months ago. The way his eyes had dark circles under them as he answered the video call, and the way something plummeted into the pit of my stomach at the sight, and I just knew. I knew it was never going to be Will; it was always going to be Carter Abrams. Will and everything else in my life has been a steppingstone to this moment. To becoming who I want to be and accepting the love I know I deserve.

This is my tomorrow. I want to continue going down this path, seeing what life has in store for me, because I know it's going to be beautiful. Not perfect, because there is no such thing, but always beautiful.

I let out a squeal of laughter as Carter picks me up, spinning me around once more. Looking down at the wide, bright green eyes, something settles in me. A comfort I never thought I'd have. I look around at Bryce, who's rolling his eyes, then to Josie and Mia, who are taking pictures, and finally to the police officer lingering with a small smile. This moment is everything, and it's mine.

"I love you," I whisper down at him.

His grin softens as he lowers me back to the ground. "Katrina Dalton, you don't even know how crazy I am for you."

But I do because I feel it, too. And I hope I never stop feeling it.

Epilogue

Katrina

September 2024

There's music pumping through the speakers of Adair Swim Club's outside deck. I greet people with a warm smile, offering them a cool beverage and a packet containing all the information they could need. Bryce and Carter are each somewhere, taking perspective families on tours of the facility and Mia is wandering around, camera in hand to capture every moment. The sign up-sheets for the team and the lessons are rapidly filling up. There's so much going on, I can hardly catch my breath, but it's the best kind of adrenaline rush. The open house is turning out better than any of us anticipated, and I couldn't be happier for the guys.

The last few weeks have been a flurry of activity as everyone settled into the post-Olympic life that was awaiting us. Carter finished all his required media appearances before officially moving into his own condo here in Columbia. Josie and Bryce are moved into their finished home and the club is officially open. These were the moments I never really got to be part of when I was with Dalton Enterprises, watching as something I helped build came to life and fulfill its intended purpose. I'm probably a little biased, but these were two of the projects I'm most proud of and it's only made more special when I see the smile on my boyfriend's face.

Carter is a natural in this environment. He gets down to the height of the kids, so he can have real conversations with them about swimming and the importance of water safety. He can smile and charm his way in with the parents, easily getting them to sign their kids up for lessons or a clinic. It's a good thing Bryce and Carter have some coaches in mind to bring in. Something tells me they'll need them sooner rather than later.

When Carter turns toward me, I catch his eye, and his grin gets impossibly wider, his eyes alight with joy. He says something to the father he's talking to and motions to me, which means he's talking about all the work I put into the construction of this place or Bryce and Josie's remodel. He's my biggest cheerleader, just like I'm his. Something warm twists in me when the father looks my way and offers a polite smile. I smile back. Then my face flushes when Carter winks.

"Josie, Bryce, and I have a bet on you guys."

I startle slightly as Mia appears next to me. "What kind of bet?"

"How long it'll take the two of you to move in together."

I fully turn to her, rolling my eyes. "Give us a second to breathe!" My tone is teasing as I hand a bottle of water to a harried-looking mother with a smile. "We both opened businesses, and he signed the lease on the condo. We haven't been together long."

"A condo that's definitely big enough for two." Josie joins in from my right. "Besides, what does the length of a relationship have to do with anything? If it's meant to be, you just know."

"Maybe don't listen to the girl who moved halfway across the country with a guy she'd just gotten back together with," Mia advises.

"Oh, shut up." Josie swats her. "You know what I mean. Besides, we literally bought a house together. I think we're going to be fine, just like the two of them."

Looking around the crowded space, I know she's right. We'll all be fine. We have each other, and an amazing place to build up. I've already got projects booked months in advance for my company. Mia's getting paid by both Adair Swim Club and Effervescent Renovations, giving her more than enough reason to stick around for the long run. The pieces have fallen together and created a beautiful picture before us.

Josie pulls a full sign-up sheet off the clipboard and adds it to a growing stack. "There's no way they're going to be able to handle all this."

Mia looks over at the stack, her eyes widening. She takes them from her best friend, flipping through the pages. "No way. They're going to have to hire someone as soon as possible."

"I wonder who they'll hire?" I ask.

Bryce is calling Mia over, probably wanting pictures of something. She snatches up her camera, giving us a fleeting glance. "As long as it's not Ronan O'Brien, I'm good."

Josie laughs as her best friend walks away, but nudges me as soon as she's out of earshot. "If it is him, maybe we'd finally find out what happened."

By now I'd heard the story, how they all used to be so close until a meet in 2017 when the friendship between the two of them stopped. Mia gave him the cold shoulder; he acted like he had no idea what happened. No one could get any information from them. He retired soon after.

"Do you think it could be him?"

Josie shakes her head. "No way. I don't think he has anything to do with the sport anymore. Besides, Bryce would tell me."

As Josie turns to focus on a new batch of people wanting to sign up, my gaze drifts back to Mia. The last person in our little group needs happiness. It doesn't have to come in the form of love, but I wish I could see her settle into something she loves and stop looking over her shoulder like the past will come back to bite her. I've learned better over the last few months, though. Mia marches to her own drum and trying to get in her way will only leave you feeling foolish.

I need to let her march. My urge to fix things has to be set aside, trusting my friends will find happiness. Just like I did.

The End.

If you loved Carter and Katrina's story, be sure to leave a review!

You can leave reviews at The StoryGraph, Goodreads, BookBub, and/or wherever you bought the book.

If you missed out on Josie and Bryce's story, get *Maybe One Day,* now! Book #3 in the series (lovingly called YIC currently) is coming! No set date yet, but it'll be early 2025.

For updates on upcoming releases, be sure to follow me on social media and sign up for my newsletter. All new subscribers to my newsletter will get a BONUS scene from *Maybe*

One Day.

Scan the code and come say hi!

Acknowledgements

Holy shit, I wrote **two** books! In less than a year. If the first book was a shock to me, then you can probably guess how I'm feeling about this now.

As always, I want to start by thanking YOU, the reader. Whether you're new to my books or returning, welcome and thank you for giving this book a chance. Authors probably shouldn't say they have a favorite book, but this one is always going to hold a close place in my heart. Since I started writing *Maybe One Day,* Carter has always been a favorite character of mine. I wanted to make sure I gave him someone good and give his story the spotlight it deserves. I can't thank you enough for helping me make this happen.

Next, I will always give credit where credit is due, because I wouldn't be here without some truly amazing people. Enni, my amazing cover designer from Yummy Book Covers. This cover absolutely blew me out of the water (look how pretty it is)! I gave her some general color palettes, told her the mood and setting, and let her do what she does best. In return, I was given a physical manifestation of my beloved characters. Next, I want to thank my incredible editor, Ashley, at Earley Editing, LLC. Her quickly filling availability caused me to challenge myself to write this book and I'm so grateful for that push. If it weren't for her, I'd probably still be piecing together the story and being the queen of procrastination. Her encouragement and incredible work continue to strengthen my stories and make me a better writer in return.

Again, hey Amanda and Claire! The memories we share have helped shape these stories, and I'm grateful for each one of them. We've been in this world of writing together for a long time and you've seen me at my worst and best. I'm grateful every day to have such a supportive group of friends beside me.

Last but not least, my family. I am so lucky to be surrounded by parents and a sister who love and support me in all of my creative endeavors. They've never once told me what I can and can't do, instead they continuously push me to new heights. I am who I am today because of them, and I'd be lost without them. I love you guys. More than you will ever know.

About the Author

Ashlyn Harmon writes books with a little bit of sass, a whole lot of swoon-worthy moments, and characters who are real, and relatable. She loves writing the kinds of female leads she wished she had more access to: unapologetically confident in their bodies and who they are.

She was born and raised in Omaha, Nebraska, and is still daydreaming of getting out one day. When she's not writing, she continues to grow her freelance editing business, where she specializes in all things romance, watching ghost hunting shows, hanging out with her corgi, or with her nose buried in a book.

She's always working on a bunch of new stuff, so be sure to follow her on social media or sign up for her newsletter, to stay in the know.

www.ingramcontent.com/pod-product-compliance
Lightning Source LLC
Chambersburg PA
CBHW022016310726
48972CB00006B/1678